# OFFSEASON

# OFFSEASON

A Novel

Avigayl Sharp

Astra House New York

Grateful acknowledgment is made for permission to reprint the following material: Lines from *The Prime of Miss Jean Brodie* by Muriel Spark. Copyright © 1961 by Muriel Spark. Copyright renewed 1989 by Muriel Spark. Used by permission of HarperCollins Publishers and David Higham Associates. Lines from "P.S." from *Walking to Martha's Vineyard* by Franz Wright, copyright © 2003 by Franz Wright. Used by permission of Alfred A. Knopf, an imprint of the Knopf Doubleday Publishing Group, a division of Penguin Random House LLC. All rights reserved.



Astra House
A Division of Astra Publishing House
astrahouse.com
Printed in the United States of America

Library of Congress Cataloging-in-Publication Data
Names: Sharp, Avigayl author
Title: Offseason : a novel / Avigayl Sharp.
Description: First edition. | New York : Astra House, 2026. | Summary: "A blisteringly funny and transcendently deranged debut novel following a young woman who takes a job at an all-girls boarding school in a small coastal town to teach English literature—and to try, desperately, to escape the trap that is herself"— Provided by publisher.
Identifiers: LCCN 2025046882 | ISBN 9781662603501 hardcover | ISBN 9781662603495 epub
Subjects: LCGFT: Novels | Fiction
Classification: LCC PS3619.H35643 O34 2026
LC record available at https://lccn.loc.gov/2025046882
ISBN: 9781662603501
First edition
10 9 8 7 6 5 4 3 2 1
Design by Alissa Theodor
The text is set in Warnock Pro.
The titles are set in Carlton Std.

*For Jason*

Attend to me, girls. One's prime is the moment one was born for. Now that my prime has begun—Sandy, your attention is wandering. What have I been talking about?

—MURIEL SPARK, *The Prime of Miss Jean Brodie*

I cannot discover this "oceanic" feeling in myself.

—SIGMUND FREUD, *Civilization and Its Discontents*

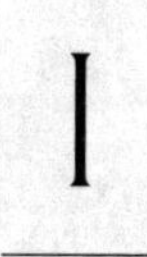

# I

I arrived at the Academy on a Tuesday in early September, one of the last weeks that the ferry would be operating for the season. My journey involved a train ride to a major coastal metropolis in the Northeast, then an hour's trip by boat to the remote tourist town in which the school was located. I departed early in the morning and watched through the train windows as the sun came up over virtuosic fields of subsidized corn, obese cows, miserable horses, so-called rivers—green, rank, oily with pollution. My seat smelled strongly of old coffee and hard-boiled eggs. I fell asleep with my cheek pressed against the glass and awoke to the sensation of my right foot being squeezed through its shoe in a firm and rhythmic pulsing motion, as in a resuscitation. The man occupying the seat next to mine was leaning forward, torso folded at the waist like a collapsible chair, his face amazingly close to my knees. Upon noticing that I was conscious he jerked upright, lay back in his seat, and pretended to be asleep himself, putting on a series of ostentatious little gurgling noises, his head, with its hair the color of an unripe peach, lolling floppily upon its neck. I knew this was all a show designed to trick and tranquilize me, but the man's babyish sounds were nonetheless soothing, and I was lulled easily back into sleep. I hadn't had sex in a long time. There were certain thinkers who might claim that I had never had sex, though I was not one of these thinkers. I was pretty sure I had had sex on many occasions. I was twenty-eight years old. When I woke up again, the man was reading a magazine whose glossy cover featured a photograph of an aging celebrity, seated in a pool chair with her legs spread, wearing a striped tankini. In large yellow lettering, the caption read: I DON'T GIVE A D*** IF YOU CALL ME A FATTY.

I looked out the window at a tent city and some wet black birds strung out on an electrical wire. The birds unhinged their beaks as if to make a loud sound. Then they were gone. I looked away from the window. I couldn't think of another place to look that wasn't my seatmate, so I looked at my seatmate. He grinned back, as though his face had always been waiting for me in just this position, with its broad pink cheeks and its green eyes and its very straight teeth. His smile said that we were two people who knew one another, not intimately but socially, and that we had each consistently made a pleasant impression on the other. The man appeared to be in his sixties, around the same age as my parents, his hair fried by dye but showing its gray at the roots, where it had been lifted up and over his skull using a firm pomade. Inside my brain it was like an empty glass was being filled with water. I looked at my seatmate's crispy hair and his delicate hands, and then I realized that we did in fact know each other, not intimately but socially, in that he was the father of my elementary school classmate Megan O'Donald, who had been the most beautiful girl in my grade.

I had not seen Megan O'Donald or this man, her father, Mr. O'Donald, in fifteen years. When I knew her, Megan O'Donald had taken Irish dance classes four times a week and performed at nearly every after-school assembly, wearing a stiff sequined dress and a golden wig of tightly coiled ringlets. Mr. O'Donald would stand in the front row, yipping and slapping a hand rhythmically against his thigh as his daughter tossed her tiny legs high above her waist, and many rows behind him Mrs. O'Donald would sit with her hands folded neatly in her lap, as if she were in church. When Megan O'Donald danced she wore a special green crown and the boy I loved stared directly up her skirt, panting. I hated Megan O'Donald's guts. I did not at that time have the wherewithal to overcome my personal feelings for the sake of political solidarity with the cultural symbols of Irish nationalism, because I was eleven years old. But I had been fond of Mr. O'Donald, who had once given me a standing ovation during our drama club's performance of *The Pirates of Penzance*.

The entire time I'd been looking at him, Mr. O'Donald's grin had been stretching more widely across his face, like a balloon filling with air. I opened my mouth to say Hi, Mr. O'Donald, how have you been, and in that moment it became clear that Mr. O'Donald had no idea who I was. When he smiled at me now, he was not remembering my luminous gender-bending sixth-grade performance as the Major-General in *The Pirates of*

*Penzance.* His mind was living in a place that was totally inaccessible to me. He was thinking about the shape and heft of my foot, or he was thinking about his daughter, Megan O'Donald, images of whom I still occasionally saw on social media, like all the other elementary and high school classmates I no longer spoke to, or he was thinking about something else. There was no way for me to know.

Megan O'Donald, I remembered from a photograph I had recently come across online, was pregnant now.

I closed my mouth and turned to look once more out the window. I saw what may have been a second or a third tent city, and then I pretended to fall asleep. Some time later I woke up. Mr. O'Donald was gone. His magazine remained splayed across the empty seat cushion. I put it in my backpack.

My ferry trip was comparatively uneventful, though there were rough seas and the top deck lay coated in a film of human vomit, like chowder.

My subsidized faculty housing would be ready for move-in the next morning; in the meantime, I was to spend my first night at an inn two blocks from the bay. With both hands I dragged my luggage toward my lodgings. The afternoon light sank into the blue harbor as the last tourists of the season ambled down the shoreline, grim-faced, confused. I had never before lived near the ocean. Fishing boats sat docked along the pier, bouncing on top of the water like a row of jolly babies. All around there was the pleasant rotten smell of dead fish in open air. It was low tide, and beyond the pier I could see the strip of beach where the water had receded, leaking seagrass and vacant crab claws.

I checked into the hotel, removed one sweater from my suitcase, pulled it on, went out, picked up dinner in a Styrofoam container, and slopped it into my mouth standing over my hotel room dresser, watching through the dirty window as darkness started to blot the sky. I switched the television set on and off, then lay down in my clothes over the bedsheets, which were embroidered with lacy orange conch shells. On my phone I reread a portion of an email my father had sent me two years earlier, in which he described the qualities of every item of clothing he had purchased that afternoon at the outlet mall. When I woke up it was night and my shoes were still on.

I put on my coat and walked down to the Old Pilgrim, a bar on Main Street that I had noted on my way in and hoped I might frequent during the school year. It was situated on the ground floor of a building that resembled every other building on the block: white wood slats with the paint peeling in spots, a squat triangular roof like an American toddler's drawing of a house. On my way I passed the library, the post office, the town hall, signifiers of a shared civic life, low-ceilinged rooms where the homeless and the elderly might congregate, holding their paper tissues and their linen handkerchiefs. All closed for the evening. I could not find the moon. I kept my head bowed against the wind, my hands stuffed deep into my pockets. Stray bits of hair escaped my ponytail and stung my eyes.

Inside the Old Pilgrim the patrons all looked like fishermen, or what I imagined fishermen might look like. The men looked like fishermen and the women looked like fishermen. There was one child there with his mother, sitting on her lap, sucking at his thumb, and he looked like a fisherman, too. A redheaded woman who looked like a fisherman worked the bar. She seemed to dislike me instantly for reasons I could not ascertain. Was it the way I moved my body, floppily, twitchily, like a seal having a panic attack? That I stuttered when I ordered my beer? I put down a generous tip and watched as her face contorted into an expression of sincerest repulsion, lips flinching in their downward curve.

I settled with my drink at a table in the back corner, leaning against the wall to prevent myself from sliding off the stool. My glass was dirty and my beer was warm. A soggy light seeped into the room from the old-fashioned streetlamps outside, trickling through the front windows, thick with grime. I downed my beer and ordered another. At the surrounding tables patrons were talking, laughing, slapping one another heartily on the back. I tried to laugh, too, but whenever I made too loud of a sound those at the table closest to mine would stop speaking and glare at me. So I smiled silently, and nodded, and took dainty sips of my beer, picking it up with both hands, like an image I had once encountered of an adorable raccoon nibbling on something inappropriate—a pre-packaged toaster strudel, perhaps. This is my favorite bar, I whispered to myself. The fact that it was disgusting and that everyone obviously wished I wasn't there made me feel it was a genuine working-class establishment, by and for the people, and that I too was one of the people, undeniably one of the people here tonight.

Beneath my feet, I noticed, the floors were so heavily slanted that they appeared to have been constructed for the convenience of someone who had one leg much shorter than the other. It was really nice, I thought, that a person with one very short leg could finally have somewhere to go that was comfortable for them. Tears filled my eyes. I was already a little drunk. My own legs were of equal length. But when it came to the world of the mind, it was almost as if one of my legs was much shorter than the other—in some psychic or spiritual sense, I mean—and I wondered if there would ever be a place where I could walk, metaphorically speaking, with ease.

Someone at the next table bought a round of shots for all their friends. I watched as they slugged back the tiny glasses, slammed them down on the table, and cheered. I went to the bathroom and purged the pulled chicken enchiladas I had eaten for dinner. They came up slimy, green with tomatillo sauce. When I returned to my seat, a faint citrus smell was wafting through the room; someone had dropped an overripe tangerine, which rolled until it hit the back wall, leaking a rivulet of juice around which a colony of hungry fruit flies swarmed. I pulled out my phone. In my family group chat, my sister had sent a series of images from the previous Saturday, when she had insisted that we go out for dinner before I moved away, to "catch up," "just the two of us." There was a photo of her platter of steak frites; a selfie in which she displayed a forkful of rare beef adjacent to her smiling mouth; an image of my empty chair, which she must have taken during the five minutes I had been in the bathroom between courses; and a final composition that featured my bowl of French onion soup, behind which slumped my body in its seat, photographed only up to the shoulders, so that I appeared to be decapitated.

Beautiful! my mother had typed.

I swallowed the rest of my beer and went outside to smoke. It was colder than it had been on my walk over. The air was damp and briny, a clammy towel on my skin. Sheets of fog hung low in the sky, obscuring what stars there might have been, haloing the streetlamps. I pulled my coat tighter around me and spent a moment engaging in vivid thoughts about my life, my future and my past. I thought about my mother and father and the city in the middle of the country where I had grown up, from which I had first departed ten years prior, swearing that I would never, no matter the circumstances, return, and where I had been living for the past six months, with my parents, in my childhood home. I thought about several events that had taken place in my adolescence and several other events that had taken place in my adulthood. I contemplated the black eyes my sister received during her training as a semiprofessional MMA fighter, which she would display coquettishly to our parents when meeting them downtown for ice cream, giggling as the man who worked the scoop counter stared in concern. How hard, I wondered, would I have to punch myself in the face in order to form a black eye of my own?

After a moment I realized that the whole time I had been outside, I had been gawking directly at a human being, a man who was seated on the curb across the street. In response to my eye contact, it appeared, he was grinning and saluting me repeatedly with two fingers. I was unsure if I should salute him back. I decided to salute him back. He stood and shuffled toward me. He wore a camouflage cap and torn brown khakis, open-toed sandals despite the weather. The big toenail on his right foot was painted lavender.

The man greeted me with great politeness and asked if I could spare a smoke. Of course, I said. I loved giving away cigarettes, due to a vague sense I had that those who accepted them were thereafter bound to me for an indeterminate period of time by an undeniable duty and obligation—a belief that provided me with a shivering spasm of well-being, similar, I thought, to what others must feel when they disrobed in a sauna or sank into a fragrant bath prepared for them by a loved one. I watched the man's face as it bent over my lighter, sucking. His eyes were closed, as in a kiss on the mouth. The skin across his cheeks was shiny, stretched tightly over his bones, with the hardened, leathery quality that signifies countless hours spent outdoors. From inside the Old

Pilgrim, the murmur of voices sounded like a television show streaming in another room. A pickup truck rolled past, and from farther away there came the pulse of the constant undulating waves, lapping at the shore like some untiring, enormous-tongued animal.

The man introduced himself as Billy. I told him my name and explained that I had just moved to town that day. I'm teaching over at the Academy, I said. I gestured in the opposite direction from the water, where the narrow streets sloped slightly upward.

Oh, yeah? Billy said. Nice up there?

Yes, it was nice up there, I told him, though in truth I had only seen it in photographs.

Did they give you housing?

They gave me housing.

All those girls? he said slyly.

Yes, I said, all those girls.

He nodded the nod of a man who knew a good deal that he could not reveal about housing and girls.

What subject? he asked.

English literature, I said. I explained that I had been hired late in the season, remotely and hurriedly, as a yearlong temporary leave replacement. I did not know who had gone on leave or why. It didn't matter to me. I was grateful to have an income, health insurance, and a reason to move away from the city in which my father, mother, and sister lived.

He nodded again and asked where exactly I was from. He told me that he was also from the middle of the country, although he had been moving around for a good while, and it had been many years since he had been back. He had spent some time in the city in which I had grown up but had found it inhospitable. I said that I had also found it inhospitable. I realized it was possible that Billy meant inhospitable in the sense of the high cost of living and the long and terrible winters and the cops who liked to strut around the parks at dusk, looking for people who were asleep so they could beat them awake with their batons, whereas I was referring to the fact that whenever I was back in that city I felt pretty sad.

Billy took a deep drag.

What kind of smokes are these? he asked.

I named the brand with a flash of pride—expensive, organic, additive-free.

You ever smoked perique? he asked me. Perique tobacco?

I admitted that I had not.

That's the stuff, Billy said. He puffed out his chest, gull-like, filling himself up with cold air. Under the flaps of his jacket there was a small tear in his T-shirt, directly over his left nipple, which protruded like a knot of purple rope. That's the good stuff, he said. Full-bodied, full flavor. Real wet. You can only grow that stuff in Louisiana. I used to live down there, in New Orleans, he said. You ever lived down there?

I hadn't, I told him, then added that I had visited once for Mardi Gras.

Crazy down there, he said, shaking his head.

Years ago, Billy said, he had known a man in New Orleans, a wealthy lawyer who had come down after Katrina to try to do his part, to give back to the city in some small way. This man took time off from his job and worked hard every day, he did his part, he really got in there to help clean up the city, and then he developed a staph infection from the filth and the rot and the sewage and lost both of his legs and one arm and now his eyes were permanently rimmed in green goo.

I never saw anything like that, Billy said accusingly. Green goo is what it was.

The lawyer, he continued, hadn't been able to keep his job because no clients wanted to entrust the law to a man with no legs and only one arm who had green goo rimming his eyes, and his wife left him, and he was impotent, and he could only rarely see his little daughter now, due to the limited rights of men—fathers, especially—in this country.

I told him that this was a horrible story, a sad story. It was tragic, I said, the havoc Katrina had wreaked on the people of New Orleans.

Yes, Billy said, it was a tragic and horrible story; but it was also, importantly, a story with a moral. He paused and looked at me hard, as if to confirm that I understood the concept of a universal moral system. Two pedicab drivers, leftovers from the summer season, pedaled past, blasting dancehall music over the speakers they had strapped to their handlebars.

Mind if I have another cigarette? Billy asked. Once more he leaned over my lighter. I felt his breath on my hand. His lips, I saw, were flecked with white foam.

The former lawyer, Billy continued, had been an inspiration to him, because he had maintained his joie de vivre and commitment to the betterment of society even after he had lost both legs and one arm and acquired loads of green goo all over his eyes. He had been the leader of Billy's rehabilitation group in the hospital—that's how Billy knew him—and had struck such a cheerful and energetic figure there, in spite of his undeniable tribulations, that Billy had vowed never to forget him. Here Billy paused to demonstrate what the lawyer had looked like when leading the rehabilitation group, leaping off the curb and squatting down in the street—I imagined to replicate the lawyer's lack of legs—then pinning one hand behind his back and pumping the remaining arm up and down several times to the rhythm of an imaginary music before returning, out of breath, to standing position.

Billy had been hospitalized for three weeks in New Orleans, he explained, after having been thrown off a bridge by two meth-heads. He paused again to show me all the places on his body that had been wounded, bruised, or broken by the meth-heads. He grabbed my hand and slid it under his jacket, along the side of his torso, to demonstrate how the bones in his ribs had been crushed to dust by the fall from the bridge; he extended his arm and rolled up his sleeve and gestured at the soft skin on the underside of his wrist, which had also been broken by the meth-heads. Then he did a little hop and kicked out his right leg, which I assumed meant that his leg had been hurt in some way when he was thrown over the bridge, although he did not say so specifically. That's terrible, I said. Billy explained that one of the meth-heads was white and one of them was black. I nodded, feeling appreciative of his commitment to pointing out racial diversity among meth-heads. Billy told me he was a nationalist. Oh, I said. I wondered if I should have understood this already from the camouflage cap he wore over his matted, pale-brown hair—but to make an ideological judgment based only upon someone's choice of hat seemed to be against my values. He was Polish, he told me. It was the white meth-head, Billy said, who had given him the final shove over the bridge. He maintained a magnificent level of eye contact as he spoke. I began to fear that he might be falling in love with me. I told him I was Jewish.

Do you want to hear a Jewish joke? he said.

Yes, I wanted to hear a Jewish joke.

He cleared his throat.

A Jewish boy, Billy said, asks his father if he can borrow twenty dollars. His father says, Ten dollars? What are you going to do with five dollars?

He looked down at the ground, suddenly bashful.

I'm not very good at doing the voice, he said. It's better with the voice.

I repeated the joke back to him, doing the voice. He clapped his hands together, delighted.

That's it! he cried. That's it!

I told him it was my mother who was Jewish. My father had grown up a middle-class white Christian in Texas, and this was less interesting than my mother's tragic foreign upbringing and might even implicate me in the history of violent racism in the American South, so I did not talk about it often. But my mother was from Vilnius, which had at one time, I reminded Billy, shared a ruler with Poland, back when Poland was a glorious kingdom, and which had later been annexed by the glorious Second Polish Republic. Billy nodded approvingly. I did not tell him that my mother had, at the age of eleven, fled with her family from the Soviet Union to the relatively new state of Israel, and that before immigrating to the United States she had done her mandated years of IDF service, as this might implicate me in the ongoing genocide of the Palestinian people, and so it too was something I did not talk about often. I told him I loved kielbasa and potatoes and all kinds of meat- or cheese-filled dumplings and that I hoped someday to forage for mushrooms. I had always found Stalin attractive, I said, specifically in that well-known photograph people referred to as Hot Stalin, if Billy had ever happened to see it online, that photograph in which a young Stalin wears a checkered scarf and gazes smolderingly into the camera? With one eyebrow cocked? It was a controversial image because it had been retouched for propagandistic purposes—that was the claim—to remove the pockmarks that disfigured Stalin's face, scars from the smallpox he had contracted as a child, which had rendered him terribly ugly, people said.

I started to cry.

Since when, I shouted, do we call people ugly just because they have facial disfigurements from having contracted smallpox as children? Would we call someone ugly if they had, for example, one leg that was much shorter than the other? Or if they had no legs at all? Whatever happened to the concept of a radical interior beauty? Wasn't this, in fact, the point of Billy's story about the wealthy legless lawyer in New Orleans? That there can be such a thing as an interior beauty so fine and so strong that it radiates outward like a bright light from something we might, for argument's sake, call the soul? That a pure nature, an ethical and self-sacrificing nature, might shine through any physical so-called ugliness?

I began to describe the plot of *Bleak House*, which I hoped to teach my students that semester, even though it was way too long to teach to high school juniors, and even though I assumed my students, whom I had yet to meet, could probably barely read due to the devastating psychic effects of daily technological overstimulation and having been exposed to iPads as babies. I told Billy about the tragedy of Esther Summerson's disfigurement after she contracted smallpox halfway through the novel, and how Allan Woodcourt, the handsome doctor with a heart of gold who tended selflessly to the impoverished and the mentally ill, and who additionally saved many British lives after the events of an awful shipwreck (though not, to be fair, in narrative time), loved—adored!—Esther Summerson in spite of this disfigurement, and so her engagement to her much older legal guardian and father figure John Jarndyce, who had earlier proposed marriage via handwritten letter and appeared to expect a response via handwritten letter in spite of the fact that he and Esther Summerson lived in the same house (the titular Bleak House), had to be broken off. But this was all her guardian and father figure's own doing, John Jarndyce was delighted to break off the engagement, he had a kind soul, an earnest and noble soul, he wanted only Esther Summerson's happiness, he even decorated to Esther Summerson's tastes a little house for her to live in with Allan Woodcourt, a house that he decided to *also* call Bleak House, which seemed to me like it might eventually get confusing, but of course this was all at the end of the novel so really there was no "eventually," I wasn't one of those morons who believed that the characters in books were real people with lives, dreams, futurity beyond the page, and I did understand the emotional and thematic resonance.

I was still sniffling but had mostly stopped crying. Billy nodded emphatically. It was true, he said, that he had been smoking a little bit of crack when the meth-heads threw him over the bridge. Yes, he acknowledged, spreading his palms open like a mayor at a podium, he had undeniably been doing a little bit of crack back then. But only the good stuff, he explained, not that nasty stuff they sometimes sprinkled on the ends of his cigarettes. I told him that I had never done crack, and he told me that he was living on the beach, but that soon it would be too cold, and then he would have to move along.

You should come on down sometime, he said. We're in the alley behind the post office.

I thanked Billy for his offer, though I didn't know to whom "we" referred. I looked at the sky. The fog had rolled off. There was a moon above us now, waning. Through the alley I saw it cast its cold, pathetic light onto the water that sucked at the sand below. It pulled up the ocean, people said, which flooded the basements here, which rotted the wood and turned Main Street on some winter nights into a canal, as in an old European city. I watched Billy, who gazed lovingly into the Old Pilgrim. The bartender was waving, gesturing for him to come inside. Her red hair in the darkness resembled a beautiful bird's nest lit on fire. From a nearby dumpster there came the sweet and musty smell of decomposing seafood.

I waited for Billy to say goodbye to me. As he turned in my direction, I thought about how I respected the moon, but I feared it, too, like a man wearing the clean, crisp uniform of a hegemonic nation-state.

# 2

*

The topic of my seminar for juniors was The Literature of the City, a subject I had chosen because it was so vague. I could list many novels that were set in cities; it had taken me thirty minutes to write the syllabus. We were not in the city here, and therefore I could ask my students, if conversation flagged, to make astute observations about the ways in which this remote coastal tourist town was different from an urban environment. What is your favorite city, I might ask, and why? Later in the semester I would have the class compose sonnets about their most beloved aspects of contemporary urban life in the global West, such as cars, boutique salad restaurants, or hostile architecture in public spaces. I planned to offer the same remarks about all of the novels we read, plagiarized directly from texts I had been studying before I dropped out of graduate school. *"Country" and "city" are very powerful words*, I would say, *and this is not surprising when we remember how much they seem to stand for in the experience of human communities!*

My students, twelve of them, sat in the semicircle of desks I had arranged around a central whiteboard that hung from the classroom's rafters. Each wore the Academy's uniform: a knee-length pleated maroon skirt, a white polo shirt, patent leather shoes. The Academy had been founded in the 1970s, rather late for a boarding school, and now it put a great deal of effort into exuding an aura of continuity and tradition that strictly speaking did not exist. Its pervy prep-school uniforms were part of this endeavor, as were the historic wood cottages that made up its main campus. My classroom was located on the second story of one, under a steeply pitched roof, where children had likely slept when the building had been a family home. The cottages, I had learned during my orientation, were not original to the town, but had been purchased on the cheap from a sandspit deemed uninhabitable by the federal government, its shoreline sloughing off at a dangerous rate. The buildings were pulled by tugboat across the strait, then planted like shrubs on the Academy's freshly purchased parcel of land. Here the ground was soggy sand. Every year the cottages sank another inch into the earth.

A few of my students were gazing down at their notebooks; the rest whispered amongst themselves in trios and pairs. I turned my back on the group and wrote WHAT IS A CITY? across the whiteboard. It was a blustery morning, and from where I stood I could hear an object smacking repeatedly against the window, though the shade was drawn so I couldn't tell what it was. I feared it might be something evil. I had been on a double dose of my prescribed amphetamine stimulant when I came up with the course topic, and I was on a double dose of my prescribed amphetamine stimulant now, for the first day of class. My prescribed amphetamine stimulant was not a methamphetamine, my psychiatrist had hastened to inform me. I should not be concerned that my stimulant was a methamphetamine just because of its name. I should think of it, he said, as methamphetamine's cousin. I told him I was really happy to be prescribed methamphetamine's cousin. In general I tried to be cheerful and encouraging during my monthly telehealth appointments because I worried that my psychiatrist might be depressed and suffering from suicidal ideations. In between statements about dosage and hydration, he would often sigh loudly and gaze at an object beyond his laptop that I couldn't see. Over time I became convinced that he was looking at the image of a person he had once loved who had been brutally murdered by a repressive state, or perhaps who had cheated on him with another, more successful psychiatrist. Sometimes during our appointments he would excuse himself, stand up, and shuffle out of view of the camera, leaving me to stare at his empty desk chair until he returned, one to two minutes later, and began speaking again as if he had never left. Every time my psychiatrist prescribed me a new medication, he would say, You won't get addicted to this, right?, and then we would share a nice laugh. I was glad to provide my depressed psychiatrist with some moments of levity in what seemed to be an otherwise desolate existence.

I had taken a double dose of my stimulant before class because I knew, deep in my heart, that I was a horrible teacher, prone to irrelevant and rambling digressions about my personal life and the childhood maltreatment of Iosif Vissarionovich Stalin at the hands of his drunken shoe-cobbler father; that when I did manage to lecture on the topic of English literature, my lectures were boring and made no sense; and that I had a bad case of dry mouth. I knew all this deep in my heart because I had read each point verbatim on an internet forum where college students anonymously rated their instructors, back when I was teaching undergraduate classes as part of my fellowship, before I dropped out of my PhD program, left the state where I had been living with my ex-boyfriend and two roommates, and moved in with my parents. The stimulants did not make me any better at teaching, but they did stop me, I told myself, from living a "fear-based life." When I took a double dose of my stimulants I remembered that for every student who insulted me on the internet, there was likely one more who was afraid to speak their mind, but who had been as moved as I was by the story of a young Iosif Stalin's mother working tirelessly as a laundress to support her beloved son, protecting him from the alcohol-fueled rages of his father so that he could one day become a man of history, a man of steel.

I looked out at my students. They stared back at me with the vacant curiosity of idiot fish whose aquarium had just been tapped by a finger. I bid them a warm welcome to The Literature of the City, then asked for a volunteer to introduce herself and tell us about one book she had read over the summer. A pimpled girl with lank sheets of blond hair raised her hand, her eyes fixed in the middle distance, as if at the veil between worlds. She announced that her name was Anita. For some reason she had decided to stand when she spoke to me, as though I were her commanding officer in the military.

This summer, she said, I read a book called *The Trial*. It's about a man named Kafka who gets arrested for apparently no reason. Bad things keep happening to him, and he keeps saying he doesn't know why. Anita shifted her hair from one shoulder to the other and crossed her arms in front of her chest. Honestly, she said, it didn't make sense to me. When things happen in my life, I *know* why. I try to take responsibility. I think it's important to have those kinds of values, to instill them in your family, to see them reflected in your country. This guy Kafka kept acting like everything was out of his control. I didn't feel sorry for him. I thought, why don't you take a little initiative, buddy?

I started to thank Anita for her comments, but she ignored me and continued to speak.

For example, she said, that summer she had experienced a terrible incident. She was in Los Angeles visiting her infertile aunt, who lived with her new husband in a big Spanish Colonial on the west side. One night, Anita said, she was going to meet some friends for dinner a few miles from her aunt's house. She requested a car to come pick her up. She saw that the driver had a 4.9-star rating and had successfully completed 378 rides. As a woman, she said, she thought it was important to keep an eye on those statistics. Pretty soon the car was caught in traffic. That was when the driver asked where she was from. She felt uncomfortable with his question because in the app she had selected "quiet preferred," not "happy to chat." The driver repeated his question—so where are you from?—as if she hadn't heard him the first time. She could see his phone lodged in its holder next to the wheel, and "quiet preferred" was clearly highlighted on his app, too. She decided that the best way to handle the situation was to pretend that she was deaf, so she shrugged and pointed at her ears and shook her head to make it clear that she was medically incapable of hearing the driver talk to her.

Everything, she said, seemed okay after that. She was enjoying her ride, looking out the window, thinking about how sad it was that she'd have to return to the Academy in another month. It was raining, and all along the road the car lights reflected off the asphalt, which made it feel like there was no ground beneath her, just more lights and more cars. Then she noticed that her driver had started talking again. He wasn't looking at her, she said, and at first he spoke so quietly that she couldn't make out his words. But he kept getting louder. Eventually she realized what he was saying. Blow job, he said. Blow job, blow job, blow job. He didn't meet her eyes in the mirror. Since she had pretended to be deaf, she couldn't admit that she heard him. She felt caught inside of something and was overcome with the sudden, sickening sense that this was only the first of many times in her life when she would be caught in exactly this way. It was a trap, a knot, a bind, Anita said. It was a terrible situation. Blow job, blow job, blow job. The driver continued to say it until he dropped her off at the restaurant, where he waved goodbye as if what had taken place was normal.

If this had happened to Kafka, Anita said, he would probably have run around in circles, pulling out his own hair and screaming. But she wasn't going to do that. She had a different set of values from Kafka, who didn't seem to have any values at all, and she was going to exercise them. She believed in agency, especially in the agency of women. She believed in women taking initiative; you couldn't, she said, just let things happen to you. You had to make something happen back. So as soon as she got out of the car, she called her mom, who called their family friend, who happened to be the CFO of the rideshare company, and thankfully this story had a happy ending, in that the driver had been fired and permanently banned from signing into the rideshare application on his phone or computer. Unfortunately, it was difficult for Anita to hear the words "blow job" any longer without flashing back to that terrible evening.

When she had finished speaking, Anita sat primly down at her desk. She was sucking in her mouth so that she appeared to be chewing a sticky candy, but after a moment I discerned that she was only gnawing on her own cheeks. I thanked her for her comments. In my brain there was a pleasant buzzing sensation, as if a group of bees were participating in an orgy at the front of my skull. The classroom's heater was on, releasing months of dust into the air, particles that shook wildly under the fluorescent overhead lights. Students exchanged impregnable glances. I was having trouble deciding which parts of Anita's story I should address. In particular, I was unsure if I should ask Anita to in the future please refrain from using the phrase "blow job" in class, even in representative dialogue. I wondered if she felt any curiosity as to whether or not her driver had believed that she was deaf, or if she had considered that her story was actually two different stories, the story in which the driver suspected she could hear him, and the story in which he believed she could not. But she seemed to have no interest in this, or in the fact that for the rest of her life she would never know what was real. I thought this was really good for her. She had made a decision, and that was the narrative she was living by now. Most likely she had chosen the story that was more flattering to herself; many such forks in the road would continue to present themselves in her life, and at each one she would continue to choose whichever option flattered her most, and then eventually she would have something called a personality. I knew this to be accurate because I myself had approached many forks in the road where the stories about what had happened to me seemed to thicken and diverge, and I had chosen every time to believe in the narrative that painted me in the best light. Typically this meant accepting that people were fundamentally malevolent actors who wished more than anything to violate me, bring me down, and ruin my life. Occasionally the thought would enter my mind that the people who had violated me, brought me down, and ruined my life may have done so by accident, without sinister intent or design—but this was the worst thought I had ever had, and each time it emerged I would drag it quickly into the trash file of my brain, because that was my personality.

I told Anita I was sorry to hear that her driver had made repeated references to fellatio after she pretended to be legally deaf to avoid talking to him. It was good news for women everywhere, I said, that her family friend was the CFO of the rideshare company and had the power to fire people at will. *The Trial,* I continued, turning to face the rest of the class, is a wonderful book about authority, bureaucracy, and alienation. It's a text that deals with the latent violence of modern life, an issue that impacts us all, and I'm so happy, Anita, to hear that you enjoyed it! One teeny correction, however, is that Franz Kafka is the *author* of *The Trial.* The protagonist is a man named Josef K.

I wrote "Josef K." on the whiteboard.

I assumed his name was Josef Kafka, Anita said. She began to weep openly. Tears ran from the corners of her eyes down to her mouth, where her tongue flicked out automatically to lap them up. The girl seated beside her, who had a mop of bright violet hair, gave her several firm but gentle pats on the back, like she was burping a baby. The other students ignored the outburst and chewed their nails. Outside, a seagull screamed.

That is a really fair assumption! I said. I quickly tried to think of tender remarks that would make Anita stop crying so that I would not get fired and have to once more move back in with my parents. I told her that I appreciated her sharing her logic with the class. In fact, she had done me a great service by demonstrating for her peers an example of "close reading." This year, I said, addressing the other students, I was going to be asking them all to focus on articulating their arguments by pointing to evidence in the text. Anita had given us a perfect example of that. I saw that Anita's shoulders were still heaving gently, but she was no longer licking the tears from her face. She showed us, I went on, how she reasoned that Josef K.'s last name was Kafka due to the following evidence: a) we know Josef's last name starts with the letter K because that is the initial given to us in the text, and b) we know the author's own last name is Kafka. Though Anita's ultimate deduction was not one hundred percent correct, it was nonetheless a fine attempt at rigorous textual analysis.

*The Trial*, I said, relates to the topic of this course in that it is set in an unidentified *city*. I gestured at the word CITY on the whiteboard. You can tell because it features an *impoverished neighborhood*. I wrote down "impoverished neighborhoods." I noticed that my hand was shaking. My phone illumined itself on the desk. I had two missed calls. The part of my brain that was stimulated by methamphetamine's cousin told me that my students would probably be pretty interested in hearing about my family background right now. The other part of my brain said, *maybe not, maybe they will write that you have narcissistic personality disorder on your end-of-year evaluations,* but that part of my brain was not so buff.

Franz Kafka's *The Trial*, I said, also happens to be the book that my mother was reading when she first met my father, in an elevator, at music school in New York City, shortly after she immigrated to the United States. I asked the class if they knew much about the Baltic nations. No one responded. On the white-board I drew a blob and divided it into three sections, which I labeled Estonia, Latvia, and Lithuania. I shaded in another blob to the left of the first blob and wrote "Baltic Sea." I explained that these three countries were annexed by Iosif Stalin's Soviet Union first in 1940 and then again, after a brief occupation by another nation, in 1944. I pointed to Lithuania on the map. My mother was born in Vilnius, a *city*—I gestured once more to the word CITY on the board—at one time known as the Jerusalem of Lithuania, due to its vibrant Jewish intellectual life, but her parents were originally from other parts of the country, villages to the north and the west.

My mouth was getting very dry. With each word I could hear the smack of my tongue sticking against my palate. I took a sip of water from the glass on my desk and peered at my students' shoes, all identical Mary Janes, then up at their faces: feral, shiny with highlighter and gloss, dark blush, dewy concealer, makeup designed to make them look like wet babies with brain problems. I understood that looking like a wet baby with a brain problem was sexually attractive to men. A hot spasm of fury ran through me—not fury with men for being attracted to the physical traits most commonly associated with infants, but fury with myself for no longer looking remotely like a two-year-old. I had wasted my life, I thought. By "my life," I meant the years in which I had looked most similar to a baby. My fingers moved unconsciously to graze my own cheeks, undeniably the cheeks of an adult with a chronic fungal infection who woke each morning to find flakes of yellowish skin piled on the pillow, like fish food.

I asked the class if they knew which country had briefly occupied Lithuania in between its two annexations by Iosif Vissarionovich Stalin's Soviet Union. The girl with the violet hair raised her hand.

Germany, she said. It was Nazi Germany.

Excellent! I cried. On the whiteboard I drew a flag with a swastika on it and an arrow pointing toward the blob that represented Lithuania. I asked the student for her name. Thales, she replied. She had been named after the first known Greek philosopher, Thales of Miletus, who thought everything was made of water. She knew, she said, that this was really weird.

Thank you, Thales, I said. I turned back to the board, crossed out the swastika, and drew a hammer and sickle in its place. Did anyone in the class know the term "collectivization"? I asked. Had anyone ever heard of a "Russian kulak"? I wrote down "economic power of the kulaks." I realized that no one was listening to me except for Thales, who nodded continuously, mouth slightly agape, with the showy enthusiasm of a born bootlicker. In the rest of my students' faces, I observed an identical slackness behind the sheen of their makeup. Anita was rocking back and forth in her chair, no longer weeping, and instead whispering what appeared to be a self-soothing incantation into her shirt collar.

My eye landed on a third student who had not yet introduced herself. She sat at one end of the semicircle, her chair at a subtle angle away from her classmates. She was plain, with a square jaw and a thick, slovenly appearance that put one in mind of a thumb. Her body stretched its shirt with a natural heft that I knew, intimately, was worse than fatness, in that no amount of calorie-cutting, intermittent fasting, purging, laxative abuse, volume eating, or overexercising would ever make a meaningful impact. I could not read this student's expression, and yet it felt familiar to me, as when encountering an object once seen in a dream. It wasn't the bored disinterest of her classmates, nor was it excitement; it wasn't distaste, it wasn't distraction; there was nothing cheerful about it but nothing exactly sad; and she appeared focused at least, not lost in a daydream. I wondered if maybe she needed to take a shit. Then it crossed my mind that what I was looking at was only the facial manifestation of a constant, lurking, low-grade fear, and I relaxed.

I glanced at the clock, swallowed another sip of water, and suggested to the class that we continue with introductions. I would tell them about the economic power of the kulaks, I said, at another time. I smiled at the big, plain girl, whose expression of what I now understood to be constant low-grade fear continued to ride her face like a crippled donkey, and whose entire life, due solely to the accident of her birth, would likely be characterized by repeated scenes of rejection, false hope, and humiliation—very sad—and asked if she would introduce herself next and tell us about one book she had read that summer.

If she was surprised that I had singled her out, she didn't show it. She first cast her eyes reflexively down at her hands, which she was lacing and unlacing in a stringless cat's cradle, then met my gaze and offered a closemouthed smile. When she spoke, her voice caught me with its firmness; it was a beautiful voice, in fact, its syllables long and round, lending her speech a weirdly old-fashioned transatlantic quality.

Hallo, she drawled. I'm Cordelia. This summer I read Thomas Mann's *The Magic Mountain*. In general I'm interested in thinking about the citification of literary production in relation to America's urban sprawl and ever-expanding hinterlands. So I'm looking forward to the class. She hesitated. On a different note, she continued, her voice ringing out even more clearly, I was curious if you knew where Mr. Nelson is?

When she said "Mr. Nelson," Cordelia's cadence took on what seemed to me to be a defiant aspect; the more closely I scrutinized her, however, the more difficult her affect was for me to read. When she was silent, she exuded fat, sullen insecurity, which felt appropriate. But when she spoke her tones were lilting, husky, and grandiose. And yet her neck was wide and short; her head, which rose from her shoulders like a dense, concrete dome, loomed above her; inside of her shirt, her large, sloppy breasts were too adult for her childish face. This combination of beauty and ugliness disturbed me, as I had been disturbed in my youth whenever I went to the opera, where my mother played in the pit during the winter season, only to discover that the romantic soprano was aging and obese. I could not assimilate the contradiction, and it had been one of the major reliefs of my life when, as I got older, the company at last began to hire sexier singers.

At the reference to Mr. Nelson, several students smirked while several others looked down at their desks. Cordelia's eyes remained fixed on me. I was certain that I wasn't wrong about her constant, lurking, low-grade fear, even if it was currently submerged beneath some other performance, because since the day I was born I had moved through my own life like an animal biologically destined to be prey, and Cordelia looked exactly like me. But there was an elusive quality about her, a remainder I couldn't identify. It was clear, I thought, that Mr. Nelson was the teacher whose temporary leave had allowed me to secure this job so late in the season, and I also assumed, based upon Cordelia's tone and the reaction of her classmates, that she was or had been in love with him. It was possible that he had encouraged her affections. Perhaps he had seduced and molested her. Another student may have anonymously reported their relationship in a fit of concern or of envy, and Mr. Nelson might now be the subject of an internal investigation, leading to my hiring for the year. If he were to be found responsible, then perhaps I would be able to keep his job for the rest of my life.

None of this was unusual. It was so not unusual that it was banal. Thinking about it, and about how not unusual it was, was also banal. I remembered a friend I once had, before I stopped speaking to everyone I had ever met before the age of eighteen, who had accused me of being "obsessed" with pedophilia. Please stop coming to parties, taking six shots of cherry-flavored vodka, and screaming "everyone is a pedophile," she had said. Please stop screaming "women be getting date-raped" at each party you attend, because it massacres the vibe, and people aren't certain if you mean there are women getting date-raped at that particular party at that particular moment, if they should go try to find and rescue these women right there and then, or if you're offering a more systemic critique, in which case they can continue partying. I explained to her that I was not "obsessed" with anything, but that if I *were* "obsessed" with something, it would not be pedophilia, but ephebophilia. No one cares about the difference between pedophilia and ephebophilia except for you, my friend said. This was exactly the point, I said. The point was that people should care. It was an essential distinction. Often when people said pedophile what they really meant was ephebophile, in that they were referring to adults who were sexually attracted to post-pubescent adolescents, not pre-pubescent children. Why did that matter, my friend said. Obviously, she said, everyone got the point, whether or not you specified the child in question's proximity to pubescence. It *mattered*, I said, because language mattered. I was a student of English literature, I reminded her. I believed in the power of language. I believed in the supremacy of speech-acts. Didn't she care, I said, that when we were in high school—this conversation had taken place one or two years after graduation—six of our teachers had been fucking students? That all around us, people were illegally thrusting and humping and fucking and feeling each other up and exchanging nudes? People who shouldn't have been engaging in any of those behaviors? Didn't she ever wonder, I asked, why none of those students had been herself? No, my friend said, she didn't wonder that. Some of those teachers, I went on, ignoring her, had been pedophiles, and some of them had been ephebophiles, and you could tell which was which based upon the age and absence or prevalence of secondary sex characteristics in the students they had molested. If my friend wanted, I could explain to her my theories about which of our teachers, exactly, had been pedophiles and which had been ephebophiles. I thought I had a pretty good sense at this point, because in the years since the scandals broke I had closely studied the physical traits of each victim. I had thought about their bodies, I said, almost every day. No, my friend said, she did not want me to explain my theories. Then she asked me if, when I talked so much about pedophiles, sorry, she corrected herself, ephebophiles, it was because I actually wanted to talk about the thing that had happened to me at Benjamin Leichter's seventeenth birthday party, when Benjamin Leichter's parents were out of town in Costa Rica, that thing that had happened after midnight, when Benjamin Leichter and I went into his parents' bedroom? No, I said. It was insulting, I said, to imply that I would only take a stand against the rampant pedophilia and ephebophilia that infested our educational system because of something that had happened to me one time in Benjamin Leichter's parents' bedroom and another separate but related thing that had happened to me several years later. It was true, I admitted, that neither my friend nor I had technically been one of our school's numerous victims of pedophilia or ephebophilia, but nonetheless all of that illicit sexual activity had been *in the air.* Surely my friend couldn't deny the pungent whiffs of pedophilia and ephebophilia that had wafted through *the air we breathed.* My friend told me she was sorry that I was sexually frigid and incapable of experiencing orgasm-with-partner. Female pleasure was beautiful, radical, and politically subversive, she said, and when she thought about how I was a fundamentally sexually frigid person because of what happened to me when I was a seventeen-year-old virgin in Benjamin Leichter's parents' bedroom and the other related thing that happened to me several years later, it made her want to cry. I asked her if she had ever actually cried about it, and she said no, she had never literally cried about it using her face, but that inside of her, the part of her soul that attended to female empowerment often wept about the things that had happened to me and what those things had done to my capacity for sexual pleasure and my personality more generally.

Thank you, Cordelia, I said to the class. *The Magic Mountain* is a very long book about disease and death, both physical and spiritual, that does not take place in a city. It takes place on a mountain, in a sanatorium.

I turned and wrote "spiritual death" on the whiteboard. I paused, then said, I'm not certain about Mr. Nelson—maybe you can ask your advisor.

I suggested that we take a short break to rest our minds and stretch our legs, after which we would go through the syllabus, beginning with the class's first assigned text: *Bleak House* by Charles Dickens—one of the finest novels of the city. A few students left for the bathroom, heads bowed, murmuring. I hurried down the stairs, ducking to avoid a low wooden beam, and stepped outside, where the wind was lifting freshly raked leaves from the courtyard and distributing them to other areas of the lawn. A pale sunshine fell upon the buildings that emerged like teeth from the Academy's hill, their facades facing the bay in a state of expectation. The light here was sea light: forbidding, austere, not very nice. From campus I could see where the town tumbled toward the ocean, houses coated like candy in cedar shingles. Thick ivy crawled up the sides, withering into filmy yellows and browns. There were front yards, green shutters, blue shutters, flower boxes. Blah blah blah, I thought. Once this had been a fishing village. Men sailed out to deep waters and slashed at whales with long harpoons, lancing hearts the size of kindergartners and binding the dead animals to their ships, rendering blubber in massive pots, stinking up the place. The oil went into lamps and, later, into the new American manufacturing. Schoolteachers got paid in vats of it. Now the town's economy was the summer money of city people. There were fudge shops, CBD shops, small-batch ice-cream stores. There were T-shirt emporiums and golf-cart rentals. Children took turns mounting the monstrous sculpture of a humpback whale that sat out on the old fishing pier, grasping its sides between their thick legs, shoving damp fists into its mouth. As for me, I consumed fish oil as a dietary supplement, two juicy capsules each morning, to maintain my mood and my energy levels.

I watched as a student not in my class, swaddled in a puffy jacket, trudged from one building to another. Her head was down, as if she had lost something precious in the grass, something I was sure she would never find. I suddenly thought of winter evenings in the city where I had grown up, when I would sneak out of the house, coatless, and stand in the street, staring longingly up into my own bedroom window, where I could see my bed, my desk, my chair, all illuminated by a warm golden light.

I put my phone to my ear. The wind moved against my face, moved my hair back.

When my sister looked back on our childhood, her voicemail told me, she remembered the happiest days of her life. Personally, she would have loved nothing more than to return to the womb, emerge again from our mother's vagina, and live out each day of her adolescence for a second time. My sister wasn't certain why I said the things about our parents that I said, why I did the things I did. Mama and Papa were her very best friends in the world, the voicemail said. I was also, the voicemail reminded me, her very best friend in the world. She was concerned, as were my parents, about the direction my life was taking. I was too old to behave in the ways that I did. I was almost thirty, said the voicemail. The wind picked up a crumpled candy wrapper hanging from my pocket and carried it to the other side of campus, where it spun, writhing, a shiny bird showing off. Sometimes the only conclusion my sister and parents were able to come to about me, the voicemail said, was that I was biologically off-balance, mean-spirited, and mentally ill. Was this true? the voicemail asked. Why else, the voicemail asked, would I not also wish to re-enter my mother's vagina like crawling up a waterslide to slip out for a second time? Why had I dropped out of graduate school? Why was it that I no longer spoke to anyone I had ever met before the age of eighteen and so few people I had met after the age of eighteen? The voicemail went on for several minutes, during which I mostly zoned out from what my sister was saying and instead thought about the long, handwritten letters I used to leave under her pillow while she purged her dinner in our shared bathroom, when she was seventeen and I was thirteen. Because my sister was older, she had the right to purge first, our own special form of primogeniture, and by the time I took my turn kneeling before the toilet, the air would already be filled with the sweet, sulfurous smell of her intestinal juices. In my letters I wrote that my sister had an enviable body, slim in all the right places, with perfect, aquiline nipples, and that I would do anything in the world to make her happy. It was like in Dickens's most ambitious novel *Bleak House*, I realized now. My sister and I had lived in the same home, but still I left letters under her pillow instead of speaking to her out loud.

# 3

*

The Academy's Director of Facilities was a balding, middle-aged man named Petar. Already I had grown accustomed to seeing him dash around campus clutching a metal toolbox, a denim sherpa-lined jacket flapping open over his impressive belly. He was a big man, but light on his feet, as if his limbs were filled with compressed air. What hair he had left sat on his skull in a smooth swirl, like a frosted cake. I had met him briefly at orientation, where he spoke at length about the beauty of this town, his love for oceanic bodies in general, and the delicacy of the Academy's septic tanks, an ecosystem in themselves. There had been a digression, I remembered, about spa resorts on the Black Sea, their outrageously affordable deals for tourists, which, as it went on, sounded more and more like an advertisement. Now he had come to my Academy-provided faculty housing unit to take a look at the pipe beneath my kitchen sink, which had been leaking for the entire three weeks since I had moved in—a slow, silent drip discernible by the puddle of murky brown water that swelled each hour on the linoleum floor. In the mornings I stared at it from my armchair like a Rorschach test. I saw apocalyptic goo, a mushroom cloud, a snail wearing a top hat, a swastika. When the puddle reached a certain size, I would wipe it up and toss the sodden paper towels into the trash can, where they would land with a wet plop, and then, hours later, the process would repeat itself.

When I let Petar into my unit he immediately began to bustle about, ignoring the pipe to demonstrate the superiority of my apartment's amenities with personal satisfaction, as if my living quarters were the beautiful new wife he was at last introducing to a cousin with whom he had always competed sexually. I trailed him into the bathroom, where he pumped ardently at my shower handle, showing off the excellent water pressure; I followed him back to the living room and watched him hop between windows, pulling plasticky shades up and down again to prove that they were functional. Wow, he remarked each time an item worked in the way it was supposed to, then stared at me in anticipation. His accent was faintly Slavic, familiar, like an old itch. Wow, I said. Only then would he grin and move on.

Housing for faculty and staff was on a street adjacent to the main campus, in a long, three-story structure with a private courtyard in the back. The building made me think of an enormous boxcar. When I observed it from the outside, projecting the way its walls would engulf the roundness of my body, I was overcome by a simmering ontological panic, but as soon as I crossed my unit's threshold those feelings receded. From the top floor, I had heard, one could make out the thinnest sliver of ocean, which might appear, depending upon the time of day and the quality of light, greenish or blueish or grayish or sometimes a creamy, foaming white. Those apartments, in high demand, were generally occupied by deans and department heads. My own was on the ground floor, one of two wheelchair-accessible units. It looked out onto some dead bushes. A wooden ramp fitted with a waist-high metal railing sloped to the front door. The floors throughout were smooth, the pathways for movement wide and arching, reminding me of an indoor ice rink, recently Zambonied. Below the kitchen sink, there was an open space so that you could roll right under to do the dishes. You could roll right over to the couch and you could roll right into the shower. The unit's layout was such that the only way to navigate between the bedroom and the living room was via the bathroom, which formed a central connecting artery through which one could roll the whole length of the apartment in a straight line.

When I looked at the bathroom, I understood that my unit, though spacious and in some sense ergonomic, was designed for a person who would always live alone, or perhaps for a couple that enjoyed shitting in front of one another. Sometimes at night when I was coming down from methamphetamine's cousin, induced dopamine seeping from my brain, I would think about this. Couldn't a person who used a wheelchair, an adult, a living human sexual being, have a casual erotic encounter in their own home with someone they might prefer not to piss or shit in front of? At times I wished that I was in a wheelchair so that I could at last take a stand and advocate for myself.

It's a very nice space, Petar was saying proudly, opening and closing a closet door. Very large for one person, and the courtyard, you can treat it as your own. I looked through the window over his shoulder. Outside, the attractive young landscaper was raking wet leaves and heaving them into a bin with both hands, pausing on occasion to smooth the hair in his glossy, nipple-length ponytail. Above him the sky wobbled like a jelly. He wore a sweatshirt, duck boots, a mossy green beanie. I watched as he rolled his eyes at a seagull that flew from one silvery tree to another, squawking, and envisioned his penis dangling out of his pants—a long, worn-out squid, an exhausted squid that had been working hard its whole life. The landscaper's method of lifting the leaves using only his hands seemed, I thought, highly inefficient. He gave a sudden phlegmatic cough, which sounded, through my closed windows, like it was coming from inside a glass jar.

I used to live in the unit next to this one, but soon my wife and son are coming to join me, Petar said, leaning against the closet, and so I have to have a larger apartment. My son, he will be thirteen years old next month. He smoothed a hand over the curve of his stomach when he said the word "son," as if referring to a vivid memory of a pregnancy that had engorged his own body. I asked where his family was coming from. Plovdiv, he said, and I nodded to signal that I knew where Plovdiv was, though in truth I could not quite remember. In Bulgaria, he added. I nodded more vigorously. There were many Bulgarians here in town during the summers, Petar explained, who came to work, and some, like himself, who were able to obtain visas to stay through the year. Some Serbians, also, he said dismissively, but very many Bulgarians especially. The word must have gotten around, he said, chuckling, closemouthed. One comes and we all come. I laughed too. He stopped laughing.

You know the J-1 visa? Petar asked.

I think so, I lied.

For university students, he said, to come and work here, in the United States, during the summers. Many college students from Bulgaria. They come, make some money, party, go back. It's hard, he said, shaking his head. They work seventy, eighty hours a week. You know the H-2B visa? he asked but didn't wait for my answer. Temporary work. All those Jamaicans. You see all those Jamaicans? In the back of the restaurants?

I acknowledged that I had seen some Jamaicans, yes, in the backs of the restaurants.

H-2B, he said. And myself, also, H-2B, though hopefully soon EB-3. Oh, but I miss my fresh Bulgarian meat, milk, and fruit, Petar continued darkly. Then he cheered up. And I miss the gorgeous Bulgarian women! Although I also of course love American women! Who doesn't love American women! Except you touch them with a feather and they call the cops! You get a divorce and where does your money go! They haven't worked a day in their lives! But where does your money go!

We both laughed happily at that. I was relieved that Petar and I appeared to be getting along better now. He had seated himself at the rectangular wood table that sequestered my living room area from the open kitchen and was gesturing at me to take the chair across from him. I was not sure if he remembered that he was supposed to repair my pipe. I was not sure he had any idea who, in particular, I was. But that all was irrelevant. I was forming a human connection, engaging in an experience of relation. Petar had Slavic roots. I had roots similar to Slavic roots. I knew that in order to enhance community bonds it was important to find sites of commonality; it was important to affirm the other's identity, to hollow out a compartment inside of oneself, like a jewelry box, into which a person could deposit their special struggles and their special suffering. I looked forward to sympathizing with Petar about, for instance, the rampant Slavophobia in this country, then forcing him to listen to everything that had ever happened to me, in addition to all the things I feared might happen to me in the future if I continued to live my life in the way I was living it.

I asked Petar if he would like a beer, and before he could respond I grabbed two brown bottles from the fridge, set them on the table, and pried them open. It was a Friday afternoon. The light that tilted into my apartment from the courtyard had a dim and hazy quality, almost blurred. I thought of the shortening days, the disempowered sun, the slow and dizzying decay of my body. There were new shadows cast across the grass outside and drooping down from the edges of my mouth. There were mounds of dust in the corners of my living room, globbed together with bright blue fleece bits that had pilled off the sweatpants I wore whenever I wasn't teaching.

A ribbon of foam volcanoed down the side of my bottle and slid onto the table. Unthinkingly I bent my head and lapped at it like a cat. For a moment I had forgotten that I wasn't alone.

Yucky, Petar said.

I wiped my mouth with the back of my hand and attempted to think of an alluring series of remarks that would distract from what I had just done. I told Petar that I had never been to Bulgaria, but that, like him, my mother was from the former Soviet bloc, though when she moved away it wasn't yet former. She had been born in the city, I said, in Vilnius; her parents were originally from the country. Petar looked bored and spiritless. My mother and I had a complicated relationship, I went on, very complicated, very difficult. Obviously I had empathy for the things that had happened to her. I had empathy for what it meant to flee from a place and never return. I had empathy for what it meant to be born to deranged and traumatized parents, one of whom—my grandfather—had escaped his hometown and spent the war years laboring at a Soviet munitions factory in Tashkent, the other of whom—my grandmother—had been ghettoized with her family in Kovno, where her mother and twelve-year-old sister had been shot, their bodies thrown into a mass grave, which I had visited once when I was vacationing in Eastern Europe with my ex-boyfriend, although my mother herself had refused to ever return to her home country. My grandmother, who had at the time of the war been seventeen, continued on to Stutthof, and later perhaps Buchenwald—my mother could not remember clearly, my grandmother was dead and could no longer be asked—while her father journeyed to Dachau and then Auschwitz, where he was gassed to death, and it was only after the liberation of the camps by the armies of Iosif Stalin that my grandmother ended up in Vilnius, where she met my grandfather, whose parents had also been murdered. Sadly my grandparents' marriage was not the happiest one. My ex-boyfriend and I, too, I told Petar, had not always been the happiest of couples—or, to be more precise, we had often been the happiest of couples, but it was a happiness that made me sick, like a man who, stumbling upon water while lost in the desert, slurps it up so eagerly that his brain cells swell and engorge and press against his skull until he vomits and dies. In any case, my relationship with my ex-boyfriend was irrelevant to the topic at hand. Rich blankets of grass and wildflowers were growing now over the mass graves in Kovno, filmy greens and balmy yellows, so lovely that several years back one killing site was rumored to have become a destination for Lithuanian wedding photoshoots and graduation parties, a story that various Western and Israeli news outlets had enjoyed reporting upon.

I understood, I said, how, in an oblique way, events such as these could bear a relation to something like my mother's mania for purchasing obscene quantities of designer purses on clearance at her favorite department stores, then forcing me to observe and praise each one in exaggerated terms, after which she would narrow her eyes and accuse me of wanting her to die so that I could have all of the purses I had just professed to love so dearly, as well as her money, her shoes, and her big diamond ring. My mother's accusations were not exactly "true," but I could not say that they were "false." Although I was not literally a refugee, I told Petar, I was pretty sure that I could relate to refugees on a symbolic level; for example, often in my dreams I found myself chased through cavernous train tunnels by men wearing military uniforms, armbands, and spooky triangular caps. I was aware that this had never happened in "real" life, that in "real" life I was an American Jew who had attended a private liberal arts college with a yearly tuition double this country's average salary in order to study the humanities, contemplate but not engage in group sex, sell my sweaty socks to pervs online for cigarette money then brag about it to all my friends, and stop shaving my legs. But I was committed, intellectually and spiritually, to the world of dreams. I had intergenerational trauma, I said. Had Petar heard about intergenerational trauma?

Across the table, Petar was repeatedly sticking a finger deep into his beer bottle and yanking it out so that it produced a wet popping noise. Mmhmm, he said absentmindedly. He appeared to be scrupulously absorbed in his finger's task. I tried to discern whether Petar and I were having an erotic encounter. Was the rim of his bottle a stand-in for my sex organs? For my sphincter? Because I was a fundamentally sexually frigid person, I did not ever seem to have the answer to questions like these.

Sometimes I got spanked as a child, I said hopefully. And my mother would call me a little American retard whenever I told her I loved her.

Outside there was a sound that may have been the landscaper passing gas or the creaking of a door, possibly the door to the shed. Petar's T-shirt rode up, exposing the fine river of hair below his belly button. I imagined it snaking into the black musky bloom of his pubes.

Did you explain to your mother about the R-word campaign? Petar asked.

Yes, I said. I had told my mother about the R-word campaign, but it hadn't made any difference.

Petar nodded. He pushed his empty bottle aside with a thoughtful air. I feel sorry for your mother, he said. Having daughters is hard. I think it is hard. Of course I do not have a daughter myself. But I believe that I can understand what it is like. For me, the girls at the Academy are like my own daughters. Each one of them, yes, he said, I love like a daughter. His voice had taken on a new texture, as though a thick ooze had swollen his tongue. My wife and my son will be happy to be here, he continued, where there are so many intelligent, sweet girls, and where there are also one million different T-shirts to buy, each in a different color and featuring a different design, so unique and so fun. Petar spread his arms wide to show me the physical volume that best represented the quantity of fun, unique T-shirts available for his wife and son to purchase when they arrived from Bulgaria. He paused once more.

My wife and I, he said, we wanted a little girl, too. Our son Georgi was supposed to have a younger sister, to be named Simona, after my wife's mother, but she was born, I don't know how you say it in English, she was born dead.

Stillborn, I said.

That is a nice way of putting it, Petar said.

The sun blazed through a window and tossed itself between us on the table, warming my throat. In the patch of light, a fly landed. Petar slapped it against the wood, then brushed its carcass onto the floor. I knew I would never sweep it up, that my best and only hope was that someday a fatter, more vicious insect would find and digest its corpse. I finished my beer and looked anew at Petar's large arms, encased like liverwurst in their denim tubes. It was clear that he did not give a shit that I had intergenerational trauma. Unfortunately I did not feel that I had much else to offer in terms of sexual charisma.

Do you know all the students here well? I asked aloud.

He nodded. Of course, some better than others, he said. But they are good girls, really very good girls.

I was surprised to hear him say this. No other member of the staff or faculty had so far come close to claiming that the students at the Academy were very good girls. The school's origin had been outlined to me on several occasions. In 1971, the story went, Robert D. Elwood, the only son of an oil mogul, had dropped acid on the site of a former commune in New Mexico and epiphanically determined, while tripping, that it was one of his life's several purposes to dedicate time, funds, and energy to the cause of women's education by becoming the sole founder of an all-girls boarding school on the Eastern Seaboard. In his own youth Elwood had been educated at the company compound in Dhahran, but he chose to build the Academy here in this remote tourist town because his first childhood love, Martha Rose Schorheimer, had once mailed him a postcard featuring the image of its lustrous seaside on a sunny day. Some months later, Martha Rose had been killed in a gruesome accident at one of her father's munitions factories in Missouri—but the postcard, with its calm blue harbor and its calm blue sky, had imprinted itself upon Elwood's mind and rose up later in his life, specifically at the age of twenty-six, when he was high on acid in New Mexico, *where every valley*, he liked to say, *is a rich and fertile basin of light*, contemplating how best to launder his family's reputation at the end of the postwar era.

Other boarding and preparatory schools boasted centuries of alumni who had gone on to become founders of charities and dot-coms, novelists, arms dealers, surgeons, lobbyists, wives of lobbyists, painters, Silicon Valley investors, journalists, movie stars, restaurateurs, scholars, wives of hedge fund managers, bankers, wives of bankers, and members of Congress. The Academy had few such important alumni. Parents sent their daughters here because they had proven to be troubled, unbalanced, or prone to self-destructive and otherwise disturbing behaviors, such as acts of sadism involving animals or siblings. Many of these students were a flight risk, the Dean of Academics had told me during orientation, but Academy girls were not allowed to keep cars on campus, so it was nearly impossible for them to run away come winter, when there were no ferries and the sole bus that serviced the area pulled up only twice a week, almost never at the time noted on its schedule. The easiest way for a student to leave in the midst of the school year, the Dean had explained, was to have an older boyfriend with a car who lived in this town or the neighboring one. And so it was not unusual, she said, to find men slinking around campus at odd hours, college-aged and beyond, wearing sweatshirts, wearing duck boots, wearing little earth-toned beanies. Regrettably, if a student was ugly, plump, hysterical, depressive, or for whatever other reason unable to snag an older boyfriend, the most direct way for her to leave the school was to walk into the ocean at high tide and drown.

It was difficult, the Dean of Academics had told me, to put a stop to all this illicit statutory sexual activity, but the faculty did the best they could. No, you couldn't keep an eye on it all, but it was still important to do the best you could, for legal as well as moral reasons. She was certain that I, like the rest of the faculty, would do the very best I could. I assured her that I had every intention of doing the best I could. Absolutely, I said. I explained that boundaries were important to me, that I was a person who believed that only through firm boundaries, only within certain inflexible structures from which we did not stray, could we be truly free. I knew from experience, I said, what could happen to a young person when these structures, which they had taken for granted, began to bend. I understood that they were more brittle than they appeared, prone to snapping suddenly into pieces and leaving one lying beneath a pile of rubble, heaving, gasping for air. No, I admitted, I had not personally been molested by any of the shocking number of pedophiles and ephebophiles who had infested my high school, but one shouldn't underestimate the psychic impact of having had behavior of that sort *in the air*. Many things, I informed the Dean, could be *in the air* without literally taking place, and it was precisely this *in the air*-ness that our culture failed to reckon with, in large part due to its disgraceful rejection of the robust scientific insights of Dr. Sigmund Freud, the neglect of which had caused us to degenerate into a society of babies, haunted by the world of dreams—

Excellent! the Dean had replied.

Under my kitchen sink, the puddle was once more beginning to pool. I saw Petar eyeing it.

What do you think it looks like? I asked flirtatiously.

I believe it is a puddle of water dribbling from a small fissure in your pipe, Petar said. He set his large hands on the table, preparing to stand.

Actually, I interjected before he could get up, there was one student in particular I was curious about, if he knew her. Her name was Cordelia, Cordelia Altman. A junior.

Petar clucked his tongue. He settled back into his seat. That, he said, was a horrible story. His eyes met mine with an expression that made it seem he had forgotten who I was, or that he was seeing me now for the first time. I worried he might not tell me the story. But then he did.

Cordelia's father, he said, had committed suicide two years ago. There was a younger sister, too, Eliza, a current freshman. Their father had left a suicide note in which he had written that if only his daughters had loved him more, he might not have needed to jump off a bridge and be dead for all eternity. Sadly, the note said, they did not love him more, and so he really had been given no choice. Cordelia's father had written that his daughters were his precious angels, sent to him by Jesus Christ, but that as they had grown older they had ceased to treat him with the tender affection they had displayed when they were babies and toddlers, and as such he felt that Jesus Christ had forsaken him, which, in the end, he wrote, was what compelled him to kill himself. This note, Petar explained, was published in several tabloids, because Cordelia's father had sent copies directly to the papers hours before he took his own life. He had run into trouble, financially and legally, for skimming off the top of the investments he had been making on behalf of several high-profile public figures, but in the note he made it clear that he wasn't killing himself because he had been caught embezzling clients' money for decades. It was his daughters, he wrote again and again, who symbolized to him the lost love of his lord, Jesus Christ.

All the Jesus Christ talk was especially bizarre, Petar said, because the Altmans are Jewish.

While he was speaking the sun had dropped behind a building across the street, draining my apartment of light. For some time we had been sitting in a blue semi-darkness. When Petar finished his story I stood up and switched on a standing lamp. I switched on my desk light. I switched on the sconces above my countertop. Petar remained seated, the pouches under his eyes growing more pronounced with each new illumination. He asked me if I could believe that a parent would do this. Yes, I told him. I could believe that a parent would do that. Through the wall came a thin wail of hysterical laughter—my neighbor's, a history teacher—punctuated by gentle hiccups. I had finished a second beer and felt a little sick, my brain squatting dense and tight inside my skull. Petar said, Ah, and then he said, Your sink, and then he jumped to his feet, buoyant and jovial once more. I no longer had any doubt that Mr. Nelson, about whom Cordelia Altman had inquired on the first day of class, was a rapacious ephebophile who had seduced and possibly molested a bereaved Cordelia after the suicide of her psychotic, thieving, Lear-ish father. Petar clambered to his knees and nudged his head under my countertop like a goat. The soles of his shoes were crusted with mud and sand. His socks, I saw, featured a pattern of tiny pink crabs, each pinching the next in an eternal loop. Across the ankle was written: GOT CRABS? I stood behind him, watching his ass bob and sway as he used his fingers to perform acts on the pipe that I could not comprehend, and I told myself that I really, really wanted to have sex with him; I made my brain form the sentence in letters, words scrolling across the screen of my mind like a message on a blimp, a practice I undertook as someone might undertake a meditation, because I hoped for or believed in the possibility of language's total domination of reality, because I did not believe in or hope for, I told myself, a prelinguistic world behind or beyond this one. *I'd love to have sex right now*, said the words on my mind-screen, *Wouldn't it be hot and horny to have sex right now*, and what I meant by this was that I wanted an authoritative male figure, preferably one who bore a strong resemblance to Iosif Vissarionovich Stalin in his later years—after the revolution, the five-year plans, the terror and the brutal war, after the attempted suicide of his eldest son, the successful suicide of his second wife—to dig a deep wide hole in the earth, tamping down the soil so that it became hard and cool and smooth as stone, then stand me at its edge, one hand clutching the nape of my neck like a mother cat, the sun glowing murderously above us, and whisper that I had been nothing but good since the day I was born, that he was so sorry about all the people who had violated me, brought me down, and ruined my life—his lips grazing my throat, his tongue probing my ear canal like a slug—then shove me into the hole and bury me alive.

Petar got to his feet and dusted off his knees. He would need to order a replacement part for the pipe. Once it came in, he said, this should be a quick fix.

Thank you so much, I said. Thank you so much.

In the world of my mind Petar's penis was alternately hardening and softening, as if it were performing calisthenics, even as he closed the door behind him. What a fascinating, innocent, and sexual penis, I thought dutifully.

I looked out the window. All the leaves were in their bins. The landscaper had gone home an hour ago.

Down at the harbor the water doubled the stars. It was later, nighttime. From a distant pier, a green light stuttered in my direction. I sat on a bench and watched the boats shiver along the dock like big sleepy cows, their hulls made ghostly by the moon and its reflection. Footsteps approached. There were water sounds, night birds, a faint far clanging. My head turned on its neck in an unconscious paroxysm of fear—not of the dark but of what might be hidden by it—a feeling followed by the sensation that nothing could ever hurt me that I didn't see. Soon the steps clarified into the outline of a woman walking her dog, wearing a headlamp like a coal miner. Her gait quickened when she noticed me, what I must have been to her: a shape with its hood over its head, its cigarette a spot of fire in the night. I understood that she was determining if I was going to rape her. The sound of her weight moving through the blackness passed me and receded, but even from a distance I could see the rays of light that haloed her skull, like the resurrected Jesus Christ in a medieval painting I loved. I was not going to rape her. Along the shoreline I thought I heard a soft laughter, possibly an Academy student who had snuck out of the dormitory to meet her older townie boyfriend. I put in my noise-cancelling wireless earbuds.

On my phone I watched a video my mother had sent to the family group chat, a recording of herself, my father, and a bald pianist I didn't know rehearsing Rachmaninoff's G-minor "Trio élégiaque." Every few moments the sleeve of whoever was holding the phone's camera lurched fuzzily into the frame. They rehearsed in a baroque-looking performance hall, gold pillars stretching to the ceiling, the two rows of seats in front of the camera empty, and I tried to make out if I recognized the space, maybe a cultural center downtown in the city where I had grown up, but maybe not. Both of my parents still held the orchestral positions they had won in their twenties, when they were younger than I was currently, and over the past decade they had also begun minor second careers performing chamber music as a duo or, as in this video, a trio, or a quartet. They played churches, community centers, school assemblies, the occasional small music festival on the West Coast or overseas. My mother maintained a website through which people could fill out a contact form for bookings. On the website she posted photos not only of my parents performing, but also of their lives together as husband and wife—my father sitting on their new-construction townhouse's wrought-iron terrace, smiling blandly in his sweater and silk scarf, sipping a coffee topped with foamed milk. A sunny day, but probably cold.

Beyond this image, I knew, the house was bright and clean, the dust wiped away each week by a Polish woman who lived far to the west of our neighborhood, who wore her hair in a gray crop, who had spoken Russian to me when I was a child, before I forgot how to speak Russian, and who still spoke Russian to me whenever I saw her, though these days I could barely understand. All my life this woman had referred to me by my diminutive, a name almost no one called me any longer. Each year on my birthday and my sister's she would bake us special cakes, thick and sticky, fragrant with ginger, which we would scoop straight into our mouths, our hands shaped like cups, then shit out, cramping, after chugging the laxative tea our parents stored under the kitchen island; and each year my mother would hound us to sort through our old clothes, a task I would delay for as long as possible, because I enjoyed the voluptuous feeling of ownership, how it felt to own even the garments I never wore, until finally I would give in and toss into a smelly crumpled pile my excess jeans and blouses and dresses, which my mother would wash and iron and fold and pack gently into boxes to ship to the woman's family back in Poland. Early one spring, I remembered, when I was a teenager, this woman had made a pilgrimage to the Vatican to watch the papal inauguration, one of the happiest days of her life, she later told me in Russian, to be so close to God, to be that close—from which she had brought back for our family a beautiful cross the size of my hand, made of rosewood and wrapped in the most delicate tissue paper. In my parents' cabinets there were sealed canisters of loose-leaf teas from Paris, tins of imported smoked mackerel. There were jars of gefilte fish and packets of dried linguine, purchased on sale, dyed black with squid ink. Forks, knives, spoons, inherited, real silver.

On my phone I saw my father's brow furrow as he drew his bow across the bridge, down to the frog, *tempo rubato*, my mother at rest, then lifting and leaning her chin into the violin after a few measures, her sound responding to my father's like the picking up of a dropped breath. The cameraperson's sleeve continued to dip in and out of view. Behind them the grand piano loomed prehistorically, my parents' bodies bending toward and away from each other so that for an instant they appeared to be made of cardboard. The music entered me. I blushed. My face was wet; even though, I tried to remind myself, Rachmaninoff had been an aristocratic fool, a bourgeois enemy of the revolution, fleeing Moscow for America, for New York City.

The video ended abruptly, and whoever was on the shoreline ran toward the dock, two sets of barely discernible footfall on soft sand.

When I got home I could hear porn playing loudly through the walls of my apartment. A woman moaned, the low keening of a wounded animal, and in response a man grunted, sputtered, honked like a car. I did not understand why my neighbor wasn't wearing headphones. I didn't, I told myself, actually care. I pulled a reading log from the top of the stack on my kitchen table. In addition to their assigned texts, I had asked my juniors to keep a journal in which they were to jot down their musings about books they read outside of class. I did not say books they were reading "for fun" because I did not want to instill the idea that reading was a form of consumerist entertainment. I wanted my students to understand that there was a difference between art and garbage, that there was such a concept as the aesthetic good, and that if they were going to be the recipients of generational wealth, the product of violent primitive accumulation and looted surplus-value, soaked in the blood of the global working class, they should at least use some of their stolen leisure time to cultivate a meaningful artistic snobbery. My parents, for instance, I wanted to say, were two people I could never forgive, two people who, though they looked normal—almost frail, even, almost old now—and though they no longer held any power over me, a reality that was in certain ways more painful than its alternative, were nonetheless ultimately responsible, I was convinced, for all the things that had violated me, brought me down, and ruined my life. Still, when I listened to them play, for example, their Rachmaninoff, with some ugly bald pianist I had never seen before, I was forced to encounter a quality inside of them—a shimmer, you could call it, or a pulse, or a soul—that in a fundamental way rose beyond all of the things I felt they had done to me. Encountering this, I would have liked to tell my students, made me want to throw up and die, but it was also comforting, in that it forced me to confront the fact that, compared to some parts of the universe, I was nothing. I was absolutely nothing.

But I did not express these sentiments to my students, largely because I had not discovered a good way to spin them in relation to The Literature of the City. Instead I provided no instructions about their reading logs at all, except to say that they should aim toward the truth—here I pointed to the ceiling of the classroom, as if the truth were an entity that could be found up in the sky, caught on a hook, pulled down—even if it meant admitting they had never read a book outside of class in their lives. My students, however, were idiots, frauds, and liars, and I had no doubt that most of their logs were falsified. I did believe Thales was reading Mishima, as her comments in class had lately begun to take on an odd shading of homoerotic nationalist fervor. And I believed Cordelia Altman, whose log I was currently reading, despite having combed through it several times already.

Through my wall I listened to a woman shriek out an orgasm, and in the log's margins I recommended with my purple pen that Cordelia give *Lolita* a go.

# 4

*

I found Billy in the alley behind the post office. He was low to the ground, squatting over his heels like a drunk woman taking an outdoor piss: knees bent, a side-to-side wobble as if maneuvering a cord tied around the ankles. It had been a mild autumn, but with enough cold spells that most people who had been sleeping out of doors—on the beach or on sailboats docked in the harbor—had made their way inland. I was surprised to see him there. He was exactly who I was looking for. My phone's calendar told me it was almost Thanksgiving. Once more, the days were descending with unseasonable heat, a bizarre counterpoint to the trees that rustled crispy and orange outside my classroom's windows, the crumpled rose heads strewn along my apartment's entry ramp like wads of toilet paper. The air simpered, delicate and moist; the sun ambled across the sky, strong as a bear. All around there was an ambient chirpy birdsong and a steaming, fertile smell that drifted from the bare flowerbeds lining Main Street. In the driveways of the empty clapboard houses, shut for the offseason, Jamaican and Bulgarian workers rested atop ladders like sailors at the prows of ships, smoking cigarettes. They smiled in the weather, with big male teeth.

Billy held a plastic fork in one hand and, in the other, a round plastic container brimming with slick noodles—take-out from the Chinese place down the street, one of the few restaurants open through the winter. A woman I had occasionally seen around town stood beside him. I could not discern her age. She was tall and thin, black, her hair dyed green and pulled into a low ponytail. At her feet lay a large gray dog. As I approached, it hoisted itself onto its stocky legs, enormous balls swinging, tight and shiny, as if from a short rope. Its jaws hung open, revealing a set of swollen gums and the requisite teeth. Drool ribboned from its jowls to the ground. It panted sensually in my direction, a heaving mouth sound that reminded me of the porn my history-teacher neighbor liked to watch on the other side of my living-room wall.

Billy put down his lunch and rose to greet me. His hair had grown longer in the months since I had first seen him; it grazed his unshaven jawline and curled at his neck. In the sunlight his eyes looked translucent, like thimbles of Jell-O. Hello, he said. It sounded like a question. Behind him the alley led directly to the beach, where two tents were set up near a patch of dune grass, their doors unzipped and fluttering in the wind. Out on the water a pleasure boat bobbed, the air drawing its laughter inland. We were all waiting for me to explain my presence, which I could not exactly do. Instead I introduced myself to Billy's companion, who nodded and said that her name was Linda. What a gorgeous name, I lied.

I told Billy I was happy to see he was still here, that I had been afraid he might already have departed. Yeah, he said, they would be leaving soon, himself and Linda and a friend of theirs, taking the bus west and then south. But they had decided to hold out a few more days, since the weather was—he raised both hands to the sky like a minister. It was obvious that he did not remember who I was. I found him wonderfully polite in his efforts not to humiliate me. Then it struck me that they might not have been efforts. This may just have been his personality.

If you ever found yourself in a life-or-death situation, you could eat Crocs, Linda said, half to herself. The shoes, I mean. You could boil them down and eat them. I read an article about it. That's why I bought these.

She used her cigarette to gesture at the foam encasing her feet. A bit of ash fell onto one shoe and she twitched it off.

You'd need a fire, Billy said. A fire, water, a container for boiling. It's not so simple.

Don't ask me about the nutrients, because I couldn't tell you, Linda said. I know there can't be many. But it would be better than nothing.

Oh boy, I said, nodding, and with this the subject appeared to be closed. Billy returned to his lunch, noodles hanging from his lower lip like a beard. I sensed my crotch filling with a sudden slime and realized I had forgotten to insert a tampon before I left my apartment. I thought of the geese that dominated the lakefront trail in the city where I had grown up, waddling across the path in packs of six or seven, big-titted and honking, dropping worm-shaped pellets of shit behind them. Females. In front of me, the dog strained at its leash, then let out a loud fart, settled back onto its haunches, and fell asleep. I remembered Mr. O'Donald and felt his hand around my foot, the spasm of a phantom limb.

I asked Billy and Linda if either of them would like to do some ketamine. I have a bit here with me, I said, if you're interested? I reached into my jeans pocket for my tiny baglet of powder. We could? I said. If you're interested?

Isn't that stuff used for date-raping? Linda said.

I said I did not think it was primarily used for date-raping. Wealthy people with clinical depression sometimes took it intravenously in hospitals, I explained. And it had recently had a renaissance among attractive young liberal-arts graduates with edgy politics who attended parties in major coastal cities. I had never been invited to one of these parties, I said, but I had read about them online. They were full of fascinating individuals who weighed less than I did. Some people found it nice, emotionally, to snort a drug that was also given to horses. It could feel good to conceive of yourself as a big horse, or even a dumb little pony—I found myself using my hands to demonstrate the comparative size of a horse and a pony—whichever best fitted into your own sense of your personality. A dumb little pony with a broken leg, for example, I said, in great need of anesthetic. That was what I, personally, liked to envision myself as.

The horse talk seemed to intrigue Billy, who had set aside his noodles as I spoke, but Linda was shaking her head.

That's date-raping stuff, she said firmly.

You know, Billy said to Linda. Respectfully. Most anything can be date-raping stuff if you use it in a certain way. Maybe even your Crocs could be date-raping stuff, under the right circumstances. But that's not a reason to discount them altogether.

Linda shot him a look of disgust. The old ball and chain, he said, patting her fondly on the head. I was considering other tactics I could use to persuade Linda that I was not trying to date-rape her when a figure turned off Main Street into the alley. He was backlit by the sun and walked toward us with a determined, swinging gait like a cowboy's. My first thought was of the cops; but there were few cops patrolling town during the offseason. When Billy and Linda noticed the stranger's approach, they started to wave—so he was only a stranger to me. He was handsome, I saw, coiffed and slim, silver-haired. As he drew closer his features clarified, and he began to remind me for some reason of my father, although this man looked younger, perhaps in his early fifties. In fact he did not look at all like my father. From his open-mouthed grin, the soft pink tongue lying there in his mouth like a sweet, I took him to be rather jolly, whereas my father's affect ranged from a shy and tentative cheeriness to a downcast, baffled gloom, depending on my mother's mood. When the man reached us he slapped Billy and Linda on the back, then kissed Linda lightly on both cheeks, like a European. A layer of spit-covered plastic encased his teeth like Tupperware—Invisalign braces. He knelt down to commune for a moment with the sleeping dog, after which he stood and gave me his hand. Thomas, he said. I had half-expected him to speak with a Southern accent, like the one my father trained himself out of when he left Texas, but this man's voice was noticeably placeless, a nothing voice, American. Lovely to meet you, he said, lovely.

He turned back to Billy and Linda. I thought for sure you two would be goners by now, he told them pleasantly. I wondered if it was appropriate to say "goners" to two people living in tents on the beach, at least one of whom had at some point been thrown violently off a bridge, but Billy and Linda did not appear to share my interest in the question of whether or not it was appropriate. They knew this man, obviously. They liked him. They repeated to Thomas what they had told me about the warmth, the buses, going west, going south, but their tones flowed bright and easy now, each sentence burbling merrily into the next. Not leaving in this weather, Linda said, smiling. Everyone seemed to have forgotten me. I considered repeating my offer of ketamine. I was loose, porous, at the edge of things. I was too warm in my sweater. Perspiration swamped beneath my breasts, in my pits, along the folds of fat on my back. Between my legs I sensed the oncoming embarrassment of hot blood. For a few minutes I watched the three of them converse, feeling like a jetlagged tourist in a new country. There was a very robust quality about Thomas. He was small but abundant, like a dense slice of meatloaf. In his smooth, pinkish face, his eyes gleamed with simple, wet innocence; yet the apparent artlessness of his aspect was mediated by an undefinable whiff of luxury that suffused the atmosphere where he stood. I pictured the towels in my parents' bathroom, heavy and plush, highly absorbent, heated on a warming rack like buns. Where west? Thomas said. Where south? Remind me where it is your folks came from originally? And what was it like down there? I knew someone who. Oh yes I've heard. No don't get me started. I see what you mean. And how old were you when you first? And did your father also?

In general, my own attempts at sociality felt akin to being trapped in a doorless, windowless room whose oxygen would soon be used up; there was always the lurking question of who would run out of air first. I chose to save myself. I believed there was a finite number of words people could safely say to each other, after which one person risked falling forever into the void of the other. I was not about to fall forever into some loser's interior void. At least once in my life, I often thought, someone was going to have to fall forever into me. But as I watched Thomas blithely leaning his questions toward Billy and Linda, blithely receding, picking up their responses as if with a dainty dessert fork before leaning in again with his own offerings, I knew that my bind was not one to which he could relate. Thomas, it was clear, experienced conversation as an open and airy structure, a delightful palace of his own architecture, teeming with endless possible modifications or additions, never bottoming out. A stop in Virginia, Billy told him. Then down to New Orleans. Linda described a public park where the dragonflies hovered above sludge-green ponds, fat as fists. Billy spoke of his sister, sick with diabetes since childhood, the months when his mother couldn't afford insulin, and his sister only eight years old, Julia, he said, so bright, the smartest kid in her class.

I turned my head and watched a seagull along the shoreline snatch a snail in its beak, fly thirty feet into the air, then release its prey, which plummeted like a man jumping from a burning building and smacked against the rocky beach. The seagull dove to meet it, but the shell had not cracked open. This operation was performed four more times, after which the bird gave up and coasted away. I badly needed to find a bathroom in which I could stuff my underwear with huge clods of toilet paper. My feet ached from standing, my neck from nodding, my mouth from the stupid smile I had walked around with my whole life, the one I couldn't ever seem to wipe off my face. No one, I understood, was going to accept my ketamine. I envied Julia, eight years old and diabetic, for being the smartest kid in her class. I envied Thomas, who, though I could not smell him, looked like he would smell so good, and Billy, and Linda, who was prepared to survive an apocalyptic situation, to do what it might take to live, who had no intention of getting date-raped anytime soon.

I hadn't noticed that everyone had stopped talking until Thomas put a fatherly hand on my shoulder.

And you? he asked. Are you a year-rounder?

His palm felt like a large, warm toad sitting on me—in its own way comforting. I wondered if we were having an erotic encounter. I replied that I was teaching at the Academy, so in some sense, yes. But I wasn't certain that I would be back next year. It depended on whether the school chose to renew my contract, I explained. Thomas's face put on an expression of tactful but entire understanding, which made me aware that it was my turn to ask a question.

So how do you all know one another? I said.

Oh, we see each other, here and there, Thomas replied. Small town, you know, and Billy and Linda have been coming up—how many summers has it been?

Six, Billy said. Past six summers.

Thomas explained that he had been out of town for a while, taking care of some personal business. He flicked his hand behind his shoulder to indicate how uninteresting the business was. Recently he'd had to find a new apartment here, a long story, which had taken more time than anticipated. Rental prices were getting out of control. He'd only been back and settled for a few days. I was surprised to hear that Thomas was a renter, but before I could inquire further, Billy started pounding him on the back.

This is the man! he said. This is the fucking man! Linda nodded and lit another cigarette. Thomas gave a modest smile. He's a superhero, Billy said more calmly.

In what way, I asked, specifically, had Thomas shown himself to be a superhero?

Billy leaned toward me, as though preparing to pass on an illicit stock-market tip. His hair, with its sharp, friendly smell, almost brushed against my forehead. If you're about to get raped, he whispered, Thomas is who you need to be there.

That's an exaggeration, Thomas said, holding up his hands.

If I was about to get raped? I said.

Thomas shrugged. Billy was making a big deal out of a minor event, he said. It was an unremarkable incident, really. One night the previous summer he had been out walking on the beach, pretty far beyond town. This was a habit of his, when the weather was fine, and often he was the only one out there; tourists tended to stay near the center. But that night he had come across a couple standing close to the shore. The man had been leaning over the woman, swaying and yelling, a bottle in his hand. At first the woman seemed to be holding her own; she was yelling, too, and pacing, and spitting at the ground. Eventually she kicked a clump of sand at her companion. Then the man punched her in the face. She fell back. At this point, Thomas said, he felt he had to intervene. He jogged over. Hey, hey, hey, he said. Woah, woah, woah. What's going on here. The woman, it turned out, was incredibly ugly, much uglier up close than she had seemed from afar. Her eyes were bulging, puffed like jelly donuts. Her hairline was receding. There were shadows extending from the sides of her nose to her mouth, from the sides of her mouth to her chin. But of course, Thomas said, he believed that no matter how ugly a woman was, she didn't deserve to get punched in the face.

That's true, Linda said. That's absolutely the truth.

When Thomas approached, the woman buried her head in her knees, whether out of shame that she had been punched or to hide her ugliness, he was unsure. The man proceeded to try to intimidate Thomas physically. Did I know, Thomas asked me, what I was supposed to do if I encountered a bear in the wild? No, I did not know. You're supposed to make yourself as large as you're able to, Thomas explained, with your feet wide and your arms up, like a jumping jack, and then you should clap and stomp and generate as much noise as possible. This was what it had looked like the man was trying to do to Thomas. But Thomas was not a bear; he was a human being. And so he ignored the man's attempts at intimidation and calmly threatened to call the cops. At this point, Thomas said, the man reached down the band of his elastic shorts and pulled out his penis. He held it toward Thomas, cradled in his palm, flaccid and soft as a worm. I will piss on your foot, he said. He was Russian, Thomas said, I think he was Russian. I will take piss on your foot! the man said. With each narrative turn, Thomas seemed to be enjoying himself more and more; he had now begun to put on a slight Eastern European accent. Slavophobia, I thought. I wondered if he had ever had aspirations of being on the stage. It did look like the man was trying, to take a piss, I mean, Thomas continued, but he was dehydrated, maybe, or nervous, or strung out, so he couldn't. This humiliated him, Thomas said. You know how men are. I agreed that I knew how men were, although I was almost one hundred percent sure I did not know, had never known, how men were. The man, he said, was getting increasingly angry, but still he didn't try to touch Thomas. He just kept wiggling around his flaccid penis, threatening to take a piss on Thomas's shoes, which weren't that expensive, anyway—it would have been unpleasant, certainly, but not disastrous. Thomas attempted to reason with the woman, who had been sitting in the sand throughout the whole exchange. He offered to escort her home or wherever else she might want to go, but she remained mute, shaking her head like a donkey ridding itself of a fly. The situation had reached an impasse. In the end Thomas did call the cops. They arrived, and then Thomas left. That was the conclusion of the story.

Amazing, Billy said wistfully.

While Thomas was speaking, the weather had begun to shift, with a rapidity that was common on the coast but startled me each time. Out of nothing, clouds appeared, heavy as meat. A great wind came rolling in, tugging sheets of water in diagonals toward the shore and flaying the skin on my cheeks. On the bay, the boats began their slow float into the harbor. I looked up; the last pocket of blue had been swallowed by endless knots of variegated gray. I decided against remarking upon the fact that Thomas's story did not seem to be about rape in any meaningful sense. Perhaps the implication was that if Thomas had left the scene, the man would have proceeded to rape the companion he had punched in the face, though I did not feel we had enough evidence to make this claim.

I hate thinking about that woman, Linda said. She's probably still with the guy, you know. You see stuff like that. I saw it with my sister—her husband. Years and years. Billy put his arm around her shoulders. I did not wish to talk any longer about the woman on the beach or about Linda's domestically abused sister, so I said, How lucky that you were there, Thomas; it's possible you saved a life that night; many people would not have intervened; there's a well-known phenomenon called the bystander effect; who knows what might have happened if you hadn't been around to call the cops!

The temperature was dropping fast. Around us the air moistened and hummed with static. There was an onrush of new sounds: dead leaves rubbing against one another in the wind, an inhuman whistle gathering along the alleyway. At Linda's feet the dog jolted awake and jumped up, twisting against its collar. It barked once, then let out a pathetic whimper.

Aw, Jerry, Linda cooed. She kneeled and grasped the dog's jaw firmly in her hand. They looked into each other's eyes. Jerry's tail lay flat as a ruler.

Jerry has childhood trauma, Billy explained.

We'd better go take care of our stuff, Bill, Linda said, rising and glancing over at their tents, whose unzipped doors were thrashing wildly, making noises like a whip. She pulled at Jerry's leash. Safe travels, you two, Thomas said, if I don't see you before you go. It was nice meeting you, I told Linda. Billy saluted. Then they turned and hurried down to the beach, Jerry loping between them, a family.

Which way are you headed? Thomas asked me.

Main Street was emptying in anticipation of the rain. We walked side by side, past the dumpling restaurant, the closed T-shirt emporium, one shut-up bar and then another. It was early afternoon, but the sky sat so low and green above us that it felt like evening.

My new apartment is pretty flimsy, Thomas said after some silence. I think it might cave in on me if there's a storm. He grinned with practiced shyness. I have a fear of being crushed, he said—suffocation—entrapment—I know, I know, I shouldn't have moved to a place with no bedrock if I was scared of structural damage.

I asked if he liked living in town. He did, but of course there were drawbacks. Like what, I asked. Like everyone knows your business, he said, once you live here long enough. Small town, gossip, the things you might imagine. What's funny is that a lot of people who come here are trying to get away from something or someone, ties or history, it doesn't matter which. Maybe you haven't noticed since you've only been here a couple of months. But the people who live here, they're not from here, for the most part. How can you be from here? There's not even a high school, excepting the Academy, of course—he gave me a jocular half-bow—but that's not for townies. There's no economy. There are basically only summer jobs.

I could tell that Thomas had made exactly these statements in exactly this cadence to many other people many times before.

I didn't mind. It was how I spoke, too, like a recording on which I could at the appropriate moment press Play. I thought again about his flimsy rental apartment and asked what he did, then, for money. Different stuff, Thomas said. His voice was opaque. This year, especially, I'm trying to patch it together. There are some family issues, he added, that I have to deal with, and they've gotten in the way of my work. As family issues often do. He looked at me.

But you're young, he said. So you haven't experienced all that yet.

Against my will, I was flattered that he had called me young.

He hadn't cared for his old apartment when he was living in it, he went on, but these days he missed it all the time. It had been on the ground floor, it didn't get much light, it had the most bizarre layout. The only way to navigate between the bedroom and the living room was via the bathroom, which formed a central connecting artery through which one could roll the whole length of the apartment in a straight line, so that the unit appeared to have been designed for a person who would always live alone, or perhaps for a couple that enjoyed shitting in front of one another. But it was sturdy. He had spent eight winters there. The windows would rattle, and no worse than that ever happened. He asked me where I was from, and I told him. We stepped into the street to allow two men carrying a large piece of lumber between them to pass. They thanked us in accented English. Ah, Thomas said. So the winter here will be no problem for you. I nodded my assent. He said he had heard that the city in which I had grown up was a pleasant place to live. And he had enjoyed his own admittedly brief stay several years back. Had I liked it there? he asked. His eyes were as keen and interested as a weapon. It was unclear what he wanted from me, but I sensed that he wanted something, and I appreciated this, no matter what that thing might be.

I made an elaborate wobbling motion with my hands and shoulders that I hoped would convey the complexity of my feelings. The way I related to the city was probably different from many people who called it home, I said. Neither of my parents had been born there, and they had no ties to it or to the middle of the country more generally, apart from those that develop inevitably after the majority of a lifetime is spent sleeping and working in one place. They did, true, have colleagues and neighbors, and my mother was also on familiar terms with three or four Russian-speaking women who worked sales at the discount outlets of her most cherished department stores. But on the whole my parents did not have intimate friendships, due to their limited attention spans and their terrible personalities.

Though the city in which I had grown up abounded with old historic neighborhoods and diasporic ethnic enclaves, I said, my parents had chosen to purchase a house pre-construction in a relatively undeveloped neighborhood close to downtown. Of course, even this neighborhood had a history: once it had been home to the Gilded Age wealthy, and later to a series of now-dead industries and the Irish immigrants who worked them—trainyards and freight depots and printing presses, publishing companies, an influx of brothels and gambling houses that pushed the rich up north. By the middle of the twentieth century, the area was left largely vacant, until the city began its redevelopment efforts in the 1980s and '90s.

When my parents bought their house in the early 2000s—actually, what they bought wasn't a house but the promise of one, a speculation based upon a booklet of floorplans and a model of the proposed development, complete with woolly miniature trees along its miniature sidewalks—the neighborhood was filled with empty lots, overgrown by weeds and various species of invasive grass. I was a small child then, but I had a vivid memory of exploring the second floor of my parents' half-constructed home, as if standing in an open mouth. By the time I was pubescent, the area had become an upper-middle-class neighborhood of urban renewal, populated by young professionals, many of them transplants. Ours was among the newest and most unreal parts of the city; the atmosphere, when you walked the streets, was that of an upscale chain hotel. There were never any old people around. Tall blue condominiums lay surrounded by blocks of identical new-development brick townhouses, the kind you could find these days all across the country. In the winter the apartment buildings generated wind tunnels so strong that once, in a snowstorm, I had been lifted several inches into the air while making my way to school. Mostly people did not seem to go outside at all except to walk their dogs or roll their babies around in expensive strollers, like tiny caves on wheels.

Recently, I said, there had been a spate of robberies in the neighborhood, and over the past several years there had also been a few shootings near the train station closest to my parents' house. Since then they had been unable to stop talking about the unfathomable crime they were certain was leaking into their neighborhood from the economically decimated and racially segregated parts of the city in which they believed it should have been confined. They had worked hard to choose a place to live that appeared to have no past, but they had never considered that it might have a present. Now they were endlessly concerned with encroaching violence, the police force, the upcoming mayoral race. They had installed a more complex alarm system, a second lock on the front door.

My parents had a terror of the past, I told Thomas, a refusal to reckon with their own histories and therefore anyone else's. They had been unable to bear the prospect of inhabiting a home or even a neighborhood in which there were signs that others had lived before them. They cowered in fear of real-estate open houses, kitchens where they might encounter souvenir mugs, birthday cards, handmade figurines sculpted from clay or blown from glass, the crayon drawings of small children, a living elderly person. Obviously this attitude of total rejection was coupled with a simpering nostalgia that I found even more distasteful than its alternative. Acceptable portions of the past were carved off, buffed into shape, then ritualistically described in the same cloying terms, colluded upon and set in advance. Once I baked you a cake in the shape of a mouse, my mother would remind me every few months, tears writhing in her eyes. Napoleon was such a sensual man, so misunderstood, not as short as you might think! she would sigh. Napoleon was a fascinating figure, both sensual and misunderstood, and not even so short, my father would later inform me. And do you remember when your mother baked you that magnificent mouse-shaped cake? It was a trait, I surprised myself by admitting, that repulsed me, that repelled me from my parents, that I feared made it impossible for me to love them even as it made them, I thought at times, unable to love anyone but themselves, and I worried that I had inherited it.

Thomas stopped in the middle of the sidewalk. A few spots of rain hit my arm like spittle. Any interest in a drink? he asked. He pointed at the Old Pilgrim, a block ahead. It looks like it's about to start really coming down, he said, staring at the sky, and I didn't bring an umbrella.

Sure, I said.

On the other side of Main Street a pack of Academy girls came into view, running in the opposite direction of campus. They laughed as they jogged, clutching at their chests to inhibit the flopping of their adolescent breasts. I had no idea where they could be going. Among them were two of my juniors, Anita and a girl named Divya, very loud and stupid, but beautiful, with thick black hair that she often wore in braids. I hated seeing my students outside of class; the perpetual proximity was one of the worst parts, I had learned, of working at the Academy. Typically my students did not seem eager to run into me either, except in the way that all teenagers liked to encounter adults outside of their usual contexts—because it humiliated and debased the adults, I understood, exposing how flimsy the veneer of authority really was. I averted my gaze in the hopes that they wouldn't notice me, but a group of students had already peeled away from the others and was skipping toward us, beaming. I rubbed a hand surreptitiously along my crotch and glanced down to find my fingers damp, pinked with blood. The girls gave me a half-hearted wave. Then they pushed toward Thomas, jostling, squirming, surrounding him, speaking over one another to catch his attention, You're back, Divya was saying, Are you not going to teach at all this year? Anita asked, and at last it became clear to me that I was not the person they had come to see.

# 5

*

I don't think we should glamorize city life, a girl named Kyla said. She sat near a window. For the whole period her head had rested upon the glass. Now she raised it, using it to glare at her classmates. She picked it up like it was very heavy. Her voice sounded ill, full of goo. I tried to remember the grade I had given her last paper but could not. Cities have high rates of violent crime, she said. Anything can happen in a city. You leave for the weekend and your wife stays home because she has a tennis lesson that Saturday and then your house gets broken into and *bam*, your wife gets raped.

She let her head drop back against the window, exhausted from the effort of speech. Outside, the snow was coming down in its wet way—big greasy clots of it. It slopped onto the frozen lawn and the bare tree branches, which creaked under their new weight, arthritic. A mass email the previous evening had warned of high winds and possible power outages. Headlamps had been distributed in the dorms and faculty housing, in case of emergency. These days it stayed dark late into the morning. It grew dark early in the afternoon. The water was dark and the sand was dark. What boats remained in the harbor were a different shade of dark from the dark of the air, which clung darkly to the skin, cold and wet. It was the dampness that made the winter here different from that of the city in which I had grown up; still, much was the same. In both places it was often too dark for there to be any shadows.

This is racism in action, Anita said to Kyla. This is a dog whistle. I refuse to sit here and be a bystander to racism in action.

I'm black, Kyla said.

I don't care if you're black, white, yellow, or purple, Anita screamed.

I wrote "dog whistle" on the whiteboard. Next to it I wrote "urban," and below that I wrote "bystander effect? (pop psychology)." I thanked Kyla for her interesting observation. I thanked Anita for her vital intervention. Maybe, I said to the rest of the class, we can parse this step-by-step. Would anyone else like to speak to whether they believe Dickens, in his finest and most ambitious novel, *Bleak House*, the first half of which they'd all by now had ample time to read, is "glamorizing" city life?

Slumped at their desks my students looked hungry, sallow, sleep-deprived. I was afraid that comparatively I appeared well-fed. I could feel my body, piles of it, sitting on my bones. No one raised a hand; I waited them out. My authority was so minimal that this game of standoff usually ended with my answering the question myself, or otherwise with Thales volunteering to speak, unable to stomach the silence. But Thales was absent today—she could not attend class due to "bad diarrhea," her email that morning had informed me. I was relieved. Her nervous energy made me sick. She wanted so badly to be useful, good, a part of it all. She would ask endless clarifying questions about any assignment I gave, a hunted animal panic rising behind her eyes, as if she feared I was about to beat her up. Her weakness made me want to beat her up. I knew she only desired to please me, not because of who I was in particular, but simply because I existed in general. I felt humiliated on her behalf. She showed me too much about myself. I couldn't help but prefer the prettier students, who turned in assignments weeks late and barely pretended to have done the reading. Dumb, vicious, vacuous—they didn't think about me at all. But they looked so nice in their little outfits. I admired the sly way they peeked at their phones in class, the fruity smell that lingered in the bathroom after they vaped mid-period in the stalls.

Eventually Cordelia raised a hand. Her appearance that week was frightful, hair the color of tar hanging in wads from her large skull. Her eyes seemed smaller and more closely set than usual, rimmed by sagging shadows. Still, as always, she spoke to me in that beautiful voice. I don't believe Dickens, she said tiredly, is interested in *glamorizing* the city. His London is the London of chaos and alienation, of surfaces, of flatness, beneath which pulses an obscure system of interconnection, a hidden logic of social relation. Her tone had been calm, but all at once she went rigid. Do you not get that in this book a person spontaneously combusts? she shrieked at her classmates. He literally explodes?

Did you not even look it up? He explodes? There's slime everywhere? Because he explodes?

Thank you, Cordelia, I said loudly. She looked at me. Her body returned to its slumped position. Then she barked out a laugh, throaty and sensual, rare from her. Sorry, she said, glancing around at her classmates. Don't mind me. I'm awfully tired.

A gust of wind pressed against Kyla's window, rattling the glass. There was a feral energy in the room, a tension like a thickness in the air, as if my students were already elsewhere, leaving behind only the meat of their bodies and their most primary instincts: rage, hunger, fear. I decided it was pointless to continue talking about *Bleak House*. Instead I asked if anyone had winter break plans they were excited about. Yes, they did. They were going skiing. They were going to stay in an eco-casita on the coast of Mexico. They were traveling to London to visit family. They were traveling to New York City to visit the 9/11 museum. A shy girl named Sasha politely asked me if I had plans. No, I said, I did not have any plans. I would stay in town, enjoy the quiet. Will you do the polar plunge, someone asked. I did not think I would do the polar plunge. It's so healthy to do it, though, she said. I was unsure if she was implying that I looked unhealthy. I let the comment pass.

I was not going to assign any homework over the break, I told my students, but I did hope they would continue to be diligent about their reading logs, which I would collect when classes resumed. They should think of it as their Christmas gift to me. My family celebrates the Winter Solstice, Anita said, not Christmas. I explained that I did not celebrate Christmas either, because I was a Jew, but that I was using Christmas here as a kind of metonym. I defined "metonym" on the whiteboard.

Even if you only read one book over break, I said, it's an excellent practice to get into, one that will serve you well later in life. I tried to contort my features into an arrangement that showcased how well I had been served, spiritually and intellectually, by the cultivation of my own literary habits. Sasha asked if I had been reading any good books lately. The period was so close to being over. I felt a wave of methamphetamine's cousin crashing over the soft curve of my brain. Yes, I said, in fact I was currently reading a tremendously interesting book, an out-of-print biography of the leader of a former world power, a man of history, the son of a house cleaner and a shoe cobbler. Over the years this man had been labeled many things, I told my students, including, it was true, "mass murderer" and "demon dictator." Yet he had other qualities, as well—a tongue-in-cheek sense of humor, a fine attention to detail, a nearly photographic memory. Some people found him quite handsome, with his exceedingly kind and gentle brown eyes. As one admiring ambassador from our own country put it, *A child would like to sit on his lap and a dog would sidle up to him*. In his youth he wrote poems, bad poems, undeniably, but that they existed at all demonstrated that he had been a sensitive and creative young man. He had been physically weak, marked by disease, smallpox and, later, blood poisoning; he spent his childhood abused by his booze-soaked father and coddled by his mother, her only living son. At the time of his death, his library contained over 20,000 books, I said, many with notes in the margins, phrases that we could all probably imagine our own pens scribbling, like Ha ha or Fool! when remarking upon the writings of one of his enemies. He was fond of Thackeray's *Vanity Fair.* He adored his sweet red-headed daughter. He did, yes, have a habit of having his enemies murdered, tortured, surveilled by secret police, and forced into labor camps. Yes, there were other atrocities—purges, etcetera. There was a certain infamous nonaggression pact signed with another important political leader of the time, a pact resulting in the division of land that allowed this man to annex the Baltic states. He did, admittedly, in fits of malignant suspicion and rage, exile his daughter's Jewish filmmaker lover and imprison his eldest son's Jewish ballerina wife. Still, I found the biography comforting, because this leader, in his personality, his method of political repression, his brutality, and his paranoia, reminded me very much of my mother, who had coincidentally spent her childhood in one of those nations he annexed, where she would sneak into the funerals of his state officials, truly distinguished affairs, she claimed, grand and elegant. We could not control what attracted us, I said to my students, listening to the weird tremor in my voice like it was coming from another room. We could not, I said, control how our desires were inscribed.

I looked out at the class. Only Cordelia appeared to be listening to me, her eyes narrowed into an expression whose meaning

I could not fathom. The others were twitching, practically, with desperation to leave. The window upon which Kyla rested her head was entirely frosted over, an inch of snow crusting its sill. The outer world had become a haze of light. Beyond this room there was nothing to see.

I squinted at the clock. On that note, I said, clapping my hands together, I'd like to wish you all a happy break. Safe travels, I called out as the room dissolved into relieved spills of laughter, a low murmuring chatter, the groan of metal chair legs against the floor. I watched my students zip and button their coats. They wound long, woolen scarves around their necks, tugged knit hats down over their delicate ears, protecting themselves from the cold. Their bodies were so newly adult, like costumes, worn with mingling shame and pride, as pungent as a smell. It was almost impossible not to feel a tenderness toward them. And yet I managed it. I felt my age like an IV dribbling through me. Someone wished me a happy holiday. Someone else waved goodbye. Bodies pushed in a cluster toward the tunnel of the stairs and descended. Still at her desk, Cordelia rummaged around in her backpack with deliberate slowness. When most of her classmates had departed, she lumbered toward me.

I'm afraid I got a bit intense today, she said. My apologies.

It wasn't a problem, I replied. Her point had obviously been correct, and well put. I finished erasing the board and turned to face her. She gazed at me coolly. I saw that she was not sorry at all. It was a very long book, she said. Did I understand that no one was actually reading it? Typically in high school, she had heard, students read *Great Expectations.* I sensed something simmering between us. It was not violence. I did not believe that it was violence. Yes, I said, *Bleak House* was long, but no longer than, say, three consecutive shorter books would have been. I could have assigned *Great Expectations*, she was correct, which also dealt with the city, and which, as she said, was more commonly read by this age group. But clearly *she* had been able to do the reading as it was, I pointed out. So I wasn't certain why she assumed her peers didn't have the same capacity. Did she believe that their brains had been rotted into mush by the endless videos they scrolled through on their phones, in which sexy teenagers of all genders performed minutely choreographed dances, joyously humping the air, each clip morphing ceaselessly into the next? If so, why did she think she had escaped the same fate?

As I spoke I had the feeling that I was communicating beyond Cordelia, into a void I couldn't help but believe was hidden within her. Her voice, I realized, sounded much like a recording I had once heard of Sylvia Plath reading "Lady Lazarus." Did she remind me of my sister? She did not remind me of my sister. I sensed her fear, what I believed to be her fear. It was like a rope that I could hold onto.

Dickens is one of the great novelists of parental abdication, I said. His father went to debtors' prison. And then he was sent by his mother to work at a blacking factory. He was only a child.

I don't know what a blacking factory is, Cordelia said.

I admitted that I also did not know what a blacking factory was. I believe it may have something to do with bottles, I said. We were both still standing, each unsure of what to do with our hands. She was tall, almost my height. We faced one another. I was overcome by the sensation that if I made any movement, her body would involuntarily mirror mine, but I did not want to find out if this were true. I stood motionless. We blinked. I heard a bird through the window; a bird in the snow.

How is Mr. Nelson? Cordelia said at last.

I told her that Mr. Nelson was doing well.

She said that she was happy to hear it. She hadn't spoken to him in a while but had heard from Divya that he was back in town. Her backpack was slung across one shoulder and looked as if it might soon pull half of her down into the ground.

Mr. Nelson was like a father to me, Cordelia said. I nodded. That's good, I said. You might tell him I said so, she said. I was not sure if I would see him, I said, but if I did I would be sure to pass it along. And that I hope all is well with him, she said. And that I'd love to hear from him. You could tell him I look forward to hearing from him.

Yes, yes, I said, I would absolutely pass along each and every one of those remarks, if only I were to see him, which it was likely I would not.

We looked at each other.

When I was in high school, I said, I had a teacher who was like a father to me.

How nice, Cordelia said politely.

I later found out he was a pedophile, I said. With boys, though.

She directed her stare behind me, at the ghostly smears that remained on the whiteboard. My apologies, she said. Her voice was calm. For a moment I had the impulse to tell her about the things that had happened to me when I was a seventeen-year-old virgin in Benjamin Leichter's parents' bedroom. But I could not discern whether I would be doing so as a warning or as a threat.

It's very painful to be betrayed by a trusted figure, I said instead.

Certainly, she replied. She gave her head a slight shake, as if to clear it out. Winter Assembly rehearsal, she said, shifting her backpack to the other shoulder. I'd better go.

Yes, I agreed, she had better go. I would see her at the assembly that night. She turned away. Merry Christmas, Cordelia, I said.

I'm Jewish, she said. Then she added, but Merry Christmas.

I walked across campus in the snow, weaving through clumps of bundled-up students on my way to the mailroom, where I picked up my packages—sugar-free barbecue sauce, boxes of laxative tea, bulk peppermint breath strips, free two-day delivery. Flakes melted where they touched my cheeks, making it feel as though I had been crying. I stopped by the cafeteria, then exited clutching a sandwich of Muenster cheese, my fingers imprinting the soft bread through its wax paper wrapper. Tomorrow the cars would begin pulling up to the dorms to carry the students back to their families. Next week I would be almost alone.

I went down to the water, careful not to slip on the new snow. My steps were tiny, like a child's. I held my arms out for balance, as if I were pretending to be an airplane or a man of faith getting crucified. I faced the bay and ate my sandwich standing, stuffing the dirty wax paper into my coat. I smoked a cigarette until my hands got too cold and I dropped it. My phone buzzed in my pocket. The vibrations moved against my thigh in a pattern so familiar it was almost biological. The phone stopped buzzing. Then it began again.

Hang on, I said. Let me put in my headphones.

Okay, I said. Now I can hear you.

Hey, the voice said. Where are you? That wind sounds crazy.

The wind was crazy. It hurt my ears, my hands. It lashed the skin between the bottoms of my trousers and the tops of my socks.

I'm by the harbor, I said. It's really windy.

Is it snowing there? he said. I saw it was snowing out east.

I told him it was snowing. Usually the waves in the bay were little ripples, I said, like a lake. Or the pond we sat next to at the botanical gardens that one time, with the koi he had admired, their whiskers droopy as mustaches, like actors in a western, did he remember? How he kept pointing to them and saying Looks like the sheriff's in town? But today the storm was making the water different. I described the wave I was watching crash against a house, a bit farther down the shoreline. The house might be on stilts, I said, but I wasn't close enough to see clearly. I could see the wave, though, a pure gray that lifted itself like a shelf, churning up and flattening against the building's first-floor windows, dissolving into a pile of foam as soon as it touched solid matter.

Let me video-call for a sec, actually, I want to show you, I said.

He picked up. His face was in the palm of my hand. It filled the screen. Part of his chin I couldn't see, the top of his forehead, one of his ears. It was a male face, the face of a man my age. I can't describe it further. It meant too much to me.

That's nuts, he said. Do you think there are people inside?

I didn't know. I didn't think so.

Okay, now show me your face, he said.

I showed him my face.

Let's go back to a normal call, I said, so I can walk.

My skin was sprayed again and again with saltwater. The wind made it difficult for him to hear me. Inside my shoes my socks were thin. My toes felt unrelated to the rest of my body, mini frozen sausages all in a row. He updated me on the roommates we had been living with before I dropped out of graduate school, left him, left the state to move back in with my parents. One of the chickens died, he said. It had a parasite. Like, worms. The roommate who kept them was devastated. And now she had become even more paranoid about hawks going after the other two. When he went out into the yard, he said, he would look back toward the house and see her face pressed against her bedroom window, just staring at the coop, keeping watch, like some kind of chicken perv. He paused. Bird perv, he said softly, testing out the phrase. I said I had never liked those chickens, but that didn't mean I was happy one had died. Did you kill it, he giggled. Did you come all the way back here to kill that chicken. What if I was the parasite all along, I said. Like, what if I was the worm. I giggled. Sorry, he said, I can barely hear you, the wind. I ran up from the bay, almost slipping, and found an awning to stand beneath, a closed children's clothing store. The tiny mannequins were dressed for beach weather in tiny shorts, tiny tank tops. Is this better? I said, out of breath. This was better, he said. I asked how his dissertation was going. It's stupid, he said, laughing. It's pretty stupid. I could hear him pacing. I could see the room, what for four years had been our room, his bowed head, his bad posture, his slippers scraping the floor as he shuffled between the bed and the desk. He would be wearing a black sweatshirt, faded boxers, calf-length white athletic socks. There would be dead ladybugs on the windowsill and under the pillows. I'm not teaching next semester, he said carefully. I got that fellowship. He paused. I was thinking. Maybe I could sublet the room here? He paused. I could come up there for a while? I felt my brain cells beginning to swell and engorge. I made a noise with my mouth. It's been almost a year, he said. I knew that it had been almost a year, I said. I paused. There were things here I had to deal with, I said, get to the bottom of. What do you mean by "things," he said. I reminded him that I was sexually frigid and incapable of orgasm-with-partner. I explained that when a woman was in love, it was essential that she produce several mind-blowing orgasms to signal that she had entered into a relationship of liberated equals. If a woman was psychically blocked from producing a mind-blowing orgasm in the presence of the person she loved due to, for example, the tragic events of her past, it was essential that she embark upon a spiritual quest of healing and self-discovery, which might involve an extramarital affair, sexual tourism in a different country, excavating repressed kinks, pursuing meaningful and latently erotic female friendships, masturbating in new positions—e.g., lying-on-belly, straddling-tall-chair—mutual oral stimulation with a much older or younger partner, violent revenge upon the men who had violated her in the past, embracing her curves, or dropping out of graduate school and moving back in with her parents. He said my name. I told him I had gotten my students to pretend to read half of *Bleak House* and couldn't be interrupted. I was making a lot of interesting friends here, I said. I said I was pretty sure one of my students had been molested by her ephebophilic English teacher, that this was the teacher I had replaced, I had recently met him, I believed that I was living in the apartment he had occupied for the past eight years, that I was sleeping in his ephebophilic bed. I explained that my pedagogy was important to me. Education, I said, is a weapon whose effects depend on who holds it in his hands. Don't quote Stalin at me, he said. I have trauma, I said. Please don't do that, he said. Do what, I said. Are you crying? he said. Yeah, I said. He said my name. He said it again. Don't you want me to come? he said. Are you crying? I said. Yeah, he said. I listened to him. He was sitting on the edge of the mattress. He was looking out the window at our roommate's chickens pecking through their trough. Tonight he would eat a bowl of whole-wheat pasta with broccoli and chicken-Asiago sausage. He would brush his teeth. He would sit at his desk and read a book before bed. He would mouth each sentence as he went along, and no one would be there to see it. There's a kid here named Thales, I said eventually. No way, he said. Yes, I said. Like, "everything is water" Thales? he said. Yeah, I said. No way, he said. Then he told me about Anaximenes, who thought everything was made of air, and Parmenides, who thought everything was one, that motion and differentiation were only illusions—all being, one sphere, he said, which people had a hard time with, because wouldn't that imply there was an outside?—and he told me about Heraclitus, who thought everything in the world was made of fire.

At the end he said, I'll talk to you next week.

I walked back to my apartment. I ate five pieces of toast spread with butter and sugar and puked into the toilet. Then I ate two more pieces of toast. I lay facedown on the couch and watched a lengthy online video compilation I had found of American politicians falling to the ground and getting back up. At some point an advertisement for a popular frozen lasagna brand interrupted my viewing. A woman around my age with a wide, sturdy mouth held forth her plate of coagulated microwaved noodles, grinning. Meaty cheesy, meaty cheesy, meaty cheesy, she chanted. Her loved ones joined her in the frame, gathering around the kitchen island without acknowledging one another's presence. Meaty cheesy, they all said to the camera. It sounded like a prayer, a plea; like they were speaking an idea into being. At the end of the video, a survey appeared. I believe the advertiser of the previous ad has my best interests in mind, it stated. I was prompted to agree or disagree, strongly or weakly. Or, if I preferred, I could select a bubble that would formally indicate my neutrality.

I picked the option that felt most aligned with my beliefs and then for an hour I drifted in and out of sleep. I had no dreams, except for the ones I always had.

I woke to darkness. I prodded my phone for light. I was late. I threw on my coat and trudged to the auditorium, where more darkness was sloshing in through the windows, big as garage doors. Hand-cut paper snowflakes had been pasted to the glass; by the janitors, I assumed. I stuffed my coat and scarf onto a seat near the back. The ceilings were high. Outside, real snow fell. In my hands I held a program containing lyrics to several hymns I had grown up singing in my middle and high school choirs. Instrumental versions of carols piped into the room via surround sound. Students made their way to their seats, blocked off by grade, led by their class deans. They walked in near-military formation. Through them the Dean of Academics wove, smiling, touching one and then another on the shoulder. She looked friendly and expensive, like the manager of a department store, her black hair pulled into a neat chignon. She wore a tasteful and festive red wool dress. I tried not to look down at my own jeans, too tight at the waist, imprinting a raw pink band around my stomach.

When she caught sight of me, the Dean paused, then hurried over and crouched so that her mouth hovered close to my ear. She touched me on the shoulder. She was so happy to see me, she said. She had been meaning to tell me how pleased she was, they all were, that I had joined the Academy's community. She had heard such wonderful feedback about my class. I wondered if she could remember my name or which subject I taught. Was I looking forward to the holiday? she asked. Was I enjoying the peace and solitude of the offseason? Would I do her the biggest favor? Her hand was still there on my shoulder. It was a bit silly, she knew, but they generally asked that faculty and staff sit close to the stage during gatherings like these. They felt it helped present an enduring, unified front to the student body—so important, these days, she said, didn't I agree—as well as a sense of care. Would I mind moving to one of the first few rows?

Of course not, I said.

I gathered my belongings, and we walked together to the front of the auditorium. I had the sensation that the Dean was about to link her arm through mine, as in a processional, but she did not. I took a seat in the third row, between my history-teacher neighbor and a woman I didn't know well, a gym coach. She nodded curtly. On either side I could feel the warm spread of my thighs pressing against theirs. My history-teacher neighbor turned to me. Sometimes I can hear you singing, he said. He was in his late thirties but had a chubby face, like a baby's. Oh, I said. I guess the walls are thin. I can hear a lot from your apartment, too. His infant expression went suddenly jackal-ish, lips peeling back to expose a set of healthy gums. Sometimes I hear you throwing up, he said happily. He wore a sweater vest the color of rust. I have Crohn's, I lied. I hear that's bad, he said. Puking and shitting, right? Remind me what you teach? I asked. Fascism, he replied. His voice was bored. You teach fascism? I said. You know, you sure do sing a lot, he said. He peered at me like someone seconds away from getting to the bottom of a long unsolved crime. Then the auditorium dimmed, and he turned his attention back to the stage.

I closed my eyes. The Head of School spoke soothingly of light and dark, the ebb and flow of the tides, the blackest nights, the brightest days, the rain and the sun—all woven into an analogy, somehow, about the illumination that a progressive women's education might bring to the shadowy, cobwebbed corners of chaotic modernity. Everyone clapped. Some teachers cheered. We rose to sing the school song, a composition in Latin, written in 1977 by the Academy's first classics instructor. I did not know the melody and mouthed the words, opening and closing my mouth like a fish. We sat. Once more the lights went out. A familiar shadow sprinted onto the stage, then staggered back into the wings, clutching the podium like a refrigerator, his panting breaths amplified through the room. I became aware of a series of strenuous shuffling movements in the two rows ahead of me but did not understand their meaning until the lights flicked on to reveal twelve male members of the faculty and staff standing onstage in a loose semicircle. At one end was Petar. He had replaced his denim sherpa jacket with a shiny black dress shirt. The auditorium fell into an anticipatory hush. A few students snickered. For some reason I found myself thinking of an air raid. A floppy-haired French teacher sounded a chord on the grand piano that sat in one corner of the stage, leaning his torso over the keys. Then the men began to sing.

I had never before heard anything like the scream that emanated from the audience in response. It pierced the room, rising shrilly to the ceiling, echoing off the walls, pooling on the floor beneath my feet. Oh my god, I said aloud. It was as though I were listening to two hundred girls being shot repeatedly through the softest parts of their flesh with poisoned arrows. My neighbor chuckled. The men sang. The girls screamed. The sound went on, so real, so primal, each individual dissolving into one voice, the shuddering collective libido of adolescence washing over me like a liquid. I feared that its purity would destroy me. When I craned my neck, I saw every mouth open, every face wet. I wondered if they were all experiencing ego death. Bells on bobtails ring, making spirits bright, the men sang listlessly. They swayed their hips and snapped their fingers. They were balding, potbellied. They wore sweaters and trousers. On a chemistry teacher's head sat an ugly newsboy cap. I felt sick, with envy and another emotion I could not identify. My history-teacher neighbor leaned toward me.

It really isn't the same without Thomas, he whispered. You should have heard them last year.

At last the song ended. I thought I was going to puke and shit. The men bowed. The room dimmed. The girls continued screaming. Then, all at once, they stopped. The auditorium sank into a terrible silence, as if it had never known sound. I looked at the snow outside the window, so nearly weightless, whirling frantically in all directions, compelled by the air.

When the lights came back up, four men remained onstage. They had been joined by eight students dressed identically in black polyester gowns, floor-length and long-sleeved, evoking a nun's habit. Each wore a string of fake pearls around her neck, fake pearl studs in her ears. Their hair was pinned delicately back from their faces with fake pearled barrettes. A small, tidy man I hadn't seen before walked out onto the stage and gave a clipped bow to the audience, then turned to his chorus and lifted his hands to his chest. He looked at them. They looked at him. He gave a precise nod. They all took their breath.

I had known that Cordelia would sing. I had known exactly what she would sound like. Her brows were arched, her mouth curled into an *O*, her tongue depressed, her shoulders gathered back. I watched the slightest wave of motion carry through her body like a shudder. It was Gustav Holst's setting of "In the Bleak Midwinter." I knew it well; I had sung it. The other altos blended to Cordelia's vowels, long and dark. They sang with one voice. It was her voice. It seemed to me that inside of the manifest sound there was another, secret, sound—inhuman, merciless, totalizing. I looked at the director, the cool twitch of his index finger, as if he were holding onto each voice with a string. They had given themselves over to him. He cradled them in his hands. He made them move. He made them sing. There was a feeling in the vicinity of my ribcage, taut as a wire, that I can only describe as rapture. They were serious, I thought. They understood what it was to be serious. What can I give Him, the chorus sang. Poor as I am. I was aware that I was weeping.

This is the boring part, my history-teacher neighbor whispered.

I stood quickly and squeezed through my row, excusing myself in hushed tones, my knees knocking the seats in front of me. I speed-walked to the gender-neutral bathrooms, pumping my arms. In the back of the auditorium I saw a silver-haired man leaning against the wall, near the doors. For a second I thought it was Thomas. But I knew that couldn't be true.

I pulled down my pants and sat on the toilet and looked at my phone. I could hear the voices from the auditorium, still singing, but muffled, as though a pillowcase was being shoved over each singer's mouth. The sound pressed in on the bathroom door. I grew suddenly afraid that I had left it unlocked and stumbled over with my pants scrunched around my ankles to check. It was locked. I dropped my phone and picked it up again. The screen felt wet. In my family group chat, my sister had sent a selfie of herself and my parents standing around my parents' kitchen island. Between them was a menorah, its shamash and first two candles lit. Each member of my family was enjoying a slice of cake on a small plate, which they had tilted precariously outward to better display to the camera.

Maybe come home, my mother had texted beneath the photo.

Five minutes later she had added, We will pay for a cab to closest airport and your ticket.

Both ways, she said.

Do you hate us, she wrote eight minutes after that.

Someone was pounding at the bathroom door. Sounds lovely, but I have so much prep to do for next semester, I typed. A high thin voice shouted, It's an emergency. Just a second, I said. I flushed the toilet. It's an emergency, the voice screamed. I deleted what I had typed.

How about Wednesday, I sent.

I turned on the faucet to pretend I was washing my hands, and then I opened the bathroom door.

# II

The long cab ride through the dark of morning, the wetlands, the hills of sand, the tall grasses sunk in high tide, the brain-dead forests, the strip mall, the gas station, the faraway hospital, the man thumb-out in the middle of the road, his knee-high rubber boots, the seasonal mansions, the spread of the ocean, the sun rising behind low thickets of cloud, the squirrel's spilled guts, the bass plunging on the radio, and the cab driver's daughter in dentistry school now, out on the mainland, the cost of living, her boyfriend an entrepreneur, the cost of a carton of eggs, his love of the Lord, the stagnating wages, the general concept of redemption, and which terminal was it again, with all of us sinners, the appropriate cash tip, my filthy socks in the security line, the down coats worn indoors, a paper cup of coffee at the gate, a sound so immense it would soon be forgotten, my seatmate's large-print e-book, my sour breath, the seatbelt sign, the low and steady dose of radiation, my complimentary drinking water, and finally, through the window, the lake, the one I had known my whole life, big and blue as the sea.

Sheets of ice fissured near the shoreline.

When you were getting born, she said, I had to *induce* you.

There were flimsy plastic coverings across the kitchen table, the countertops. I was not permitted to sit down because I might scratch the newly finished floors. They had visited a quarry to select a top for the island—a slab of matte gray stone that closely resembled, but was not technically, concrete. The backsplash would be elongated strips of vertical wood. The new flooring was pale, cool-toned. On its surface hung flat pools of overhead light.

They tried to convince me it was too early, she said. Doctors. Know-nothings. Get it out, I said. You were wet. You had a face like a peeled tomato. You had a *mohawk*. You wouldn't stop screaming. You looked exactly like a disgusting lobster!

She spoke to me using her favorite baby voice. I watched her mouth enjoying itself as it slid through the shapes of speech. Next to her, my father smiled and ate his banana.

Babies are nasty, aren't they? she said. Big slimy things. Ick! She stared at my father and then at me, waiting for us to laugh. We laughed. We were all three standing, facing one another. On the counter between us sat a plate of oranges, cut into crosswise slices, like an offering.

Oh oh oh, I was a bad mother, wasn't I? she lisped coyly.

Something special about you, my father said, is that you've always been very good at finding things. If your mother ever misplaced an object—an earring, a tiny screw, a needle and thread—we could call your name, and you'd get right down on your hands and knees and crawl around looking for it. You would root through the carpet. Sometimes it took you a long time. Sometimes it took you hours and hours. But you wouldn't give up until you found what your mother had lost and returned it to her. I thought that was simply amazing, he said. You were four years old.

You were like a vacuum cleaner, my mother said.

Her hair was dyed dark, the color of mine. Her eyes were the color of mine. Once she had baked me a cake in the shape of a mouse. Next to her, my father wore a half-zip sweater. The temperature of the house was electronically maintained at sixty-two degrees. My suitcase was upstairs. The car was in the garage. The milk was in the refrigerator. In the living room a white sheet had been draped over the couch—a child's costume of a ghost.

And when you got older, my mother said, you had such *enormous* tee-tees. She opened her eyes wide to signify her astonishment. She gaped her mouth and stuck out her neck. I couldn't believe it. Like a moo-cow. Your sister, too. Like I had birthed two moo-cows. She shuddered. Through the window I watched two children from an adjacent townhouse bicycle out of their garage, faces mummified in thick scarves, like burn victims. My mother switched to Russian. Was it possible, she asked, that my tee-tees had gotten even bigger since she saw me last? In English I told her I did not think this was possible. I was almost thirty, I said. In Russian she replied that my shirt was looking very tight over my enormous tee-tees. I was embarrassing my father, she said. I was making him uncomfortable. I was making him blush. Maybe I had gained some weight? Didn't I have a sweater I could put on? She could lend me a sweater? But it might be too small? She reminded me that she would be happy to pay for my breast reduction. Had I given any more thought to getting a breast reduction? Next time, she told me, her voice no longer the voice of a baby, I really should not come downstairs without a sweater. I had to remember that my father lived in this house, too.

I looked down at my T-shirt. It hung loosely over my breasts. My father was gazing into the middle distance with a half-smiling, sated expression, waiting patiently for my mother to return to a language he could understand.

I said that I would go upstairs and put on a sweater.

My childhood bedroom was mostly bare. Against the back wall stood the four-poster queen bed that had once occupied my parents' room. There was a white wood dresser and a mirrored side table, upon which sat a plain white lamp. In the closet hung my mother's finest summer suits. The walls had been painted beige. The windows looked out onto two tall glass luxury condominiums, around which the townhouse development formed a U-shape. What light the room received was milky and cold. Half a mile away, the lake was sitting in its basin like an aluminum pan. I didn't need to see it to know that it was there.

I jogged down two flights of stairs to the kitchen wearing my largest sweatshirt. My mother's voice rose from below.

Ow, ow, ow, she said. Don't go like a goat.

I showered this morning, I said. Do we really need that sheet on the couch?

She pretended not to hear me. In Russian she asked for a kiss. I approached and mashed my cheek against hers. I had to stoop to reach her. She was shrinking with age. Her skin felt papery beneath mine. Her breath was rancid. I could have snapped her bones with my bare hands.

I will make you an eggy, she said.

She filled a pot with water from the tap and turned up the flame.

We took you to Italy, you know, she said, but you didn't appreciate it. You were afraid of the pigeons. All you wanted to do was steal miniature cereal boxes from the complimentary hotel breakfast. You had no interest in culture. You didn't *care* about the Uffizi. You only loved those cereal boxes. Sometimes you would bite into your own arm until it bled. You would stick it right under my nose. Look what you made me do, you would say. You thought I was some kind of retard. Six years old.

I ate my soft-boiled egg standing, my teeth sinking too easily through the whites. My father had peeled a second banana. Between nibbles he stole covert glances in my mother's direction.

The renovations had been a nightmare, she went on. The contractor was supposed to finish the backsplash weeks ago. She could hardly sleep. At night the anxiety sat on her chest like a dog. The contractor had fallen out of a tree. He was Polish, my mother explained.

I am reading *Emma* by Jane Austen, my father said. He sidled over to me and poked at a paperback on the island with his index finger. What an amazing book!

We can't entertain you, my mother shouted. Across the room she had started to run the tap and clang dirty dishes together in the sink. Don't expect us to entertain you just because you're here.

Every line is astute, said my father. It's true that I am reading slowly, but I find it so beautiful. Like glass.

My mother turned on the vacuum cleaner. She doesn't want to hear about that, she said. She thinks you're a pathetic old man.

I raised my voice over the din and told my father that I would love to hear more of his thoughts about one of Jane Austen's most luminous and exhilarating novels, *Emma*. My mother jabbed the vacuum around our feet.

She's lying, she said, because she feels sorry for you. Because you walk around looking like a sad old loser.

I'm not lying, I said, though I felt I had absolutely no way to tell whether or not this was true.

Fine, then. My mother's voice went soft. She switched off the vacuum and leaned it against the wall. Her shoulders sagged. Her lower lip wobbled. Her expression was wet as cake batter.

I recalled an instance in my teenage years when I had slammed my hand as hard as I could against the island's top, but I could no longer remember what my reasoning had been.

Go ahead, she whispered. Leave me out of everything.

Oh no, my father said. He began to apologize profusely in a high, whining tone.

She wants us to die, my mother said. Get it? She's waiting for us to die. She wants all our stuff. She wants the house. She wants my most special handbags. She wants my biggest and most special diamond. Look at her face. She turned to me. She patted my left breast. Her mouth was grinning now.

But I'm going to live forever, she said.

I said I thought I might go out for a while.

I went upstairs and changed my clothes, staring at the wall that adjoined my sister's old room, pretending I could see through to its pleasant view of the avenue: the median planted with big branching oak trees and, in the summers, geometrically patterned flowerbeds; the row of brick townhouses across the way, each nearly identical to this one. My sister's windows faced west, and in the afternoons the room flooded with alternating slats of light and shadow, like a prisoner's uniform in an old cartoon.

When I came back to the kitchen, my mother was gone. I climbed a flight and knocked on the door to my parents' bedroom. I tried the knob, but it was locked. I walked down two more flights to the ground floor, where my father sat in the practice room, holding his cello to his chest like a dog on its hind legs. The doors were paneled with thick glass. I rapped on them lightly and waved. My father flapped his bow back at me, then put it to the bridge and played out a few measures of the theme to a spy movie franchise we had watched when I was a child, films that featured opaque Cold War geopolitics coupled with extended sequences in which the capitalist protagonist vigorously humped his female enemies. When my father finished, he tried to smile, but his eyes were glazed.

I cancelled and rearmed my parents' alarm, stepped outside, and locked the door behind me. It was winter. It was always winter here. A thin light leaked out of the sky like a wound. Old snow sat piled in shining drifts on the roadside, runnels of frozen slime overflowing the gutters. Somewhere in the neighborhood, children were sledding: little moon men in their snowsuits. I wore two pairs of pants, three shirts, my mother's largest coat, down to my calves, fat with goose feathers. I did not want to walk to the lake. I would do anything not to walk to the lake. I would rather die than walk to the lake. I walked to the lake. Behind me stood the supermarket, the drugstore, the train platform cutting north to south. I passed another pedestrian on the sidewalk and we both kept our heads limp, my scarf bringing the damp heat of my mouth back against my face. All over the city the streets lay wide as highways. In the transit shelters people pressed metal buttons to generate warmth. I removed a glove to check my phone. Can you try to be nice, my sister had texted, apparently you already made Mama cry. I opened another message. The image of Thomas's erect penis filled my screen, pale as a hedgehog's belly. I think you left something behind, the text said. Wow! I typed. My fingers were numb. My sister messaged again: She would see me tonight, she loved me, she had a present for me.

By the shoreline the water was a mosaic of splintered ice. At the horizon it went liquid, blue as soap. Across the lake there were cities, towns, summer homes and real homes, outlet malls, dune land, the clumsy steel structures of dead industry, but I couldn't see any of it. I walked a mile, the wind entering my ear canals, my chin tucked into my neck, and then I turned west, off the trail, into the streets, back through the frozen parks, the dead grass half-hidden by snow, the dead crab-apple trees and the dead bushes, past the outdoor bandshell, the ice rink where children clung to the railings, screaming as if they had been slapped. Here the city was flat and wide as butcher paper. A row of steel-framed buildings hulked along one side of the avenue, generating its own wall of wind. I walked through huge squares of shadow, deeper into the blue city, up the stairs to the platform, where I paid and waited, waited, shivered, got on the train.

The doors closed behind me. I sat and turned to look out the great dirty windows. Shoppers huddled in the streets like animals. Office workers on their lunch breaks scurried toward boutique salad restaurants, heads bent, hands shoved in their pockets. For more than a decade I had hated this city, corrupt and infuriating, intellectually vacant, hog butcher for the world, foul, provincial, with its torn-up prairie and every mayor an old-time gangster; but somewhere inside me, deeper than the reservoir of my contempt, deeper than I ever wanted to look for the rest of my life, I could feel the clenching of a furious pride, in these stupid lives that acted themselves out day and night, pointlessly, ridiculously, year after year, through the vicious, uninhabitable cold, people with families and people who were completely alone, who played video games, who wrote rude messages on internet forums and purchased liver-based bodybuilding supplements online, who scrolled through the same little videos that I did, or different little videos, had good personalities and bad personalities, did horrible things, glorious things, nothing at all, who had medical debt and children and aging parents, who were too exhausted to cook dinner, in a landscape that did not love or long for them, that would never even see them, much less forgive them, a cold that made it impossible to deny, I thought, that human life was a disgusting accident, an unimaginable miracle. I dry-swallowed a Xanax. The man next to me farted loudly and shifted in his seat. We churned past department stores the width of a city block, the winding murked-up river with its floating chunks of ice that resembled lumps of lard. We took the curve fast. Our coats were on. We were leaning and sweating, the train steaming with human vapor. After a few stops, a heavily pregnant woman stepped into the car, accompanied by a short man carrying several large shopping bags. They sat across from me. He set the bags on the floor. That's dirty, the woman said. Her legs were open, her swollen stomach falling between them. He picked up the bags and placed them on an empty seat. We still have to get the pot roast, the woman said. Her voice was tense. The tone hooked onto my insides. She met my eyes, then turned away. We passed above my old high school with its new additions, the empty lot where the projects had once stood, the Greek diner with the good cranberry pancakes, the supermarket with the good fried chicken, the twenty-four-hour coffee shop, the cathedral, the chain burrito restaurant, the liquor store that didn't card, the greystone in whose ground-floor apartment I had spent certain winter evenings with my high school choir director, singing Thomas Tallis as the snow came down and the streetlights flickered on outside the windows, a man, I had often told my parents in those days, a note of smug accusation in my voice, who was like a *father* to me, who *respected* me, who nurtured my *talents*, who knew I was good for more than *finding things*, though much later, long after my beloved choir director's abrupt firing for undisclosed reasons my senior year, at which time, fearful that he might sink deeper into the quagmire of alcoholism and depression that already splotched his skin and bloated his jowls, I had sent him frequent loving text messages expressing my indignation at his unjust treatment by our vindictive and malicious school board, I learned that he too had been one of my high school's numerous pedophiles and ephebophiles—just not with me.

The pregnant woman stepped off the train with her companion. I followed. She walked slowly, her feet angled outward in their winter boots, ducklike, one hand pressed to the small of her back, the other in the crook of her husband's arm. Even after fifteen years, I knew that walk. I knew those apple cheeks, that pointed chin. They were the walk and cheeks and chin of my elementary school classmate, Megan O'Donald. And there she was. She looked old. Her hair was brown. I longed for her golden wig and her green crown. Her body tilted against her hand, like she was preparing to curve all the way back into a bridge. She had been wonderful at doing the bridge in gym class. I dawdled behind, keeping my head down. I turned where they turned. We were on the city's north side. In a front yard, an inflated character from a children's movie rode in its bulbous sleigh, flailing an inflated hand. It looked like it feared for its life. This is the last year we go to Daddy's for Christmas, Megan O'Donald said. I want to do our own. She was waddling, out of breath. It's a lot of work, her husband said. You know he's going to be fucking drunk at midnight Mass, Megan O'Donald said, he always is, I can't stand it. Well, his wife died, her husband said. Yeah, sure, said Megan O'Donald. Like they'd spoken a single word to each other in ten years. I kept an even distance. They did not notice me. I was not a frightening person. Just don't think about it, Megan O'Donald's husband said, it's still a couple of days away, I don't know why you're already thinking about it. He unlatched a gate and took her hand. Together they climbed the steps to a pretty blue worker's cottage. It was a pretty tree-lined block. Someone had strung Christmas lights along the railings. They went inside the house, their house. They closed the door behind them. There were snow boots and umbrellas in the front hallway;

a long table with a lamp; a shallow bowl for keys. I walked deeper into the cold.

I took a turn, another turn, then entered a bar whose exterior sign featured a colossal neon parrot, its beak alone unilluminated, as if it had been torn violently from the glowing bird's face. It was a normal bar: dim and damp, the air mildewed. There were booths, tables, stools, chairs. There were draft taps and a lowboy fridge and dusty shelves lined with bottles of varyingly priced alcohol. Looking around, I could feel the room in its current state superimposing onto my memory, like a child's marker scribbling over a photograph, and I knew that I would never again be able to recall the bar as it had been before, that the present had retroactively reconfigured the past. I didn't care. None of it meant much to me. The bartender, I saw, was no longer the man I had known as a teenager, who had sported a fluffy gray beard and a baseball cap. Maybe the old bartender was dead. Years ago my friends and I would lurch through the front doors, frozen and drunk, and he would lift one hand to greet us, the palm rising like an object jerked by a wire, in a gesture between a wave and a heil. I had loved that bartender. He always knew what we wanted. What we wanted was a popular brand of spiked lemonade. We wanted fruit-flavored vodka. We wanted popcorn from the popcorn machine, and the boys wanted to watch the game on TV, and the girls wanted to get finger-banged by the college guys who arrived later, when the city was silent and the lights were on in the long hallways of the office buildings, miles away, downtown; and in some muddy way I believed I wanted to get finger-banged, too, but really what I wanted was to hold the hair of the girls who got sick, to kneel beside them on the bathroom floor as in a genuflection, and bring them flimsy plastic cups of water, and rub their backs in circles, and wipe up their puke when it splattered onto the toilet seat, listening to them gurgle out every hideous thing their boyfriends had done to them that week, so that for all eternity they would be compelled to remember me with an amalgam of horror, guilt, gratitude, and, I may have believed at the time, love. In those days I could have waited all night for some girl to start puking. I waited like a hound, sniffing the air.

The new bartender met my eyes. He hit his vape lazily. He did not have a fluffy gray beard. He was younger than me. A turbid white cloud materialized and dissipated, obscuring then revealing his face. This second revelation made him seem more beautiful than at first glance. At the end of the bar a middle-aged woman sat, texting with one finger, drinking a green liquid from a martini glass. After she finished typing, she clasped her hands together and raised her eyes to the ceiling, her lips incanting a sequence of words I couldn't make out. She knocked over her drink with an elbow then hastily returned it upright, scanning the room for witnesses. This was a woman of God, I thought. I watched her mop the viscous green liquid with her scarf. She tumbled off her stool and hoisted herself back on as if she had fallen from a horse. I removed my coat, my gloves, my hat, shoved them into a booth and ordered a whiskey. In my own texts I saw a photo of two living chickens, arranged outside their coop like loaves of bread. A deep golden light appeared to emerge from within them. Freaks, I typed. I took a photo of my half-empty drink and sent it across space. Lol, I wrote, I went home. He typed for a while, though when the message came through it only said Oh geez, followed by a tiny cartoon of a red face sweating. A minute passed. My brain cells had begun to swell and engorge. Stay safe out there, he said.

I drained my whiskey, ordered a beer, and sat back down. On my phone I read the headlines for an article about private equity, an article about a celebrity's carbon emissions, an article about fertility rates, an article about imperial decline. I returned to the image of Thomas's penis and zoomed in to get a better look at the neatly made bed in the background. One of his pillows was girlish and frilled. I envisioned him pacing the perimeter of the bedframe, ensuring that each corner of his quilt was appropriately tucked into the mattress before dropping his trousers and coaxing his penis into its alert and unfurled position. I thought about several nights I had spent in that bed, in the weeks since Thanksgiving, engaging in behaviors alongside Thomas's penis of which I was technically capable due to matters of physiology, musculature, and gravity. I slurped at my beer and attempted to cheer myself by affirming that I was technically capable of a huge number of behaviors, that I had engaged in these behaviors on many occasions, I was pretty sure, and not once had they caused me to literally die. There were rooms in the mind where a person could go when necessary. There were whole worlds of rooms in the mind.

There was one room I liked in particular, outfitted with a fainting couch draped in a cozy Qashqai rug, identical to that upon which Dr. Sigmund Freud had treated hysterical patients in his office, first in Vienna and then, after fleeing the Nazi occupation with his family and cherished Chow Chow, in London. In this room I had also placed a live pony, which I could stroke and feed juicy lettuce leaves, and a cupboard filled with snack cakes. The front door opened. I exited the room in my mind. A flood of cold air entered the bar and with it two men, both around my age. I watched them take off their coats, their gloves, their hats. One of the men removed his glasses, scrubbing away the fog with his shirt. He was a stranger to me. The other man was not a stranger to me. He was Benjamin Leichter, whom I had not seen in almost a decade. His parents lived right down the block. I had known this when I left the train with Megan O'Donald, at the stop where I used to get off to go to Benjamin Leichter's parties; I had known it when I passed Benjamin Leichter's parents' house on my way to the bar, pausing in the street to observe the lights on in what I believed, if memory served, was the living room. I closed my eyes, felt the stutter of my lids, and when I opened them, he was still there.

He was there. He was laughing. His bulging coat lay in his arms like a beloved pet. I recognized his ears, his nose, the width of his shoulders. There was nothing I hadn't seen before. I walked to the bathroom with my head bowed, my hair draped over one side of my face, and locked the door behind me. The walls were painted a spongy blue and coated in layers of Sharpied graffiti, an ongoing linguistic representation of the passage of time. SUCKY SUCKY SUCKY, I read. I read, LOVE'S MYSTERIES IN SOULS DO GROW BUT YET THE BODY IS HIS BOOK. I could not remember if I had written that one. The handwriting was cramped, jagged and ugly, not unlike mine. It had been scrawled near the toilet bowl, low to the ground, where I was kneeling now, puddled water soaking through the knees of my pants, and holding my own hair back with one hand, attempting to retch. Bile stung my throat, the deepest part of my nose, but nothing of substance emerged. I sputtered. I released my hair and washed my hands and rinsed my mouth under the tap. In the bottom of my bag I found a dull brown lipstick, which I smeared on, staring in the direction of my face in the mirror. My cheeks were red in weird places. My eyes were also red. I looked as old as Megan O'Donald had. It was almost three in the afternoon.

When I returned to my booth Benjamin Leichter and his friend were chatting with the bartender, whom they apparently knew. They asked if he had plans for the holidays. His father lived a few hours away, the bartender told them, in another state; he'd drive over there on Christmas Eve. He'd recently become an uncle, he said, and pulled out his phone to show them a photograph. They both cheered, then took turns hitting the bartender's vape. They wanted to buy him a drink. The bartender suggested that they all take a shot together. I watched the three men joyfully ingest their tiny tequilas, sucking at the pulp of their limes, smacking their lips. I felt myself standing, moving toward the bar to order another beer, as if I were being tugged along by some external force, which was exactly the sort of thing I was always saying was happening to me. I am a horse, I thought wildly, I am a horse being led by the bit, by my cruel and thoughtless master! I walked toward Benjamin Leichter, ready for him to fall, slobbering, to his knees, clutching at my ankles and begging my forgiveness, which I would offer with the loftiest generosity, like a monarch from her throne—whoops, Benjamin Leichter said, sorry, we're in your way! He scooted his stool to accommodate my approach. Then he registered me.

He leapt to his feet. His mouth grinned. His eyes were big and brown. He looked the same. He looked different. His hair hung longer than when I saw him last, almost to his shoulders. We were hugging, my face smashed against his neck. Dude, he said. How long has it been? We were no longer hugging. He smelled like his parents' house. I was not a horse, and neither was he. I felt the weight of his medium-sized hand on my upper arm. Wow, he said happily. Wow! I said. I reached into my wallet to pay for my drink, but he stopped me. I got it, he said, no worries. A high school friend, he told the bartender. We used to come here, back when Joey was working—did you ever know Joey? We were, like, twelve, he said, laughing. I heard myself laughing. Oh my god, I said, oh my god, we were so young. Benjamin introduced me to the bartender and then to his friend Leo. Leo was a graphic designer, Benjamin explained. Leo nodded. I said that was great. This was, in fact, all so great, I said. I thanked Benjamin Leichter for paying for my beer, very thoughtful, very gracious. I thanked Leo for his surely remarkable contributions to the field of graphic design. What an amazing coincidence, I said, and I said it again.

It had been ten years. I could feel my body pooling around me, pressing up against my clothes, the time that had accumulated in almost geological layers, as if I were an old stupid rock formation. I felt the droop of my face, my breasts, my arms, my stomach, my buttocks, the folds of baggy skin from years of rapid weight fluctuations, the cellulite, the discoloration, the fuzz that coated my upper lip, my pink head round as a balloon, the pocket of fat under my chin, the shadows and lines that curved darkly around my mouth. I looked at Benjamin Leichter. For so many years he had come to me in my most terrible dreams, performing small acts of kindness to animals, cooking soup for the homebound, putting down generous tips. He reached into his wallet. He put down a generous tip. Over the past decade he had grown even more deeply into himself, into a body that looked as though it had been waiting its whole life for him to eventually fill it. In his right earlobe he wore one tiny earring. Fear surged through me like a sickness—the fear that I was not hot enough for Benjamin Leichter to want to date-rape me again.

Benjamin and Leo sat in my booth. I faced the window, which was iced over, nearly opaque and drooled through with streaks of condensation. I could see nothing outside. The window as it existed in this particular time and space seemed to negate the general concept of "window," I thought. I am having a series of lucid and penetrating thoughts, I thought. My face throbbed. The men raised their glasses and I lifted mine, moving its rim against each of theirs. Beer dribbled onto my hand and snaked down my forearm. L'chaim, Leo said. Benjamin laughed. Dude, he said. Happy Chanukah. Three Jews walk into a bar, Leo said. Benjamin's white-blond hair looked almost pink in the dim light. Dude, he said again. His elbows were on the table. He was leaning toward me. I saw the pad of his tongue, dense and supine in its mouth. It's great to see you, he said. We were like, is she dead? He laughed. He had laughed a lot when we were teenagers. He had played ice hockey, eaten burgers, worked hard in school, treated his younger brothers with kindness. I told him I was not dead. Awesome! he said. His shirt sleeves bunched sweetly around his wrists. His forehead was as smooth as an infant's. I decided to direct the conversation away from the question of my physical or spiritual demise. I asked Leo where he was from; he named a suburb I had not heard of. So great, I said. I love it there. Oh, yeah? Leo said. Did you ever go to the cheese shop? I adored that cheese shop, I said, with its incredible variety of cheeses. Leo informed me that the owner of the cheese shop had recently been arrested for the sexual assault of minors. He had been doing all that stuff in the cheese basement, Leo said. Now the cheese shop was forever closed. But it wasn't such bad news; Leo had hated that cheese shop. He was surprised to hear I had liked it. The quality of their cheese selection had been, he said, awful. When it was revealed that the owner of the cheese shop had been raping minors in the cheese basement, it all made sense to him; the shop had to have been a front.

They didn't even have Irish cheddar, Leo said. I absolutely *love* a sharp Irish cheddar cheese, I said. I proceeded to name my other favorite cheeses: Manchego, Camembert, Taleggio. I could hear the strain in my voice like a bad violin. Gruyere, Gouda, chèvre, I screeched. I met Benjamin Leichter's eyes. He looked so happy to see me. He looked exactly like an old friend. At the bottoms of our glasses lay gentle wisps of foam, like clouds over a beach I had never in my life been to. I'll get the next round, I screamed. I had difficulty navigating out of the booth. My clumsy scooting motion nearly toppled my coat, my gloves, my hat. We all laughed.

The bartender was nicer to me this time; maybe because he had seen that I knew Benjamin Leichter, that I had known Benjamin Leichter when he was something other than the thing he would one day become. He pushed three beers toward me, wearing an expression that I decided meant he was trying to ascertain whether I had ever encountered Benjamin Leichter's teenaged penis. A horrible thump sounded from the other end of the bar. I twisted my torso; the texting woman had slid off her stool and was posed serenely on the floor, unmoving, as if she believed a supreme stillness would soon render her invisible—a feeling I knew well. She clambered to her feet. I returned to my task, maneuvering the three drinks into a manageable triangular formation and shaping my fingers around them like a rocket preparing to lift off. The woman stumbled toward me. She poked me on the shoulder. I looked at her. Incest cousin, she hissed. I looked away in case she was speaking to someone else. She poked me again. Her eyes were brown and bulging. Her spittle landed on my cheek. Don't *you* look like the incest cousin, she said. She stuck out her tongue and waggled it at me. Martha, the bartender said in a warning tone. She *does*, Rob, Martha pouted. I know she does, he said, but you really shouldn't say that. Sorry, he mouthed in my direction. No, no, no, I said, flapping my hands to convey how unoffended I was that this woman had basically spat in my face and called me the incest cousin. It's my fault, I said. I apologized to Martha and then to the bartender. The edges of Martha's skull pulsed in my vision like a heartbeat. I wasn't surprised, I said, to hear that I looked like the incest cousin—no, it didn't surprise me in the slightest, and I was sorry, truly sorry for any harm I was causing by having the face that I had, this face I had been given, that I had never wanted in the first place. I started to cry. Martha's expression softened. Fat wrinkles furrowed her cheeks like parentheses. Honey, she said, are you Lebanese? I had slumped onto a stool and was thrusting my index finger into one of the three beers like a thermometer. Martha took a seat beside me. No, I blubbered, I was so sorry, but I wasn't Lebanese. I looked behind me to see if Benjamin Leichter was watching me cry, but he remained immersed in conversation with Leo. My grandmother was Lebanese, Martha said sympathetically. She was stroking my hair. You gotta understand, she said, the incest cousin died last year. He had a cancer of the pancreas. You're not doing anyone any harm carrying around that face. That face is not a legacy, not necessarily. I'll tell you what, she said, knocking a fist against the table for emphasis, I can be harsh,

I know I can. My son always says it to me. Gee, Mom, he says, you sure can be harsh. You can be a real bitch, he says. You do behave at times like a grade-A cunt, my son tells me. Mother, he says, you are a disgusting slut, a vixen, a whore. And it's true, I can be harsh. But it's only because I've been on the run for so long. She glanced around and scooted her stool closer to mine. From neo-Nazis, she whispered. I also glanced around, to assure her that I was invested in securing the perimeter against any neo-Nazis who might be lurking in the vicinity, preparing to strike her down, and then I leaned in, until her forehead, with its soft crumpled flesh like the interior of a baked potato, was almost resting upon mine, and proceeded to relay to her in a rapid whisper the fact that I was sexually frigid and incapable of experiencing orgasm-with-partner, moving my hands in free-flowing watery shapes as I spoke in an effort to demonstrate the feelings that passed through me like a river, because of something that had happened to me when I was a seventeen-year-old virgin, I told her, plus another related thing that happened to me several years later, a statement to which Martha responded by gasping, flailing her arms so wildly that she almost fell off her stool once more, and slapping a palm over her mouth in a convulsion of utter physiological shock and horror. The bartender raised his eyebrows. He twirled a finger apologetically near his ear canal to signal that he believed Martha to be either clinically or metaphorically insane, which he hoped, his gesture implied, would not prevent me or my old friend Benjamin Leichter from frequenting this bar in the future, indulging, reminiscing, putting down generous tips, and I ignored him because, although I too believed that Martha was either clinically or metaphorically insane, I also believed this may have been the first time in my entire life that any person living or dead had reacted with the appropriate level of gravitas to the words I said out loud. Firmly, encouragingly, Martha clasped one of my hands in hers. Her skin was soft and oily, as if recently slathered in lotion. The more I spoke, the more embryonic I felt; I imagined each word pumping out a nourishing fluid to surround me, feed me, keep me safe. The week before the first thing happened to me, I babbled in a whisper, though I no longer cared if Benjamin Leichter could hear, my mother had yanked me into her bathroom to tell me I had better make haste and lose my virginity ASAP, that otherwise I would develop a chip on my shoulder and turn into a repulsive and incomprehensible lesbian; my mother told me I should let anyone do it to me, I whispered to Martha, I should allow any person to do it to me who might be willing to do it to me, I should lay there and squeeze my eyes shut and *think of England* while someone did it to me, ASAP, that terrible thing, my mother said, which would be very painful, my mother told me, I whispered, *think of England*, she had said, giggling each time she repeated it, although we were not from England, my mother was born into the Soviet Union six years after the death of Iosif Vissarionovich Stalin, fourteen years after the end of the Second World War, in a certain sense the opposite of England, I had never been to England, I whispered, and perhaps I should have voiced these observations to my mother at the time but in the reality that was my life I did not, in my real life I watched as my mother started to chant, *Let a doorman do it, Let a doorman do it,* hopping around with a plush towel wrapped in such a way that it concealed her breasts and her mons pubis, her hair stringy and wet, her strong musician's hands clapping with glee. The bathroom had been thick with the smell of roses; under the roses the smell of my mother's skin, freshly scrubbed but still musty; underneath it all the faint rich scent of shit, gurgling through the new-construction pipes. It was so specific, I whispered to Martha, and we didn't even have a doorman; who was the doorman my mother wanted to make love to me while I lay bleeding and thinking of England and attempting to remind myself that everything that happens is only time, a sequence of time, a stack of instants, unless of course you were dead, death signifying either the total loss of time or the entrance into eternal time, two concepts that may ultimately function as the same concept, and how could something that was only time *hurt* you? Time was a concept, I explained, and concepts couldn't *hurt* you. Martha asked me if it was possible that my mother was a neo-Nazi. No, I said, I did not think my mother was a neo-Nazi. From Martha's lips came a noncommittal smacking sound that implied my denial was unconvincing, but she did not further pursue her line of questioning. Who did it in the end, she asked instead, the thing that happened to you when you were a seventeen-year-old virgin? Her head was bobbing toward me, as though she were performing a complex swimming stroke upon which her survival depended.

It was a doorman, I lied. In the end, it was a doorman who did it.

It was unclear to me how long we had been talking. All the sounds in the bar remained what they had been: the radiator hum, the dopey jazz from the digital jukebox, objects encountering other objects, wood, glass, plastic, the liquid slosh in someone's mouth, maybe mine. The quality of light was the same; the window continued to negate the concept of "window"; the bartender wiped down the bar with a wet white cloth. I had finished half of my beer. The other two glasses sat untouched, divots depressing their crests of foam. Once in a dream Benjamin Leichter and I had picnicked at the edge of an algal-bloomed pond. Out-of-shape tourists pedaled boats constructed to look like big wild birds. We had shared a tuna salad sandwich. Behind my stool Benjamin Leichter's chest nearly grazed the back of my head. Martha braced herself against the bar and vomited onto the floor. Jesus fuck, the bartender said. I scrambled down to my hands and knees in an effort to contribute, clean up, make clear my prevailing use-value, though I had no towels. Benjamin Leichter reached out a hand to help me stand. He turned to Martha, who was swaying on her stool, staring vacantly at the puddle of sludge before her. How about we get you home? he said. The bartender brought his hands together in a gesture of prayerful thanks. Martha nodded. Leo joined us. We both watched Benjamin take Martha's phone, help her call a car, gather her belongings—her purse, her hat, her jacket—speaking to her the whole time in low, soothing tones, as if she were a farm animal giving birth. Leo laughed. Benjamin led Martha to the door, an arm around her shoulders to steady her as she stumbled, muttering, a dribble of vomit running onto her chin, and I followed, stopping at the entryway as the car pulled up and Benjamin helped her into the back seat, passed her her bag, said a few friendly words to the driver, handed over a cash tip. Martha didn't look back at me. Already the sun was beginning its mindless plunge, elongating the shadows that spilled into the street. The prairie sky stretched above the city like a parachute. It was a perfect winter afternoon. The car drove off. Inside the bar the vomit had been wiped up, but its stench lingered, slurred together with the antiseptic brightness of cleaning supplies.

We finished our beers in the booth. Leo described a new project he was working on, web design for a feminist cybersecurity start-up. Chill vibes, he said, they want chill vibes, they're pretty cool—woman-owned, he explained, nodding in my direction. Benjamin talked about his job: somehow related to data analytics, targeted advertising based on a set of obscure demographic variables. I tried to discuss the evasions of Esther Summerson's narration in *Bleak House*, her repeated turning away from the self, which could be taken as an irritating Victorian modesty, but might be read instead as a form of intimacy, intimacy through privacy; I should go, Leo said, my brother's flying in from California. He slapped Benjamin on the shoulder, shook my hand, it was nice to meet me, he left.

One of Benjamin's arms was draped over the back of the booth. His body sat slack and easeful, as if it had been fed a satisfying meal. When he smiled, dainty lines wriggled around the corners of his eyes like maggots. I asked him how his brothers were doing. He shrugged. Noah was fine, but Sammy had had some mental health stuff in college; he'd ended up taking a leave, never went back. He was living at home, at least for a while. It sucked, if I wanted the truth, it wasn't a good situation—not to overshare. His parents were worried, he worried too, but everybody had their shit, right, and Sammy was a great kid, he was smart and young, he still had a lot going for him. I joined Benjamin on his side of the booth. Between us the leather seating was cracked, a tuft of beige fluff sprouting out like a crop. What had I been talking about, anyway, he asked, with that drunk lady?

Just family, I said.

The jukebox jazz was no longer playing. The bartender was in the bathroom. At home, my parents would be lying on their backs like injured insects, taking an afternoon nap. I lifted a hand and moved it through Benjamin Leichter's hair, a few strands stiff between my fingers, as if they had been dipped in glue. My sister was at the gym, pinning people to the ground between her knees. Somewhere Cordelia was sitting at a table with her mother and sister, discussing her dead father, how strange the holidays seemed without him. Or maybe not. I pushed my face toward Benjamin's, keeping my eyes open so I could watch his features merge and distend in my field of vision, until he was no longer a person I knew. I poked my tongue out and slid it over his lips, prodding firmly at their seam until they parted and the smell of his spit melted into mine, meaty, sour. I felt around in his mouth and there was his tongue, enormous and soft, gritty on top with a slick wet underside like an oyster in its shell, lying limp as I pulsed the muscle of my own above and below it. I clutched at his shirt, licked his teeth, swallowed a thin rope of his saliva. Disgust worked its way through my body like a tapeworm, as it always did, and I began to hope, as I always did, that if I could push myself to descend fully into the well of my revulsion, I might eventually fall through to the other side, to a place I could almost stand on—the tightrope of my desire. Just because this had never happened before didn't mean it would never happen in the future. All the world could be different; I was embodying the infinite human capacity for change; Benjamin Leichter and I were, together, retroactively reconfiguring the past. I lifted one of my legs over one of his, so that his thigh was nestled in my crotch, and humped vigorously in a demonstration of my sexual enthusiasm, thrusting my breasts against his chest, wriggling my tongue in the direction of his uvula and emitting coy panting noises like the ones I had heard so often through the walls of my apartment at the Academy. I fought back the compressed sensation in my ribcage, my organs gasping under my skin, and reminded myself that this was only a stack of instants, a concept, that I was participating in an interesting and rigorous intellectual experiment, if I could reframe it in teleological Marxian terms, perhaps these were the necessary stages of my development, it was true that inside of me things were getting worse, infinitely worse with each passing second, but maybe that actually meant they were getting better, I sucked at his tongue and pumped my crotch against his leg, the contradictions were deepening, generating deeper crises, eventually the machinery would break, the glorious world revolution would come, I would experience orgasm-with-partner, adult sexuality, the proper entanglement of love and desire, I could feel every hair on my head screaming in its socket, and I tried to coerce into my mind an image I had once seen of Iosif Stalin and his second wife, some years before her suicide, standing side by side, staring directly at the camera, no, at me, the shadowy photograph blurring their arms together so that they almost appeared to be holding hands, although it was impossible to deny that they both looked so sad. I loosened my grip on Benjamin Leichter's shirt and plunged an arm to his lap. His face was drawing back from mine. His hand was between us, on my shoulder, his leg pulled out from under me, and I was falling in a new way now, past disgust, into a humiliation so familiar that it felt like entering a house in which I had once lived for many years. I don't think this is okay, he said, quietly and kindly, and then he said it louder, patting me on the arm like a dog.

You're super drunk, he explained.

The sky was dark. My driver carried me south along the lake. In front of us streamed a river of cars, their taillights the eyes of nocturnal animals swimming backward. The cost of this ride would be automatically withdrawn from my checking account, my location tracked and registered, my data stored. Benjamin Leichter was right. I was super drunk. Heat flowed from the car's vents onto my lap. The air smelled strongly of the fried food the driver must have inhaled between rides; the seat warmer, turned on for my comfort, made me feel like I was peeing in one continuous gush. I swallowed the urge to puke. We hit the downtown curves, my favorite part of the drive, which I had been borne through so many times, first as a child in the backseat, then drunk with friends, riding shotgun, city-side in the frenzied summers, the windows rolled down, my elbow on the sill and a hand drifting over sticky pockets of air, an action my parents had warned would lead to my inevitable maiming, but at that time I did not give a shit if I got maimed, because tearing through me as my friends debated which of our teachers might be finger-banging which of our classmates was a sensation of existential freedom and personal insignificance so overwhelming that I could not believe anyone had ever once felt as I did, entangling even my early experiences of beauty with the idea that I was and always would be totally separate from, and perhaps better, if also more depressed, than other people. If other people were real, I thought, I would die, and I did not want to die, therefore they could not be real. Some ideas were simple. We took the bend, the other bend. I wondered what Iosif Vissarionovich Stalin would have made of it all, the city's stupid decadence, its stupid squalor, and I remembered the tears that had welled in my eyes when my ex-boyfriend and I first descended into Moscow's Mayakovskaya station, a hundred feet below the street, his face grinning up at me as the escalator moved us to the vaulted platform, where, recessed into the ceiling like jewels, there were dozens of Soviet utopian mosaics—ski jumpers, pole vaulters, the joyful thrusting legs of joyful laborers—beauty available to all the noble working people, I had whispered, and he whispered back that it wasn't so easy, we needed to acknowledge the violence, the terror, the betrayal of the revolution, poor sweet Trotsky, whom he had once dressed as for Halloween, with those funny little spectacles, but then he shook his head—no, he'd changed his mind, he smiled, he touched my hand, it wasn't more complicated than that at all. Each mosaic had promised me that dignity lay thrashing right there in the beyond; that the future would be fundamentally different from the past. From the car window I saw the pier slicing through the invisible lake, and on the other side a startling vista of high-rises, their uniform white squares of American light making them seem uninhabited. Below them the parks were empty, cutting black swathes through the city like stamps. I asked my driver if he could imagine saying the words "blow job" to one of his female riders. Was there ever a context in which he could see that happening? His eyes met mine in the mirror. He looked afraid. I'm not saying that, he said, I never said that. I knew that, I told him, of course he hadn't, but could he imagine it, as a possibility, an act he might be driven to, under a particular set of circumstances? I never said that, he repeated, shaking his head. The lake was behind us. He was pulling over fast, letting me out on the wrong side of the street. Thank you, I told him, grasping at the door handle, thank you, five stars, Merry Christmas.

The evening hour was early enough that I should have seen neighbors out walking dogs or jogging, but the sidewalks were deserted. The darkness had brought with it a new iteration of cold. I crossed the street and vomited into a trash can at the end of the block, next to an ash tree I had loved since childhood, leafless, the pale interior bursting its thin-skinned bark in streaks. I sipped at the freezing air until my nausea receded, then lumbered in the direction of my parents' house. On the terrace the flower boxes were dotted with yellow lights, overflowing with drooping evergreen foliage—Christmas tree leftovers, I assumed, that my mother must have bargained for at an out-of-the-way hardware store, just as she had a habit of driving to the Russian supermarket a half hour outside the city to purchase the cheap butt ends of cold cuts, slips of turkey and ham encased in shining brown skin like leather. The kitchen lights were on. For a second I stood in the street and stared into the warmly lit room, as I often had as a child. Even then I had understood that I could only ever love it from the outside; even then I had feared that I might spend my entire life going outside so that I could love things. In the world of the mind I saw another house, another state, a bed I had shared for four years, a book I had yet to read, one dresser drawer for me and one for thee, all those mugs I had neglected to wash, tea bags fuzzing with mold. I unlatched the gate and fumbled my key in the door. The alarm went off. My fingers punched in the code, the same one I had used for years as my phone and debit card PIN, a sequence of numbers my parents had chosen at random, or perhaps that had been preselected by the security company. Upstairs someone was picking out the beginning of Schumann's *Kinderszenen* on the baby grand. I could almost feel my own right foot on the pedal, the metal sliding against the sole of my sock. I took off my boots and stepped into the slippers my mother had left for me, encased in delicate velvet roses, striped ribbons, cinched at the ankle with elastic satin. The music stopped. My sister's voice called out my diminutive. I smelled frying onions, heard my father's laugh. It was not as if I had never been happy here. Once my mother had baked me a cake in the shape of a mouse.

In the kitchen my mother was leaning over the stove, wet to the wrists with potato juice. My father uncorked a wine bottle at the island. Next to him my sister stood, smiling blandly in her finely woven gray sweater, through which I could see the curving muscles of her biceps, her lean waist, her high round breasts and the dusky roots of her nipples. She had the remnants of a black eye, faded to an elegant shade of lavender, and a bright red welt marking one of her cheeks. Along the side of her neck lay a thin bruise. Otherwise, her face was a slimmer version of mine.

She walked around the island and hugged me. I had a loose-edged childhood memory of her fist jamming me in the stomach with such force that it stopped my breath, but I could not remember if she had ever really punched me or if this was only a lie I had told once to impress my parents. It was so good to see me, my sister said. She spoke in the voice that had been hers for many years, beneath which I continued to believe she was hiding her real voice, her secret voice, the voice I had once loved. Her hair sagged around her cheeks in wispy curls. *Kinderszenen*—a brown-nosing, simpering, manipulative choice, a psyop, a plant, a transparent attempt to kneecap me with beauty so that she could go on violating me, bringing me down, and ruining my life; and of course I remembered her playing it; of course I remembered playing it myself, throughout the endless winters, my father poking at the fire, my father's brown slippers, my mother's cup of tea, my father trotting downstairs to practice his Dvořák concerto; of course I could see myself, the way I was then, sitting on the stairs, my knees tucked into my chin, out of view and listening to him play, the thick intake of his breath over and around the downbow. Almost as if he were singing.

It looks like someone beat the shit out of you, I told my sister in my most complimentary tone. People probably assume you're a battered woman!

She sighed, turned her bruises into the light. It could be awkward, she admitted, with cashiers, with servers, in work meetings.

Don't fight, my mother said, flicking water from her hands at the sink. She joined us, accepting a glass of wine from my father. Her hand was damp against the stem. We were all standing. Every chair had been removed from the room. Oil sputtered on the stove. In a wooden bowl lay floppy leaves of butter lettuce.

We never fight, my sister said.

We're not fighting, I said.

My mother smoothed my sister's hair behind her ears. Look at her, she commanded, pointing out my sister's bruises. Look at what they do to her. My sister batted her eyes.

I have two retarded daughters, my mother said happily.

My father edged over to my sister and me and offered us each a glass of wine. My sister shook her head. She couldn't understand the point of drinking. It made her feel tired, she sighed. It made her feel weird. It was difficult, to confront the fact that other people were capable of experiencing so many delectable pleasures beyond her capacity, she said. She must be missing a gene—the gene that allowed for the experience of delectable pleasures.

Not even a sip? my father asked.

Oh no, my sister said, no, I couldn't. I must be missing a gene.

Is it the calories? I said loudly. I watched the faint twitch of her nostril, and then her expression righted itself.

Of course not, she said.

Of course not! I screamed.

I yanked a glass of wine from my father's hand, thanked him, and chugged it—trying not to vomit, my throat working at the liquid—to display to all present that I was sensually and morally superior to my sister, in no way missing a gene. Excellent, I gasped.

Where were you today? my sister asked when I had finished wiping my mouth. Mama and Papa were worried you might not come home for dinner, they didn't know when you'd be back, you weren't responding to their texts.

I went to meet up with an old friend, I said. I held my glass out for my father to refill.

You don't have any friends, my mother said.

Which friend? my sister asked.

An old friend, I said, from high school, no one you'd remember.

She's lying, my mother announced, selecting a water cracker from a bowl and gnawing on it. She went to get a disgusting tattoo.

I said that I had not gone to get a tattoo. My mother shook the bowl of crackers at me. No, thank you, I said.

A tattoo? my father said, eyes widening.

Did you really? my sister asked. You went to get a tattoo?

No, I screamed, I really did not get a fucking tattoo.

My mother stared at me. You smell like shit, she said in Russian. Go clean yourself. Go brush your hair. Go wash your tattoo.

I focused on the wall behind my mother and apologized for screaming, cursing, and smelling like shit. It had been windy out, I explained, using my hands to make a blowing motion around my head, my hair got messed up, I would be right back.

Don't be too long, my sister said with a placid smile. Mama is cooking such an amazing meal for us.

I went to the upstairs bathroom. My face was puffy, streaked with eyeliner. My lipstick had moved around my mouth, staining parts of my skin a strange mauve color. The whites of my eyes were swollen and bleary. I had looked worse, I reminded myself—yes, I had absolutely looked worse. I brushed my teeth and hair, rinsed the makeup from my face, changed into fresh clothes. Over my T-shirt I pulled two thick sweaters, then bundled myself in a blanket and stepped out onto my bedroom's egress balcony for a cigarette. Across the way a luxury condominium rose up, reflecting the dark sky—never as dark here as it could be, as one imagined it must be in other places—and the sharp lines of the high-rises opposite. In a few apartments I could make out the shapes of the inhabitants, trapped in their windows as if in a computer screen. I put my phone to my ear, pinning it against my shoulder so that I could shove one hand back inside the blanket. It rang twice, and then there was the sound of his name in the voicemail greeting. Hi, I said to no one, it's me, coming at you live, you know how Stalin's eldest son tried to kill himself but the bullet lodged in the wrong part of his chest, and you know when Stalin heard the news, he was like *Ha ha ha! He can't even shoot straight!*—if we're to believe the Western propaganda, that is, the nefarious capitalist biographers, this is not a suicide threat, by the way, I clarified, I was mainly calling to say hey, Happy Chanukah, in case you had a minute to talk. I hung up and hurled my unfinished cigarette off the balcony, where it looped in the wind, dissolving into black before I could watch it hit the asphalt. I pressed the heels of my hands into my eyelids and, for a few seconds, imagined that I was wailing and thrashing about in a small, clean room, a room in which there were no signs that others had lived before me, where everything would always be completely pure, completely bare, completely safe.

A pitcher of water.

A vase of tulips on the sill.

Then I stopped imagining.

When I returned downstairs my mother was in the middle of a story about a new friend she had made, a young woman in her French class. What a perfect idiot I am, she was saying, dressing the salad with one hand, her eyes ticking between my sister and my father, to have trusted again, when life has already shown me countless times that anyone you open yourself up to will only betray you and break your heart, especially these Americans, these females, these cold fish.

I'm really sorry, Mama, my sister said. Her voice was limp. People can be so disappointing, can't they? People can be awful.

Some people, my father said, really don't appear to feel as deeply as others.

All the time she walks around with her big fat neck showing like a gobble gobble turkey, my mother said, and if you go to the restaurant with her she eats off a plate using her *fingers*. She set aside the salad bowl to do an impression of her new friend hunched over, nibbling and sucking at her hands like a rat. When she spotted me at the threshold of the kitchen, she removed her fingers from her mouth.

It's you, my mother said. You look exactly like a humongous baby!

I thanked her. She was grinning, her lashes trembling ecstatically around their orbs. Then without warning her face collapsed inward, as if her bones had been turned to jelly. It's getting late, she said. Exhaustion seeped into her voice, a quivering fragility that dripped from her lips like a gas, soaking the air—one of those rapid modulations in her tone with which I was so familiar. My body responded before I could bring forth a single thought: a precognitive jolt. Let's just do the candles and then we can eat in the bathroom, she said. I looked at my father, who was blinking rapidly in my mother's direction, panic tugging down the corners of his mouth. My sister fixed her eyes on the island, her sleeves rolled up to expose the fresh marbling of bruises on her forearms.

The bathroom? I said.

Because of the floors, my mother said.

Why not your bedroom? I said. Your massive bedroom?

We can't eat in the *bedroom*, she scoffed.

She took a sip from her glass and peered at each of us in turn. Her eyes were huge, triumphant, the turgid green of the lake in a lightning storm, boring into mine like screws. I looked away and thought of the stories she used to tell me, when I was young and ugly, about how gorgeous she had been, since the day she was born—how stunningly gorgeous she had always been, her entire life. I could feel my self slipping away from itself. For a second I clutched at it; but it was like running my hands through a pool of water.

It's the seventh night of Chanukah, my mother said. Her tone had shifted again: syrupy, melancholic, liquid. I watched my father swallow his wine and attempt to recalibrate.

My father's birthday, she continued in her new voice.

Your mother is a Jewish person, my father explained hastily.

My father's parents were killed in 1941, my mother said, by Lithuanian Nazis.

I know, I said.

That's terrible, my sister said.

You didn't know it was *Lithuanian* Nazis, my mother said to me.

I decided it was not unlikely, I said, given the timeline, given what we've learned about the extent of Lithuanian collaboration; given that Nazi propaganda associated the Jews with the Bolsheviks, blamed the Jews for the annexation of Lithuania by Iosif Vissarionovich Stalin's Soviet Union; given that Lithuania eradicated a greater percentage of its Jewish population than almost any other country; given the violent enthusiasm of the local paramilitary forces; given all of these historical facts, I decided it was not unlikely that the perpetrators had been Lithuanian collaborators rather than Nazis proper.

My father's village had only nine hundred people, my mother said, and three hundred Jews were murdered.

I know, I said.

Including my father's parents, my mother said.

I know, I said.

So horrible, my sister said.

Three hundred out of nine hundred, my mother said, it would have been people you knew, your neighbors, can you imagine.

Yes, I said.

Unbelievable, my sister said.

Your neighbors, my mother said.

Your mother is a Jewish person, my father said.

And who knows what happened to my mother's parents and her twelve-year-old sister, my mother said.

What do you mean? I said. We know what happened.

Maybe we don't know, my sister said.

But we know, I said, we know they were in the Kovno ghetto, we know your mother's sister was murdered in the Kinder Aktion, twelve years old, we know your mother's mother was killed then, too, we know they didn't make it to the camps.

I don't know that, my mother said.

We know that, I said. I went there, I went to the mass grave, I said Kaddish over a field of the dead, we've spoken about this, you're the one who told me this.

I don't know what you're talking about, my mother said.

Your mother is a Jewish person, my father said.

I am also a Jewish person, I said.

You're an American, my mother said, laughing, you're a little American girl.

I am a part of the Jewish diaspora! I screamed.

It must be terrible for you, Mama, my sister said, that we'll never know what really happened.

Kinderlach—my mother's voice soared like a bird, swooped, hovered—I should tell you, I am going to go back to Vilnius. She pressed her hand over her heart as though preparing to break out into nationalist song.

No, you're not, I said.

Wow, Mama, that's a big deal, my sister said. That's amazing.

Late this spring, my mother said.

No, you're not, I said more loudly. You haven't been back since you were eleven years old, you've sworn up and down that you would never, no matter the circumstances, return, that you would never set foot there again, that it was too much, that you couldn't take it.

I am going back, my mother said, glaring at me, and then I'm going to go again and again and again, lots of times before I die.

Your mother has made a courageous decision, my father said, a beautiful and important Jewish decision.

I am confronting my past, my mother said.

No, I said.

Things change, my mother said. You get older. Life is amazing.

No, I said.

Stop crying, my mother said. You look ridiculous.

This isn't about you, my sister stage-whispered.

You've constantly been crying, crying, wah wah, your whole life, putting on a show, trying to make me kill myself, my mother said.

Jewish people like your mother have intolerable histories, due to the Holocaust, fleeing the Soviet Union for the nation of Israel, cruel parents, estranged sisters, and other miscellaneous factors, said my father.

I stand with the Bund, I shouted, I stand with the long history of Jewish anti-Zionist struggle, I stand against the invocation of the Holocaust to justify the genocidal project of an ethnostate, I stand with Karl Kautsky, I stand with Rosa Luxemburg, I stand with Albert Einstein—

And then we will go to London and Paris and Amsterdam, my mother said, away from the harsh and provincial East, back to the cosmopolitan West!

I think you have some vomit on your chin, my sister said.

Baruch atah, Adonai Eloheinu, Melech haolam, asher kid'shanu b'mitzvotav v'tsivanu l'hadlik ner shel Chanukah, we all said.

The menorah was an entangled mass of silver rope. In it I saw my face reflected, a shiver of fragments crowned by the tiny flames my mother had coaxed into being.

When I was little you used too much soap on my vagina in the bath and it really stung, I said.

We piled our plates with latkes, salad, sour cream, my mother's homemade apple sauce, the skins loosed from their flesh in curls of blushing pink.

The renovations look fantastic, my sister said.

There were wooden chairs in my parents' vast bathroom, arranged around a plastic folding table I had not known they owned.

I'm teaching a seminar called The Literature of the City, I said.

These latkes are delicious, my sister said.

My mother said that my father would be playing a solo next season.

The Elgar? I asked.

That's right, my father said, the Elgar.

I love the Elgar, my sister said.

Me too, I said.

Two sinks, white ceramic, clean as teeth.

My sister said she was competing soon, down south, the first time in a while, she was nervous.

Have you heard Jacqueline du Pré play it? my father asked.

Vaginal pH is delicate, I said, and too much soap can be disruptive to its ecosystem.

What do you know about the city? my mother said.

I'm sure you'll do great, I said.

I hope so, said my sister.

There was a drop of wine on the table.

The way she interprets it, my father said.

Beat them up, my mother said in Russian.

Less soap, less firmly applied, less stinging, I said.

My sister handed me a package of red tissue paper.

There were two drops of wine.

I have a present for you too, I lied, but it got delayed in transit.

Where did this table come from? my sister said.

My father would have been one hundred and one years old, my mother said.

A delicate golden necklace, pretty, with a charm in the shape of a whale.

I asked my parents if I could have money for Chanukah.

How much, my mother asked.

You know that calling Albert Einstein an “anti-Zionist” is a serious misrepresentation, my sister said.

Two hundred dollars, I said.

Behind me the toilet made a gurgling sound.

My mother’s framed photograph of Simone de Beauvoir.

Fine, my mother said.

The gurgling stopped.

One hundred and one years old, my mother said.

Would you like cash? asked my father.

Cash would be great, I said.

It started to snow, beyond the bathtub, beyond the window.

I hate Tchaikovsky's endings, said my mother. You hear one beautiful melody and then it's just on and on ad nauseam and it's like, get over it.

These latkes are delicious, my father said.

Look at the snow, my sister said.

You don't hate Tchaikovsky's endings, I said.

I never said I did, said my mother.

# I

*

I returned to the Academy on a Wednesday in the first week of January. My journey involved a short flight to a major coastal metropolis in the Northeast, then a cab ride to town, over an hour's drive without traffic. I departed early in the morning and watched through the plane windows as we heaved above the runway, the rows of empty aircraft parked in their slots like animals in a manger, the winding highways and the winding train tracks. Below us lay squares of square houses, same-heighted, dense with light; commuters in their kitchens, readying for the drive downtown. We carved through a sheet of cloud, and the city ceased to exist. The sky was a soupy blue. There was nothing else to see.

Fifteen minutes after takeoff, the woman occupying the seat next to mine fell asleep. Twice her head drifted toward my shoulder but twitched away before contact, as if she could sense my proximity in her dreams. Some time later I too fell asleep, my cheek pressed against the glass. When I awoke my seatmate was sipping at a complimentary ginger ale from the beverage cart, her plastic tray extended over her lap and notching into her stomach. Upon noticing that I was conscious she wriggled an arm under the tray, retrieved a second can from her seatback pocket, and thrust it toward me. She had asked the flight attendant for an extra, she explained, when she saw that I was sleeping. I began to thank her profusely, but she interrupted me. Years ago, my seatmate said, she had fallen asleep on a plane—very early into the flight, perhaps even before takeoff—and the trolley had passed her by. For the first time in her life she had failed to procure the ritual ginger ale to which she routinely looked forward when flying. In general she was not a superstitious woman, but on that particular day she had been certain this was a bad omen, and until landing an obscure sensation of disorientation and unease had coursed through her like an infection. She experienced her lack as a presence, she said, a physical presence inside of her. A present absence. At intervals she had been forced to unbuckle her belt and bolt to the bathroom, even during periods of turbulence, each time apologizing to the poor gentleman in the aisle seat until, at last, he offered to swap places. Because I had the runs, she confided. She leaned closer. And that day, she whispered, was September 10, 2001. She spread her hands and raised her eyebrows. I thanked her again for the ginger ale. Narrow as a telephone booth, she said, shaking her head. Like taking a shit in a telephone booth.

We drank our sodas side by side, streaming different shows on our individual seatback screens. Halfway into my episode a male voice piped simultaneously through the plane's loudspeaker and from my wired earbuds, announcing our imminent descent. The plane landed without issue. When the wheels touched down, my seatmate whistled and applauded, stamping her feet. I alone joined her, to demonstrate my gratitude for what she had done for me, clapping my hands and softly whooping. Before we disembarked, she explained to me that her father had been a military pilot in Vietnam. He had been killed, she said, when she was a teenager. I was sorry to hear that, I told her; it was horrible to imagine all the lives lost in such a senseless war. Her father had not actually died in active duty, my seatmate said. Years after his military service he had crashed a small personal plane while flying in inclement weather. He had built the plane himself from a kit, a two-seater, assembled in their garage. How awful, I said, to lose your father so young, under such tragic circumstances. That day, she said, the passenger seat had been occupied by her father's underage mistress—one of her classmates, the most beautiful girl in her grade—who was also killed in the accident. My seatmate told me that when she was a child, her father used to kick her in the head, throw chairs at her, and pinch her lower lip until the skin broke. As a teenager she had been proud of her long hair, until one night her father wrapped it around his forearm like a rope and lopped it off using her mother's sewing shears.

I took a cab from the airport back to campus and paid the driver with several bills from the stack my parents had handed me before I left. A week of break remained. The student dorms were closed; only one of the faculty housing units had its lights on. Over the Academy's hill the low clouds sat like a ledge. I felt pinned, mounted. I had a vision of the clouds sinking further and further until they suffocated the church steeple and the peaked roofs, the holly tree in the courtyard, the old cemetery, the ocean, me—pressing us all deep into the earth like a machine. Just because this had never happened before didn't mean it would never happen in the future. I rolled my suitcase up the ramp and felt for my key in the torn lining of my purse. Inside, my apartment was cold and stuffy, the bed half made, exactly as I had left it. I adjusted the heat and cracked a window, then went to pee, closing both bathroom doors. A trail of ants maneuvered around the sink faucet, one lugging a thin yellowish flake on its back. On my phone I searched *do ants eat skin*. Maybe, my phone told me; maybe sometimes ants eat skin.

I walked down Main Street and sniffed at the mist, my face damp, though it wasn't raining. I could smell seawater and all that creeped within it. Between the crowded buildings, the alleyways were slashes of light, each opening onto the bay, which melted into the spread of fog above. There were no cars. I took the middle of the street as if it belonged to me. When I reached the Old Pilgrim, I saw that the windows had been freshly washed. Cleaning residue traced conspiratorial circles on the panes like the mucus of a large slug. The mesh screen door dangled violently from its hinges, scraping the sidewalk with each gust of wind. Inside, strings of colored lights the size of peppers had been tacked along the ceiling. It was the newest year yet. A naked plastic evergreen leaned in one corner and next to it sat Thomas, his phone awake in front of him, maybe glowing with a message from me. I would be there soon, I had said, and I was.

Thomas told me he had spent the holidays in town. His daughter, he explained, had recently gotten involved with an older woman, and she had chosen to celebrate Christmas with her lover and her lover's two young children. The relationship was too new, his daughter had claimed, for her to feel comfortable inviting him. Too new, the contours as yet undefined, a shared language in the making but incomplete. He assumed that part of his daughter's discomfort was due to the age difference—or, more precisely, the age similarity between himself and her lover—but he couldn't be sure. Maybe she merely thought he was homophobic. He wasn't homophobic. But maybe she thought so. She had texted him several photos on Christmas Eve: the handsome tree with its skeletal popcorn strands, the glazed ham, the platter of cookies chaotically gooped with colored frosting—which had at first confused him, inducing a grasping fear that his daughter may be damaged, unwell, mentally regressed, until he realized that the cookies had been, obviously, decorated by the children. His daughter had also sent a selfie of herself, her lover, and the two young boys, who cowered under the sweep of their mother's arm like the victims of a crime they could never forget, with his daughter standing on the other side, holding the phone in such a way that her distended arm was caught in the frame and made obese by perspective. Her smile was a twisted cord on her face, her body stiffly posed to maintain distance between herself and the children, perhaps so that it would not seem like she was trying to get inappropriately cozy with them. You mean like in a pedophilic way? I asked. No, Thomas said, he hadn't meant in a pedophilic way—just that one wants to give children a certain amount of space when they've begun, with their babyish sexuality, to sense that a new adult in their lives is making love to their mother. His daughter lived far away, in any case, he continued, out west, it wasn't easy to get to her. For Christmas dinner he had cooked a duck. He had eaten duck alone. He and his daughter had never been very close, even when she was a child. A lone duck, he said.

I asked Thomas how much older this woman was than his daughter. He wasn't sure; he imagined she might be around his age. I told him I found the term "lover" disgusting. Perhaps he should stop saying "lover." "Lover," I said, was an abnormal and disgusting word for a father to use. I asked if he wanted a beer. I asked if he had ever been with a younger woman. He laughed. You mean apart from you? he said. I turned away, toward the jaundiced afternoon light that pushed against the windows. I asked if he thought it was a coincidence that his daughter was consorting with an older woman, around his age, while he was consorting with a younger woman, around his daughter's age. Did he think his attraction to me had anything to do with his relationship with his daughter? I looked from the window to his face, which crumpled and smoothed itself like a piece of cloth being ironed. No, he said coolly, it's your huge tits. He paused. Consorting? He paused. I was a bit older than his daughter, he said, actually.

I ordered two beers at the bar. The redheaded bartender filled a glass halfway with foam, dumped the foam, and filled the glass again. Her hair had expanded since I saw her last. I thanked her, and she released the tap over another glass. I told her the decorations looked fabulous. I asked if she had any New Year's resolutions. What? she said. Do you have any New Year's resolutions? I said. I don't do that, she said, I've never done that. She slid the beers across the bar, through a skin of dust.

The table Thomas had chosen was near the back, in one of the more steeply slanted sections of the Old Pilgrim. I carried our drinks with careful mincing steps. We sat at the short end of the bench, where the floorboards must have been digging below sea level and our beers could be steadied against the wall, the liquid a urine-colored tilt in each glass. Thomas grimaced. Pardon me, he said, obscuring his face with one hand while sticking his other fingers into his mouth and tugging at his back molars. His Invisalign braces trailed threads of spit as he arranged them neatly in a round black case. He sanitized his hands and offered me a squirt. I felt a subterranean tremor of surprise as I watched him. I could never remember what Thomas's face looked like unless it was directly in front of me. As soon as I blinked, his features would begin to disintegrate and reconfigure themselves in my brain; whenever my eyes opened onto his real face, it was like I was experiencing a minor visual hallucination, as if, I thought, I had eaten psychoactive mushrooms—though I had never eaten psychoactive mushrooms. It wasn't that Thomas's appearance was bland or unmemorable, but in the world of the mind, I nonetheless tended to unconsciously replace one of his features with that of another person I knew. This was why, I understood, he had reminded me of my father when I first met him; it was why he had reminded me of so many different people since then. At times he appeared on my mind-screen with the marvelous hooked nose of my childhood piano instructor, the pulpy lips of my mother's estranged sister, even the soppy, heavy-lidded eyes of my history-teacher neighbor. But when I encountered his true face, with my own eyes open, it reminded me of nothing, and I felt afraid. I wondered if this was how Cordelia had experienced him, too—if she had looked away, at times, and seen in Thomas someone other than himself.

For years, Thomas told me, he worried that his daughter was still a virgin. He had separated from her mother when she was a toddler but remained in the same city until her senior year of high school, when he moved away to teach at the Academy. He had been concerned that the divorce may have had an impact on his daughter's sexual development. His ex-wife had dated a string of boyfriends through his daughter's childhood and adolescence; the apartment in which she resided with their daughter had been small, a two-bedroom floor-through. He worried that at night his daughter could hear her mother and the string of boyfriends having sex: primal scene after primal scene. The boyfriends,

Thomas told me, were all different heights, weights, and ethnicities. It was as if his ex-wife had been attempting to prove how unconstrained her erotic needs were, that she could be satisfied by any man, practically, apart from him. His ex-wife was gorgeous, brilliant, and sexually adventurous. She was a teacher, too—they had met in graduate school—as well as a translator of Japanese literature, mostly contemporary stuff, though she had been working in her free time on a translation of tanka composed by courtly women of the eleventh and twelfth centuries, which she hoped to publish with a small feminist press. He did not wish to talk too much about his ex-wife. The point was that her sexual appetite was unlike any he had encountered before or since, and he feared that this libidinous energy, which oozed from his ex-wife's pores like pus, may have had an adverse impact on his daughter, who, unfortunately, was quite ugly. She had been a lumpy, sullen child, and as a teenager she developed awful acne: yellow bumps that scabbed her hairline and threaded across her chin; swollen cysts in the thick flesh of her cheeks; assorted crusts, caverns, and stains, each dripping with the sewerish odors of the body's interior. Her figure was oddly proportioned, which she didn't grow out of or into, her legs and arms short and squat, her stomach bloated like that of a starving child. She had mild lordosis that grew more severe when she hit puberty, and when he picked her up from school he would watch her waddling toward him with her lower back swayed, her ass sticking out behind her and the bulge of her belly thrust forward, like a goose. When his daughter came to spend weekends with him, he tried to praise and encourage her, but because he was a natural truthteller he had found it difficult. He told her what a lovely woman she was becoming, white lies, how long her hair was getting, how stylish her clothes. He often asked if she had any boyfriends, and his daughter would shake her head in the negative, responding to his flattery by folding further over her body in her armchair, the one piece of furniture he had brought to his new apartment from the home they had once shared—it had been a gift from his mother, who had passed before his daughter was born—creating a cave within herself, a place inaccessible to him. But years later, in her adulthood, his daughter had revealed that she had in fact been a rather promiscuous teenager. A slut, she had called herself, a whore.

I told Thomas that as a child I had envied my own mother's beauty, a quality she had endlessly emphasized to my sister and me. As I grew older, however, I came to realize that I could not ascertain if my mother was genuinely beautiful or if I associated her with beauty only because she had told us to. It had been hard, when I was growing up, to know what was real. In my mother's household, truth was managed under a system of brutal but arbitrary control; for years I had tried to unearth the hidden pattern, the secret web of meaning I believed to be lurking beneath the events of my life, but eventually I was forced to abandon this project. What had been established as real one day was made unreal the next, mediated by my mother's moods and enforced by a collusion in which my whole family was energetically involved. I found that when I said things I knew to be true, they did not *feel* real, as if they had been neutered by their emergence into language. Maybe this was why I had been a compulsive liar when I was younger, though the lies I told were generally related to easily verifiable facts, so I was caught every time. Like many liars, I said, I felt a desperate hurt whenever I was discovered. It was as if my lies were the most honest words I had ever communicated, and I often experienced myself as a person martyred and falsely accused.

For instance, each autumn my family would go apple picking, and the next day my mother would bake a pie, after which I would sneak into the kitchen and eat half the pastry with my hands, hunched over the island, shoveling crust directly from the pan into my mouth. At the time I was in the habit of watching television dramas about sex crimes, and I had become invested in the concept of "physical evidence"; I must have believed there would be less "physical evidence" if I did not use a utensil. The following morning my mother would point to the edge of the pie, ragged from my clawing, and I would start to cry, insisting that my sister was the real culprit. No one respects me, I would weep, no one ever believes me. Occasionally on my way home from school I would buy large quantities of candy and cookies and chips, stuffing them down my throat at night until I vomited, then hiding the wrappers in my desk drawers, although I was not permitted to store food in my room. On the weekends my mother would search the drawers and discover the wrappers, and I would sob that they were my sister's. No one respects me, I screamed, no one ever believes me. When I was very young, my sister and I had taken baths together, during which, soothed by the warm lapping of the water against my skin, I would occasionally shit out a healthy log of excrement. My sister would yelp and leap over the edge of the tub, dripping onto the tiles as the outline of my feces began to dissolve and cloud the bath. I would remain in the water, weeping, until my mother or father came to investigate, and then I would howl that it had been my sister, my sister had done this nasty thing in the bath. No one believes me, I choked out, no one respects me. I suffered from insomnia, and many nights I would beg my sister to let me have a "sleepover" in her room. Once in a while she would acquiesce, and we would fall asleep together in her twin bed, tangled like puppies in her sheets. In the middle of the night, I would wake in a panic and pick my nose and smear sticky ropes of snot on the wall; when my sister rose in the morning, she would emit a guttural shout and push me out of the bed while I wailed that it was her snot, she had plastered her snot all over the wall in her sleep, it was disgusting, I had tried to stop her but hadn't had the strength.

Later, as an adult, I told Thomas, I informed my mother, father, and sister about an event that had taken place in my late adolescence and another separate but related event that had taken place in my early adulthood. I had long imagined the momentous impact these revelations would have upon each member of my family. At night I would lie rigid in bed, mentally careening between states of abject terror and excruciating desire as I envisioned the catastrophic explanatory power of "my truth." For years I had sensed that the things that had happened to me were all connected to a certain loss of language, an inability to speak during which I ceased to exist and for which I felt my parents, who had declawed and defanged me in childhood, were solely to blame. I was a teacher of English literature, I reminded Thomas. I believed in the power of language. I believed in the supremacy of speech-acts. It followed that to name out loud the things that had happened to me would be a display of spiritual resistance and self-assertion so potent that it would necessarily unleash a deluge of empowering and sexy consequences, including mind-blowing orgasms-with-partner and the psychic deaths of all my family members.

Of course, as Thomas had perhaps already predicted, when I did at last speak "my truth" to my mother, father, and sister, the impact was negligible, on them as well as on myself. As in childhood, the words I said out loud did not *feel real*; the language I used to describe to my family the things that had happened to me tasted pathetic and putrid in my mouth, sickeningly false, devoid of meaning. It was a degrading experience for us all, one about which we would never again speak. Not long after, I told "my truth" to a person I lived with and loved, a person whose reaction was far from negligible, but still, no matter his response, "my truth" did not *feel real*—and so in desperation I began to bring up "my truth" with greater and greater frequency, I brought up "my truth" each time we ate lunch or went for a walk in the botanical gardens, before and after class I brought up "my truth," when we read side-by-side in bed I set my book down on the pillow to discuss "my truth," when he studied for exams I vocalized "my truth," he cooked me dinner and I railed about "my truth," on his birthday and my own I whispered "my truth," we tossed bits of bread to the koi we loved and I sniffled about "my truth," until over time I began to accuse the person I lived with and loved of not even *caring* about "my truth," not *investing* in "my truth," surely if he really *cared* about "my truth," I would weep, if he really *believed* in "my truth," then "my truth" would begin to *feel real*. No one believes me, I would sob to him, no one respects me.

But all that was in the past.

Thomas took a large gulp of his beer. A muscle moved in his neck like a trapped insect.

I had already told him these anecdotes, he said. I had told him about my childhood compulsion to lie, and then I had listed these same examples: the pie, the candy, the shit in the tub, the snot on the walls. I had gone on to discuss how my lies all seemed to revolve around consumption or excretion. I had spoken about oral and anal fixations, polymorphous perversity, aggression and anxiety in babies, true selves, false selves, cathecting and introjecting, the question of whether an iPad could be a good-enough mother. I had relayed my feelings about several events that had taken place in my adolescence and adulthood, as well as my feelings about my family's negligible reaction to learning of "my truth." Three times I had referred to a person I loved, though never by name, muttering something about "intimacy through privacy," then abruptly changing the subject, claiming that my "brain cells were swelling" and that soon I would "vomit and die." I had told him that my mother used too much soap on my vagina when I was a child with no concern for the delicacy of my vaginal pH, that my mother's and sister's beauty had been difficult for me to bear, that I had not been breast fed, that I could not remember ever having witnessed a primal scene but did recall once walking into the bathroom and encountering my mother's mountainous pubic hair corkscrewing over the toilet, which stimulated and frightened me. I had explained that my mother's mother had been interned in several concentration camps, between which she had traveled by death march and cattle car, that my mother's father had spent the war years working in Tashkent while his parents were murdered by Lithuanian collaborators, that my mother had lived in the Soviet Union until she was eleven. I had asked if he was intrigued by the concept of "intergenerational trauma." I had not mentioned my father's background or my mother's place of residence directly before she immigrated to the United States. I had told him that I had always found Stalin attractive and pulled up an image on my phone of "Hot Stalin," pointing to places on the photo that had been retouched to hide the General Secretary's smallpox scars, then describing in depth the arc of the smallpox plotline in *Bleak House*. Dickens is so back, I had mumbled twice.

All of this had happened here, Thomas said, at the Old Pilgrim, at this table. We had been sitting in this exact configuration, with me facing the door and him facing the back. It had been raining, and as I spoke, he told me, the bar had started to flood, initially only in the lower sections of the slanted floor, but the water kept rising, displacing dust and washing the wood clean of old beer. I had been caught up in my story and had not noticed the flooding had reached us until my feet were submerged in an inch of liquid. Thomas said that he was telling me this not to humiliate me. He did not want to humiliate me. He himself had occasionally been immersed in a long, pleasurable conversation with a friend or colleague over wine or tea, returning home bloated with feelings of intimacy and well-being, only to realize that in the course of the evening he had relayed a detailed tale he had told his companion before, often nearly verbatim. When this occurred, he felt deranged with distress. And he was saying all this to me now because he wished to spare me that agony.

The last light was sapping from the sky, the Old Pilgrim's windows boxes of shadow beside us. I could still taste the stale plane air on my breath. I thanked Thomas for sparing me the experience of humiliation. It started to rain, at first a few fat drops that splatted the windows one by one, tracing the curves of the cleaning residue, then sudden billows lashing the glass, the panes wobbling in their frames and making a sound like a child's howl. Behind the bar the redheaded bartender muttered under her breath. I thought of Billy and Linda, warm and dry in another state. I asked Thomas if he wanted to go to his place or to mine—though he had yet to come to mine, to the apartment that for eight years had been his, and I suspected that he was not allowed on campus.

Let's go to mine, he said.

We drained our glasses, gathered ourselves, zipped, gloved, hooded, the rainwater pooling at our feet and frothing like a sink. Bye, Deborah, Thomas called. The bartender lifted one hand and continued to stare listlessly at the floor, ready for more flood.

Outside the treetops were darker than the sky. They moved against themselves with a noise like fabric tumbling in a dryer. At the ends of the alleys, I could see the wind flattening the dune grass, the water swelling against houses built too close to the bay, which would someday have to be lifted and moved from the shore like toys. My cheap zebra-print umbrella snapped inside out and filled like a bucket, once, twice. Thomas offered to trade; I don't mind getting wet, I shouted. A face was pressed to a window, open-mouthed and taking in the rain. Out of the corner of my eye I saw an Academy student and her older townie boyfriend sheltering under a tree, sopping, feeling each other up. We made our way to Thomas's apartment complex, his second-floor unit with its view of the motel swimming pool, covered in a tarp for the winter. I raised my voice over the wind, tasting water, and asked Thomas if he planned to return from his leave and resume teaching the next school year. It depended, he shouted, his father was still very ill. We sidestepped into the street, around three drunk men huddled on the sidewalk, smoking under an awning. Ma'am, one of them shouted, excuse me, sir, would you tell me, excuse me, is there a liquor store open? Thomas shouted directions. It closes in an hour, I shouted. My hair was wet, the mesh toes of my sneakers, my arm where it clung to the umbrella. The rain was so cold that it should have been sleet. I was curious, I shouted to Thomas, as to why he was living in town, when his father was that ill? Surely it would have made more sense to rent an apartment in the city where his father was in and out of the hospital? Why, I shouted, would he have taken a leave only to stay where he was, especially when it was so difficult to travel during the offseason? Why had he spent Christmas alone rather than with his ailing father? I'm giving up on this, I shouted, my umbrella inside out once more. I held it against the wind, as someone had once taught me, until the nylon flung itself toward my shoulders. We sprinted the rest of the way to Thomas's apartment, heads bent, his wet hands slipping on the key, my wet shoes filling with rain, and he pushed his torso against the glass door until at last we stood in the entryway, panting. Across the street, one corner of the tarp had come away from the pool and was beating madly against the deck. I wrung my hair over the wall-to-wall carpeting and followed Thomas up the stairs.

The apartment looked lived-in, despite the sealed cardboard boxes stacked under the windows, each labeled in Thomas's neat teacher's handwriting: kitchen, bedroom, books, miscellaneous. Orange laminate coated the cabinets, reminding me of kindergarten cloakrooms and cubbies, corners made safe with foam. What few objects Thomas had set out hummed with implications I couldn't follow, places and people I didn't know, attended to and left behind: a pottery bowl with a turquoise glaze, a vase in the shape of a dalmatian, flat-weave kitchen towels, cornflower blue. On the desk there stood a photograph of a woman around my age, pretty in her red cardigan, with cropped black hair and a shy expression. Her face was closed to me, like a loose fist. I had seen it all before.

I dribbled onto the living room floor, afraid to sit on the couch in my dripping jeans, until Thomas threw a towel at me and I buried my head, wrapped up my hair. My father, he said, is a piece of shit—you look like a wet dog right now—a dying piece of shit. I can't be there all the time, can't or won't, one of those. I closed my eyes and let Thomas's face transform into someone else's. When I opened them, he was standing next to me, taking hold of my towel and scrubbing gently at my hair. Wet dog, he said again. He dried my ears, the back of my neck. I asked him who his favorite student at the Academy had been. I was very fond of Cordelia Altman, he replied without pause. Very fond? I said. A brilliant kid, he said. She's gone through hell and bears it with dignity. He slung the damp towel around my neck as if I were a boxer. When she was a freshman, he said, her father committed suicide. She had been in his American Lit survey course that year. It was horrific, the tabloids—I know, I interrupted, I know what happened. I told Thomas that I had also gone through hell. Yeah? he said. She's in my class, I said, Cordelia. That's good, he said. In fact, I said, she had asked after him. It seemed she hadn't been told he was going on leave. It seemed no one had been told. It was sudden, he said. I said he could have emailed her. He said he had lost access to his Academy email. I said he had another email, no? I said that student emails were easy to recall, weren't they, lastnamefirstinitialclassyear? Unless he wasn't supposed to be in contact with students during his leave? But that seemed strange? Given the circumstances?

The Academy is an incomprehensible place, Thomas said.

We peeled off our clothes in the bathroom, tossing them into a soggy heap near the toilet. My socks squelched. I could feel my fungal infection spreading beneath my bra strap like a handful of hot sand. The trash was filled with trimmings of what would have eventually become Thomas's beard. I thought of the ants in my apartment, bringing dead bits of me to their queen.

Pancreatic cancer, he said, my dad has pancreatic cancer.

He slid down his trousers and boxers, his penis dangling friendly and limp between his legs. He walked naked to the bedroom closet and put on a clean pair of underpants, then passed me a set of flannel pajamas. He told me he was not feeling sexual tonight. Was I feeling sexual? No, I said, I was not feeling sexual tonight. He asked if I wanted a bite to eat. There were leftover chicken thighs in the fridge, he said. There was a squash we could roast. There was a head of cauliflower and a jar of duck fat, rendered from the bird he had prepared and consumed on Christmas Eve. The way he named each food conjured images of casual health and abundance that felt absolutely exclusive of me. I considered the possibility that Thomas's desire for my company, which he sought with some regularity, was borne less from erotic interest than from the urge to be witnessed in complete control of his life by a woman obviously not in control of hers.

I fucking hate squash, I said.

Thomas shrugged. I'm not so hungry either, he said.

I left him to cleanse his face in the bathroom and returned to the kitchen, retrieving a chicken thigh from the refrigerator and rinsing it under the tap, flushing away its coating of cold jellied collagen. I pulled at the skin, flabby and stippled as if with goosepimples. Poor chicken, I whispered in Russian, poor chicken, are you scared? I stooped over the sink, gripping the severed femur, and ripped the meat away from itself with my teeth. A ribbon of tendon lodged between my molars. Poor chicken, I whispered, are you feeling sexual tonight? I did not know the Russian word for "sexual," so I said that part in English. Once I had finished eating I wrapped the remnants in paper towel and buried the bundle under a layer of trash in the bin, a habit retained from childhood.

Thomas was already in bed, the quilt tucked tidily under his newly cleansed chin. When I came in, he sat up and the cover dropped away. I felt the sink of the mattress as I clambered to join him. My flannel pajama bottoms strained; the drawstring, rough as a shoelace, dug hard into my navel. Thomas was shirtless. The puff of his belly looked so tender and sweet, like something I could eat with a spoon. I rested my head on his upper arm and began to produce the satisfied cooing sounds of a person for whom the experience of sharing a bed was a simple daily pleasure, noises I based upon those I occasionally heard myself making during the consumption of a nice ham sandwich. In a room of the mind I was stroking a pony's mane, tough and wiry as pubic hair. Thomas switched off the light and closed his eyes. The thought that he might fall asleep and leave me alone with everything I still needed to say made me feel suddenly ill. I propped myself up on his frilled pillow.

My trip back to the city in the middle of the country where I had grown up, I whispered into his ear, and where I would most likely, barring extenuating circumstances, never return, had surprised even me. Perhaps by returning to the diseased, degenerated, and noxious city of my youth, I had unwittingly embarked on a spiritual quest of healing and self-discovery? Perhaps I was confronting the tragic events of my past? Perhaps diffuse experiences were coagulating, like a gelatinous meat stock placed out to cool on a winter day? It was possible that someday soon I would become a person who used words like "cock" in earnest. If so, Thomas would be one of the primary beneficiaries. He stood much to gain, didn't he think? Unless his sexual proclivities lay primarily in other directions?

Thomas's eyelids twitched. He snuffled deeper into the covers.

Back home, I continued, if you could call it that, I had encountered an old friend, quite by accident, in one of those systematic coincidences that characterize city life, whose echoes of meaning gesture toward an unspeakably complex imbrication; an intestinal tangle without beginning or end; the sense that everything is inscribed in everything else. This was a person I had not spoken to in many years. He had looked both the same and different. He'd been so happy to see me.

Thomas released a long, shuddering sigh and smacked his lips.

My friend and I had shared a delightful kiss, for old times' sake, I said, though nothing more than that, due to the fact that I hadn't been feeling sexual that night.

A string of drool leaked from Thomas's mouth into my hair. I reached toward him and rested two fingers on his breast, above his nipple.

The way I chose to make meaning of this experience might prove formative, I said.

I stroked upward, in the direction of his throat.

The negation of the negation, I offered.

Thomas's organism was unconscious but pulsing with life. I considered curling my fingers such that my untrimmed nails tore his skin open. I withdrew my hand and placed it over my own stomach and turned to face the wall.

Just kidding, I said.

Thomas breathed on me. Water beat the windows. I tapped my phone awake and felt the relief of its puddle of blue light on my chest and chin. I replied to my father's text in our group chat and said that I had made it safely back, yes. It was raining here, I added, to give my message a personal touch. Cats and dogs.

# 2

*

My psychiatrist was running five minutes late. He alerted me via direct message, five minutes after the start of our scheduled appointment, so that I was unsure whether he meant he would be arriving imminently or that he would be in total ten minutes behind. His message was unpunctuated and in it he misspelled my first name. In front of me my laptop sat balanced on a stack of books, its camera angled downward to facilitate the illusion that I was small, vulnerable, and easily crushed, which, I hoped, would compel my psychiatrist to experience himself at all times as looming monstrously over me, engendering unconscious sentiments of benevolence and patronage. I was tiny; I was tinier than tiny; I was nothing. Because I had yet to meet my psychiatrist in person, I was confident that this deception could go on indefinitely. While I waited, I stared at myself onscreen, grasping my empty coffee mug, nudging the rim into the dry flesh of my lips, pretending to drink, and setting it back down. I was afraid to step away from my computer in the event that my psychiatrist might arrive and absorb my absence as a sign of disrespect for his profession. I did not, in fact, have any respect for his profession, but I couldn't bear the thought that he might one day discover this and kill himself.

There was a slight delay, I noticed, between the world as I perceived its phenomena around me in "real life" and the world as it manifested itself onscreen; when I looked at my face in the top right corner of the virtual waiting room, I could observe myself blinking. For ten minutes the darkish slats of skin unfurled over and retracted from my eyeballs like little garage doors. Then I disappeared. In my place was a black expanse; at its center, the fatal white swirl of the loading icon. Eventually I re-emerged, smaller, in a box at the top right corner of my psychiatrist's gigantic head, which stuttered and rippled across the screen before catching up with itself. I clicked to activate my microphone. Along the bottom edge of my face-box was a name, almost identical to mine, in white type. Can you hear me? I said. Onscreen my psychiatrist's mouth opened and closed like it was gasping for air. I had misspelled my own first name, I realized, when I "checked in" to the virtual waiting room. You're probably muted, I said.

My psychiatrist was from Argentina, but his surname was distinctly German. He was middle-aged, with a swooping pile of brown hair that at times appeared, even through the screen, to be unwashed. His large, deep-set eyes drooped like a hound's; his lips, thick and sensuous in his unshaven face, brought to mind a raw coil of blood sausage. There was an undeniably meaty quality to his looks, while at the same time he had the air of a man who was wasting away, so that he at once seemed to be on the verge of total physical collapse and capable of beating me to death with his bare hands. I was very fond of him. I assumed he had been born into a family of Nazis who fled Europe for Latin America, Eichmann-like, postwar. The sight of my depressed psychiatrist filled me with pity for the fate of man and with longing for a different world, prelinguistic, behind or beyond this one. Whenever I saw him I felt pretty hungry.

He was sitting in a mesh-backed desk chair that looked to be set up in his kitchen. In the background, hulking stainless steel appliances reflected the opposite side of the room—otherwise invisible to me—in a hazy wobble. When he rolled his chair in a certain direction I could make out the tower of dirty dishes in his sink. After some brief fiddling he managed to unmute himself. He greeted me without using my name and did not apologize for being late. Suicidally depressed, I thought, an emigrant from a family of emigrants, forced daily to reckon with a genocidal family lineage, lips too large for his face, unable to bring himself to do the dishes in spite of a highly visible dishwasher, very sad—okay, my psychiatrist said, sighing audibly, then looking or pretending to look down at a document on his desk. I put on my most cheerful voice to ask how he was doing. His body gave a jerk and his eyes darted to the right and left, as if he were being held hostage. Everything is fine, he said, too loudly. I watched him shuffle through a stack of papers, but his camera was angled such that I could see they were all blank. He squinted at his screen and mumbled the names and dosages of my medications.

Everything is the same? he asked.

Yes, I said, everything was the same.

He asked if I was still in graduate school, and I reminded him that I had dropped out, although I did not use the phrase "dropped out." He sighed. Yes, yes, he said. He asked if I was still living in the city where I had been studying, and I said no. He asked if I was, then, living in the city in the middle of the country where I had grown up; I said no, and reminded him that I had been teaching English literature at the Academy since September, for our past five appointments. I had recently visited my hometown, true, but everything there had been the same as always; I had nothing of note to report. He asked if I was still with my boyfriend. I said no. We broke up a year ago, I reminded him, around the time I moved back in with my parents. A small, strangled sound escaped my psychiatrist's throat, as though he had been stepped on. I worried that he was about to burst into tears. Totally amicable, I said hurriedly. His lower lip trembled. We're still in touch, we're still close, we still talk every week, I explained. I smiled with my teeth and flashed the camera a thumbs-up. So everything is different, my psychiatrist said. No, I assured him, everything was exactly the same. He shook his head. Everything is different, he repeated softly, gazing beyond his laptop at an object I couldn't see, then standing and stumbling out of view of the camera, leaving his empty desk chair askew. Through my laptop speakers there came the shrill and insistent yapping of a small dog, but I could not tell whether the sound originated from inside or outside my psychiatrist's apartment. I leaned closer to the screen in an effort to discern the view from his window. All I could make out was a square of blazing white light. On the counter below sat two boxes of organic muesli—a brand my mother liked—and a bowl without a spoon.

After several minutes my psychiatrist returned to his chair. He appeared to have combed his hair while off camera.

The dosages are okay, he said without preamble.

Yes, everything was okay.

You do not feel addicted? he said.

No, I did not feel addicted.

You are sleeping fine, he said. You have no new depression, anxiety. Sleeping like a baby, I said, no depression, no anxiety. That's Stalin? my psychiatrist said. Hm? I said. I craned my neck. I had neglected to pull down the photograph of a young Iosif Vissarionovich Stalin that I kept taped to the wall above my desk: pinpricked, worn at the corners, smudged from the oils of my fingertips. Oh, I said, yes, for research. What are you researching? my psychiatrist asked. Stalin, I said, and my psychiatrist nodded to demonstrate his recognition of my status as a young intellectual who, despite having dropped out of her PhD program to move back in with her parents, continued to conduct personal research on academic topics such as "Stalin" in general. There was another silence. I wondered if this was my cue to remind my psychiatrist about the pharmacy I used in town, the only pharmacy for miles, but he took a gulp of air that indicated he had more to say.

My psychiatrist told me that he had been thinking of me and my studies because he had recently started a book club with some friends from Argentina. He glanced down shyly as he spoke. That was wonderful news, I said. What fabulous fun to start a book club with old friends. My psychiatrist's left hand reached outside of the frame and reappeared clutching a glass of clear liquid, at which he proceeded to suck energetically with a curly blue straw. I asked if his book club was reading Argentine literature. No, he said, postwar American fiction. They had first read Nabokov's *Pale Fire*, if you considered that American—I did, I said, of course—and were currently reading Philip Roth's *The Ghost Writer.* I felt profoundly moved by the vision of my psychiatrist and his Argentine friends, some—perhaps many, perhaps most, I thought—like him, the descendants of Nazis and their collaborators, engaging with the impact of the Holocaust on postmodern American letters. I loved *The Ghost Writer*, I said. It was an excellent choice for a book club, an excellent novel about wanting to fuck Anne Frank. My psychiatrist blinked. They had only just started, he said, he had not yet read that part. Again he looked like he was about to burst into tears. That's okay, I said, that's totally okay. I apologized for getting ahead of myself. In a soothing voice I told him that *Pale Fire* was also a favorite of mine. All of his friends had hated it, my psychiatrist said, and so had he; it was incomprehensible, an incomprehensible book. His eyes sat moist and quivering in their sockets. I said that was totally okay. Literary quality was a matter of opinion, taste, and the unique life experiences we each brought to the page, I lied. *The Ghost Writer* is about wanting to make love to Anne Frank? my psychiatrist asked. Before I could respond, he began to shake his head, running one large, fleshy hand through his hair. Anne Frank, he muttered, Anne Frank. Anne Frank, I repeated supportively, Anne Frank, because I did not wish to leave my psychiatrist alone, psychically speaking, in the midst of a spiritual confrontation with his violent familial history. The dog once more began its horrible yapping, let out a final squeal, and fell silent.

In Buenos Aires, my psychiatrist said, a recreation of Amsterdam's Anne Frank House—the Casa de Ana Frank, as he called it—had been established in a residential neighborhood not far from where he had grown up. The museum had been founded relatively recently, he said, fifteen years or so ago, in a mansion that had been used as refuge for political dissidents during the military dictatorship of the seventies and eighties. Buenos Aires's Casa de Ana Frank featured a precise reproduction of Ana's famed hiding place, filled with precise copies of certain objects from Amsterdam's "real" Anne Frank House, those "real" objects that had once belonged to the Frank family, for Argentine schoolchildren and perhaps tourists, though the latter seemed unlikely, to peruse. On the museum's website, the reproduction was referred to as Latin America's "only recreation of the Secret Annex," as if to dissuade visitors of the notion that there were dozens of recreations of "the Secret Annex" all over the world; as if featuring "the only recreation of the Secret

Annex" was an unassailable claim to archival originality and innovation. In the backyard of the Argentine Casa de Ana Frank there grew, the website claimed, my psychiatrist explained, "the original chestnut tree" discussed in Anne Frank's beloved diary entries. My psychiatrist did not care to learn what they meant by this, or how and why the museum curators had moved "the original chestnut tree" to Buenos Aires from Amsterdam. It was probable, he said, that they had simply cut a sapling from "the original chestnut tree" and replanted it. He felt it came off as disingenuous to refer to their tree as "the original," when in reality it would be more accurate to call it "the progeny" of the original chestnut tree; "the original chestnut tree's son."

Or daughter, I said helpfully.

Yes, my psychiatrist said, or daughter.

The establishment of Buenos Aires's Casa de Ana Frank, my psychiatrist went on, took place more than a decade after he had left his home country. He hadn't visited the museum, nor had any of his friends. He admitted his interest; there had, of course, as he was sure I was aware, been terrible antisemitism in Argentina—for many years, yes, including when he was growing up. He could understand why in the contemporary climate such a museum had been founded. I watched the bobbing of my head on the screen, my eyebrows knit to convey how moved I was, as a Jewish person, to witness my Nazi-descendant psychiatrist reckoning in earnest with the weight of the historical past. It had been difficult for his grandparents, he said, when they fled Munich for Buenos Aires in the thirties, though obviously the situation could have been much worse; obviously, the situation had been much worse for those who remained in Germany, in most of Europe, to be more precise. He did not wish to appear to complain; it would be obscene to complain; he did not wish to appear obscene.

No, I said, one would not wish to appear obscene.

A lock of oily hair had fallen over one of my psychiatrist's eyes. The screen buffered in the middle of his attempt to puff it away with an upward gust of breath, and I watched his frozen curled lip and my own cocked head as I assimilated the fact that my psychiatrist's surname was not German, but Yiddish. By the time his image unfroze, the hair had been flipped away from his face. There were deep ridges pleating his forehead, like the creases in my mother's finest leather handbags. There were slimy yellow granules in the corners of his eyes. He squinted at me and sighed loudly. Anyway, he said. He read out the address of my pharmacy in town. Was this still a good place to send my prescriptions? I confirmed that it was. I assured him that I would let him know if any aspect of my life became different. I agreed to make my next appointment via his preferred online scheduling platform. I expressed my thanks for his meeting with me. I wished him the best with his book club. Two Jews walk into a psychiatric session, I thought. It was difficult to avoid the sight of my big head miniaturized at the corner of his—the meaty droop of my cheeks and the wet gap between my own florid lips, too large for my face. My psychiatrist ended the call while I wagged my hand goodbye, as if one of us were pulling away on a train; as if there was still a long journey ahead. My desktop was revealed with its filth of icons: screenshots, word-processing documents, downloads. Behind them glowed a cultivated green valley. A whorl of high-definition fog—like a veil.

I arrived late to class—my students were already seated—and out of breath. Off came my coat, my gloves, my scarf. I heaped them onto a spare desk. Through the room wafted the faint directionless stench of rotting meat, a smell I had noticed before and that seemed to emanate from the wood of the rafters. The windows had been cracked, maybe for this reason, filling the room with cold air. A gust pushed itself into my mouth. I steadied my elbow against the metal border of the whiteboard. My students leaned, yawned, chattered like birds. It was comforting to remember that I would remain invisible until I addressed them. I had taken my double dose of methamphetamine's cousin too late that morning and my constant, lurking, low-grade fear was stuck in my throat like a lump of dry bread. Did I fear the Third Reich? I did not fear the Third Reich. Did I fear that someone was going to rape me? I did not fear that someone was going to rape me. I feared that I was going to rape someone else; I feared that I had already raped many people; that I had perhaps spent my whole life accidentally raping those weaker than me, of whom there were few; but also those stronger than me, of whom there were many; I feared that I had raped my mother and my father; that I had raped my sister; that I had raped Benjamin Leichter; that I had raped both Thomas Nelson and Cordelia Altman; that I had raped my depressed Jewish psychiatrist that very morning; that I had raped many, many times the man I loved. I looked at my students and tried to determine in a rational fashion which of them I had raped the most often. It was Valentine's Day. All my girls wore red satin bows in their hair. They wore pink socks, pink cardigans. The skin on their faces glistened, as if freshly buffed at a car wash. Their mouths churned around their teeth, which lay in neat, tight rows, like new developments in a tiny city. If I hadn't raped them yet, I feared I soon would.

I clapped my hands together once, then twice. I coughed. Good morning, I called. My students quieted, crossed their legs at the ankles, and blinked. From the open windows, a smudged morning light pitched pale rectangles onto the hardwood.

I would like to encourage you all, I said to my students, to consider the upcoming exam as an *opportunity* to synthesize what you've learned about The Literature of the City, rather than as an *obstacle* to overcome.

Thales unzipped her pencil case and lined up an orderly row of colored pens on her desk. Next to her, Kyla was fast asleep, her head slack against the windowsill. Her lower lip was as round and damp as a baby's.

I wrote "obstacle or opportunity?" on the whiteboard.

Have any of you ever encountered an *obstacle* that you later understood to be an *opportunity*? I asked.

Like trauma? Divya said. A celebratory gold foil heart had been pasted to each of her cheeks.

Not necessarily like trauma, I said. I meant more along the lines of getting your driver's license, or volunteering at a nursing home.

Trauma can be an opportunity, Divya explained, to enact restorative justice.

I said that was an excellent point.

Trauma can be an opportunity, she said, flicking her braids behind her shoulders, to take a stand against the revolting and pernicious "Trauma Olympics."

In my periphery Anita nodded eagerly, hand jabbed high in the air. She was wheezing. Her thin hair clung to her skull. I ignored her and thanked Divya for her contribution. Once more I clutched at the whiteboard's metal border. Outside, a seabird was screeching. The clock's second hand twitched manically. My knees popped; my knuckles cracked; my throat engorged inside my neck. I feared my imminent and inevitable collapse. Then, at last, I felt it: methamphetamine's cousin hopping through my bloodstream like a frog. In an instant I was incredibly alive, strong as a cow. I let go of the ledge. My feet ticked beneath me. My mind screamed Brahms. I could have waltzed. Instead I started to pace.

Many people, I announced, would doubtless agree with Divya's astute observation regarding the so-called "Trauma Olympics."

Many would affirm that the "Trauma Olympics" were designed to divide rather than unite! To destroy rather than build! To pit against one another those who should be standing shoulder to shoulder in triumphant solidarity! However, I went on, my strides lengthening, I would encourage us all, for the sake of intellectual curiosity—let's not forget, one of the Academy's core values—to take seriously the *alternative* position.

I wrote "Trauma Olympics—what if good?" on the whiteboard. Thales scribbled fearfully in her composition book. Her writing hand trembled. Cordelia, who had been leaning on her desk with her hand smashed against her cheek, sat up.

I would encourage us all to consider, I said, the possibility that some things are worse than other things. As a thought experiment, it may be useful to construct one's own personal rankings of how comparatively bad particular things are.

I turned to the whiteboard.

I wrote "Holocaust > pedophilia > ephebophilia."

I wrote "violent rape > date-rape."

I wrote "Gulag > legal refugee status > mean mom."

I wrote "kicking a child in the head > lack of breastfeeding/babyhood skin contact."

Now, I said, we can of course see how difficulties might arise if we were to attempt to combine our terms.

I wrote "Holocaust > pedophilia > violent rape > Gulag > legal refugee status > ephebophilia > kicking a child in the head > date-rape > mean mom > lack of breastfeeding/babyhood skin contact."

I saw that two more of my students had fallen asleep.

This is not to say, I continued amiably, that the psychological impact of an event on an individual is equal to the measure of that event's objective moral status. Obviously, I said, the psyche is infinitely complex, oceanic, mysterious, burdensome, frothy as a foam, dense as a rock, sublime and ridiculous, vertiginous, totalizing, obscene, exquisite, disgusting—like a gargoyle, I explained—like a mountain—like a tunnel—like a cave—like a long, cold river—like a cornfield—obviously the psyche collapses all the past (historical and personal) and all the future into the present; obviously in the terrain of the psyche, an event which for one person may feasibly have no discernible impact (ethically, spiritually, or psychologically), which may appear so negligible even to its perpetrator that he might, for instance, *not recall that such an event ever took place*; obviously this same event, meaningless to one person, may leave another wrecked and wracked—I scribbled "wrecked and wracked" on the whiteboard—sexually frigid, incapable of orgasm-with-partner, violated, brought to her knees—I made a sweeping arc with my hand—life-ruined, spiritually sick and morally warped, due not necessarily, I babbled, to the "actual" moment of the event itself, but rather to all that came before and all that may come after, to the eternal time that might occupy one singular moment, until *the moment becomes a container*—I wrote "the MOMENT = container" on the whiteboard—so that in this way we perceive that every moment is in itself meaningless, I said, meaningless in isolation, we see that every moment can only begin to "mean" when time dissolves inside of it, like Alka-Seltzer, I was yelling now, we comprehend, as did Marcus Aurelius, that *He who sees the present has seen all things, both all that has come to pass from everlasting and all that will be for eternity—*

I stopped speaking. The window had blown shut. The majority of my students were asleep. I could not remember what I had been trying to say. My tongue ached. My heart thrummed in its cavity. I called on Kyla, who had awoken and was raising her hand listlessly, elbow propped on the sill for support.

Is this going to be on the exam? she asked.

Yes, I said.

I called on Divya.

So which one do you have? she asked.

Which what? I said.

Which type of trauma, she said, like specifically?

I clarified that I had been speaking not personally but theoretically.

Domestic violence trauma, she listed, childhood abuse trauma, war trauma, neglect trauma, bullying trauma, overly-strict-upbringing trauma, porous boundaries trauma, sexual assault trauma, cult survivor trauma, historical trauma, or near-death-event trauma?

I asked Divya where she had learned this categorization.

You can choose more than one, she said kindly. That's called "complex trauma."

I called on Anita.

Is John Jarndyce supposed to be a pedophile? Anita said. I asked what she meant by "supposed to be." Was Charles Dickens a pedophile? she said. No, I said; neither John Jarndyce, Esther Summerson's legal guardian, father figure, and, briefly, fiancé in the novel *Bleak House*, nor Charles Dickens, eminent Victorian author and social critic, was a pedophile. Charles Dickens, I explained patiently, cared for the plight of children because of his own life experiences with a loser debt-ridden father and mean mom, who sent him to perform child labor at a blacking factory; some scholars might even claim that in certain respects Charles Dickens remained a big fat baby his entire life. Many other influential historical figures, I said, were also the victims of child abuse or neglect: picture delicate, pox-ridden, poetic sons bludgeoned in the head by shoe-cobbling boozehound fathers. As for John Jarndyce, he was simply a wealthy man with a kind and noble soul; also, I said, he was a fictional character, which meant that he was not real, had no body, and could not exhibit sexual preferences. Why have we only read one book this whole year, Anita asked, when every other class has read four? I said that all the information a person would ever need about The Literature of the City could be found in the 989 pages of *Bleak House* by Charles Dickens. *Dickens's ultimate vision of London*, I plagiarized, *lies in the form of his novels: in their kind of narrative, in their method of characterization, in their genius for typification. It does not matter which way we put it: the experience of the city is the fictional method; or the fictional method is the experience of the city!* What? Divya said. Is Esther Summerson a lesbian? Anita asked. Is fog going to be on the exam? Sasha said. Is Esther Summerson a lesbian who never had the chance to be herself? Anita said.

These were all thoughtful questions, I announced. I was delighted to see the class's level of thoughtful engagement with the text in preparation for next month's exam. This depth of thought, I said, would serve them well, today and far into the distant and impenetrable future, in whichever career path their passions guided them toward, whether business administration, SEO strategy, LLM modeling, or even UX design. I suggested that my students spend the next fifteen minutes in pairs, compiling lists of any remaining points of confusion about *Bleak House* and its relation to The Literature of the City. In a quarter of an hour we would come back together as a group. In the meantime, I told them, I would leave them to it; I was sure that as juniors they could be trusted to work diligently without my surveillance. We're all adults here! I said. Before they split up, I pulled out my phone and snapped a photo of my girls sitting with their red bows, their glossed hair, their acrylic cardigans.

Smile, I said after I had taken the picture.

I left the classroom.

I had no plans or direction. I only knew that methamphetamine's cousin was eager for me to be outside, to be marching along to the speed of my blood, to be looking and looking at my phone. I walked across campus, past the cafeteria, the auditorium, the student dorms. My calves spasmed on the incline. The wind invaded my nostrils. Fauré's Requiem was shrieking through my wireless earbuds. The day was freezing, all the plant beds in the courtyard long dead, the grass dead, the trees, in a manner of speaking, also dead, though the holly still waggled silver in the sunlight, as if dewy. *Libera me,* I thought. *Domine.* I thought it in song. Under the holly tree the handsome landscaper teetered high on his orange ladder, clutching a huge pair of scissors. His gloved hand made a fist around a branch and all the birds flapped off, bleating like sheep. *Requiem aeternam dona eis, Domine,* I thought. The sea sky pressed into me. The wind was salty on my gums. I unhinged my jaw and ate the air like food. Cordelia sat in the foreground of the photograph I had taken, staring into the camera, her arms huddled over her large breasts as if she could invert them into her ribcage. Her expression was sullen. I stood shivering in the cold and sent the image to Thomas.

Happy V-Day, I wrote.

Above me the landscaper was jerking and bucking his head like a blinded horse. I prodded at my screen, navigated to my messaging application, scrolled down slightly, and touched Benjamin Leichter's name. I reread his most recent message. Great to see you yesterday! it said. I read it once more. It continued to say, Great to see you yesterday! I rubbed my thumb against the screen and read Benjamin Leichter's second most recent message, sent eight years earlier, to which I had never replied, asking if I had plans to come home that summer. I had been twenty years old at the time of its sending, three years older than my juniors were now. It was almost a third of my lifetime ago. In almost a third of my lifetime I had never once considered deleting my correspondence with Benjamin Leichter, though I had deleted many other messages to free up what my phone cloyingly referred to as its "memory." I had no idea what I had done that summer, I realized suddenly, the summer I was twenty years old. I had no idea whether I had gone home or not. Had I held an unpaid internship? Had I worked the counter at a café? My vision blurred from the effort of summoning an image of myself at that age. Had my hair been long or short? Had I dyed it pink? Had I been shaving my legs in those days? Had I been wearing makeup? Was I still in touch with my friends from high school then? Had I read Dostoyevsky yet? Had I longed for someone? Was I eating? Had I been having those dreams? Was I choked, just choked with longing? Did I ever go for a swim? Did I miss my parents? Did I call my sister? Had I been taking pills? Did I wear a bra? Was my grandmother still alive? Had I started smoking? Had I been singing, was I singing, had I still been singing then? You good, Miss? the handsome landscaper shouted down at me. I had been standing directly beneath his ladder, staring at my phone for ten minutes.

I'm great! I said. I'm great! I'm just texting an old friend!

Nice, he said. He buried his face once more in the tree.

I started to walk back to my classroom, still looking at my phone, and opened my family group chat, where my mother had uploaded an image of her and my father. They must have asked someone to take the photo; it depicted them from head to toe, their insulated coats, the limpid lake disintegrating into the limpid sky, the distant planetarium, the concrete ground beneath their feet, smeared with goose feces in delicate shades of white and gray and green. In the camps, my mother texted, they probably made your grandmother shovel shit with her bare hands. She sent a digital representation of a tiny, angry face. She sent a photograph of a raw chicken on a sheet tray. We are having a roast chicken as our Valentine! she said. I reacted to my mother's first message with a thumbs-down and to her second message with a thumbs-up. Thomas replied to the image of my juniors with two question marks. There was a pause. He typed; he was no longer typing; he was typing.

I don't think V-Day means what you think it means, he said at last.

When I returned to the classroom, my students had risen from their desks and assembled into a swaying mass by the windows, now closed and latched. Their backs were to me, their foreheads pressed against the glass. They did not notice my entrance. I stood behind them, unable to see past the wall of their bodies. I had no idea where they would be in three years, when they were twenty years old. Would they hold an unpaid internship? Would they work the counter at a café? Would they have whole worlds of rooms in the mind? One by one they gasped, as if singing in a round. The sound came from their bellies. I stood on my tiptoes and inhaled, squeezing oxygen down into the deepest part of my lungs, into my stomach, my diaphragm contracting, the muscles between each rib prying the bones apart and opening me from the inside, until I was filled and tautened. My navel rubbed against the metal button on my trousers. I thought about how long I might be able to sustain a note, if I were to open my mouth. I thought about the slow leak, the palatal hum. Somewhere inside of me I heard my pedophilic high school choir director's voice—you're pinching a balloon's neck, he told me. You're widening your fingers. A millimeter.

Slower.

A half of a millimeter.

I opened and closed my mouth and emptied my lungs, soundlessly, of air. In front of me, someone pointed out the window and laughed. Someone made a noise like a car whooshing through a tunnel. One by one each student made a retching sound. That's disgusting, someone said. Someone said, that's illegal. Someone covered their eyes with their fists. Someone was plugging their ears. Someone was buckling at the knees. Someone was reaching for someone's hand. Someone was weeping. I thought of mountains I had never seen, coastal geographies, blind curtains of snow, a dairy cow, a pond filmed with ice, birch forests, green fields of the dead, my own name in the diminutive. I would kill myself, someone said, if anyone saw me like that. Look at the legs, someone said. This is fascist, someone said, and someone said, please make it stop.

What are you all looking at? I asked.

My students turned. Their hair drooped. Their eyes dulled. They hung their heads, lurched to their desks. Nothing, they mumbled. One by one they slid into their seats and opened their notebooks, yawning.

I walked to the window and pressed my own forehead to the glass. My eyes were wide open. I was looking; I was really looking. But there wasn't anything there.

# 3

*

The Dean of Academics's office was situated on the second floor of a cottage dedicated to administrative work. The building's exterior was, like that of all the Academy's other acquisitions, shingled, salt-sprayed, the cedar cracked and showing the weather, but its interior, unlike any other part of campus, had been renovated in a weirdly anachronistic Gothic style. Along the ceiling line snaked ornate moldings of deep wood. Persian rugs dampened the administrators' footfall through the hallways. The windows had been re-paned with Tudor latticework, and in the afternoons the sunlight that spilled in from the west scattered across the floor as diamonds. From the walls looked out nineteenth-century oil paintings of austere females seated in practiced repose—portraits that implied storied connections between the women depicted and the institution itself, when in reality they had probably been purchased in the 1980s from the antique warehouses that stippled the highway along the coastline. Slabs of overhead fluorescent light cast hard shadows onto the women's sallow skin. This was a school. The stairways were linoleum. The smells were antiseptic citrus. Next to the gender-neutral bathrooms hung fire alarms, red as candy, and next to these, plastic sheaths that housed epinephrine pens and nasal sprays brimming with Narcan. Laminated diagrams were tacked to the wall above, demonstrating proper usage: a stick figure plunged a needle into another stick figure's thigh; a stick figure's hand hovered over a stick figure's distended nostrils, squeezing, portending something, possibly doom.

Between two portraits of middle-aged women clad in severe white bonnets, the door to the Dean's office imposed itself: heavy mahogany with an etched brass knob. I had the sense that when it opened, I would be crossing the threshold into the nave of a church. I took a seat in a carved wooden chair in the waiting area, my spine straight as a tree, the chair back in contact with my head. Across the room, the Dean's assistant typed and coughed; looked at me; typed and coughed. She sipped her water from a paper cup. Ice clacked against her teeth. Behind her, a little red bird slammed into the window and fell to its death. She didn't turn around.

After several minutes the door swung open and out stepped the Dean, her kitten heels driving into the carpet, followed by my history-teacher neighbor. Her hand, prominently knuckled, was stroking his back. His hair hung babyishly over his dainty ears. They were both laughing, though my neighbor's eyes were bloated and pink, as if he had been weeping. I could have plucked those eyes, I thought, like berries. I rose from my chair. My neighbor dabbed at his cheeks with a handkerchief. When he recognized me he leered, showing off his pretty teeth. He clapped a hand on my shoulder. The singer, he said, chuckling. The Dean's hair was pulled into a glossy French twist. Her elegantly pressed pantsuit reminded me of my mother's upstairs closet, lined with linen garment bags—like clothing wearing clothing, I had always thought. La la la la la! my neighbor said. He patted me affectionately. You two are hilarious, the Dean cooed. She called across the room to her assistant: It's springtime, Donna, and faculty friendships are blossoming. Donna typed and coughed; looked at me; typed and coughed. On the windowpane, the bird had left a smudge the size of my thumb. I'll see you later, my neighbor said. He squeezed the fat on my upper arm as though we were two adults in love—with one another's adult bodies, one another's adult brains. I made a mental note to discuss with my students the intimate connection between psyche and soma, how their physical lives might be rendered more legible if they were to conceive of all that had ever happened to them as originating first in the world of the mind; for example, I would tell them, I had once smashed my skull into the lip of a car door, concussing myself, in what was obviously an unconscious plea for the love, pity, attention, and skin contact I had been denied as a baby. Did I receive it then, my students would ask, and I would say no, I had not received it then, but for weeks afterward when I tried to read, the words had flipped and squirmed across their pages like tadpoles. What does that have to do with this class, my students would say, aren't we supposed to be talking about *Bleak House* by Charles Dickens? And I would be unable to answer their question.

For a second my neighbor's infant face continued to leer, shining with aimless glee, after which he abruptly turned around and walked away. I watched the shifting of his buttocks as he left and wondered, not for the first time, if the porn he watched each evening—at what, given the quality of the sound as it traveled through my apartment's wall, could only have been his kitchen table—provided him with a deep and abiding joy; a private feeling, for him alone, that no one else could touch.

Have a seat, the Dean said.

She clicked the door shut behind me. I sank into a leather armchair across from her desk. Its cushion was too deep, and my ass dropped horribly low to the ground, my knees thrust toward the ceiling and splayed, my elbows jutting to reach their rests, like an animal butchered and trussed for consumption. The Dean crossed her legs easily in her rolling chair. I tracked her eyes as they slanted to take in her desktop monitor—whatever information it must have held about me. On the wall behind her was a framed photograph of a man, tall and wiry, posing in a field of sunflowers. His hands were resting lightly on his hips, his shirtsleeves rolled up to expose a pair of tanned and muscular forearms. The top two buttons of his shirt sagged open, and from the floppy chambray collar emerged a head almost entirely wrapped in thick bandages, so that beyond the layers of gauze one could only make out a pair of pale blue eyes and a small pink mouth. The image had been captured on a bright day; the bandages caught the sun and glowed a pure and luminous white. I was not certain whether the photograph had been hung only recently, or if I simply hadn't noticed it before.

My husband, the Dean said upon registering the direction of my gaze. I waited for her to make mention of the bandages, but she did not.

So handsome, I said admiringly. He looks exactly like Paul Newman!

The Dean offered a tinkling laugh in acknowledgement of how attractive her husband was—possibly, I thought, the survivor of a house fire, or maybe the veteran of some endless imperialist war. Then she coughed.

So, she said.

The Dean asked me how I had been finding my months at the Academy. Her knees uncrossed and recrossed themselves. Her hands lay folded in her lap. I told her it was remarkable, the way time slipped by here: the rhythmic churn of the academic year, the opening days, the reports, the comments, the trainings, the meetings, the vacations, all kinds of weather. Repetition, I said, and variation, like music. Like Bach. I could hardly believe that it was already the exam period, already essentially springtime. All year, I said, I had felt that I was drifting through a viscous amniotic fluid, untethered and galactic. Time moved around me; time seeped. I was twenty-eight years old, I explained. That's wonderful! the Dean said. And how had I been finding my students? My students, I said, were very impressive. I was so struck by their exemplary attention spans, their profound intellectual curiosity, the crystalline quality of their minds. That's wonderful! the Dean said. She looked at her monitor, then back at me.

I thought we might chat about your contract, she said.

My contract, I said.

She asked if I had been having any thoughts about my future.

My future, I said.

Two fat pigeons landed on the windowsill adjacent to the Dean's desk. One began a languid strut toward the other, its chest inflating and pushing out toward its ruffled neck.

Did I see myself, she asked, for example, pursuing a career in education long-term?

I believed that quality women's education mattered now more than ever, I announced. The pigeons purred from their perch. Now more than ever, I repeated in a tone of great conviction. Yes, the Dean replied mildly, she agreed, though she had been asking less about the concept of women's education in general and more about my own personal career trajectory. She knew—again she glanced at her screen—that I had been working toward an advanced degree before joining the faculty here. Did I have any ambitions with regard to an academic career of my own? No, I assured her, I did not have those ambitions any longer. The academy had been so cloistered, I lied, an ivory tower, cordoned off from all that was real in this world; I preferred my work to touch people directly, to be intimately engaged with the public, the polis. The Academy? the Dean asked. No, oops, sorry, I said, I meant the academy, lowercase. Her expression cleared. Of course, she said. She paused, rolled her chair further under the desk, and leaned toward me, allowing her breasts, surprisingly robust for her frame, to spill across the wood.

The Academy's English department was, as I knew, she said, quite small. She spoke in a voice that suggested we were two close friends who had once, long ago, survived a military coup together. As I knew, she went on, I had been hired on a temporary basis—which wasn't to say there was no chance of my contract being renewed, but she did need to acknowledge that she could not at the moment offer any guarantee. There were certain affairs, she said, that had to be settled before it could be determined whether a position would be vacant in the department for the next school year; and she couldn't promise that, if such a position *were* to become available, it wouldn't be posted publicly, in an open call. But there was no need to get ahead of ourselves, she chuckled. I chuckled, too. First, she hoped to establish whether I even had any interest in remaining at the Academy long-term. She thought we might have a brief chat and clarify the situation for all parties.

I thanked the Dean for her commitment to clarifying the situation for all parties, then asked if she was implying that it was still uncertain whether the teacher who was currently on leave would be returning in the fall. Yes, she confirmed, that was not yet one hundred percent clear. Was there a more accurate percentage she would be comfortable naming, I asked, if not one hundred—for example, was it eighty percent clear? Or maybe forty? She said she did not have a specific percentage in mind. I admitted that I found this curious. I didn't mean to pry—of course not, the Dean said—but it did seem odd, given that it was March, given that contracts were at this very moment being disseminated, discussed, negotiated, that the status of this teacher's return remained precarious. Perhaps she was on an extended maternity leave? I offered. Perhaps there had been complications in the birthing process?

He, the Dean said.

Ah, I replied in a shocked little voice, as if I had never before heard about the existence of men. An accident, maybe? An unexpected disability? A surgery? Perhaps his recovery process had not been as linear as anticipated? That can happen, I informed her. I began to relay the story of the concussion I had once given myself in an effort to receive male attention, but she interrupted me. She appreciated my investment in the teacher's well-being, the Dean said, but wished to remind me that the Academy took matters of confidentiality seriously. She was certain I could understand the School's obligation to protect its faculty's privacy. She gave a friendly laugh. Naturally, I said. I gave a louder and more friendly laugh. I would never, I assured her, want to invade a faculty member's privacy.

Particularly in the case of a devastating family illness, I murmured.

I watched her.

Or a mental health crisis, I said.

I whispered, Suicidal ideation?

Something illegal?

Something immoral?

A criminal act?

Something heinous?

Disgusting?

Perverse?

A trespass for which the School could be held liable? I suggested.

Shall we discuss your juniors? the Dean said.

On the windowsill one pigeon had clambered upon the back of the other, who lay below in squashed quiescence while its companion's talons kneaded the flesh around its folded wings. I observed the upper pigeon's clumsy thrusts, the scratching feet and frantic eyes, the throat pulsing, puffing, gulping. I turned away and attempted to recalibrate my position in the armchair, but each effort to scoot my torso into a more upright formation only led to my sliding back down into the lowest recess of the cushion.

I gave up and confirmed to the Dean that I would be delighted to discuss my juniors.

She smiled. Give me one quick second, she said. Her fingers flew across her keyboard. She lifted the office phone to her ear. From the other side of the mahogany door, a high ringing sounded.

Donna, the Dean said into the receiver, will you tell my four o'clock that we can use the conference room? I sank further into the chair, my chin tucking more deeply into my neck, like I too was a bird getting fucked. She hung up the phone. Sorry about that, she said, where were we. She looked at the screen. Ah, she said, okay. The Dean scooted her chair away from the computer and cleared her throat. It was obvious, she told me, that I was a highly committed educator. My responsiveness to my students' needs, my intuitive hands-on approach, my interdisciplinary bent—all these qualities were more than evident from my students' comments. She blew her nose and placed her used tissue on top of her keyboard. Excuse me, she said. She admired, she continued, my dedication to modeling for the Academy's young women how comprehensively the personal and the political were intertwined. The Dean wanted to thank me for the incredible amount of work I had put in this year. Teaching could be a thankless job, she knew; the labor of women, in particular, she knew, often went unnoticed in institutions like this one. We both shook our heads wearily in acknowledgement of our shared status as females. The Dean wished to recognize, she said, those low-light, post-class hours she was sure I had spent providing emotional support for my neediest students throughout the year; the surrogate mothering; the caretaking; the mentorship. It was important to her that we took the time to name my unnamed labor. She wanted me to really *feel* the Academy's gratitude. The Dean paused to give me a chance to feel the

Academy's gratitude. I felt it sitting on my skin like frosting. You're welcome! I said.

Satisfied, the Dean turned once more to her monitor. I do have a few questions, she said briskly, about certain aspects of your pedagogy; I wonder if you could clarify some of your methods. I told her that I would be delighted to clarify some of my methods. We've received a few comments, she said. Mm, I said, nodding. The Dean asked if it would be accurate to assert that I had on several occasions spent class time—she glanced at the screen—sorry, she said, "sexualizing" Joseph Stalin? Iosif, I corrected her. And your department head, she said, brought to my attention repeated changes to your syllabus; would it be accurate to say that the only book your juniors read all year in advance of this week's exam was *Bleak House* by Charles Dickens? I explained that, as an educator, I thought it essential to encourage an ethic of rigorous and sustained attention in teenagers whose lives had thus far been primarily mediated by ceaseless rapid-fire digital communication—repeated class-time references to the coming of global communism? the Dean interrupted. The end of history? she asked. An age of no alternatives? Pointed discussions of suicide? Pointed discussions of pedophilia? Mentions of rape? Repeated references to the fact that your family "got Holocausted"? Impassioned defenses of Freud's gender politics? Warning your class that "true love" might cause their "brain cells to swell" until they "vomited and died"? An exercise in which each student was asked to approach the whiteboard and rank in order of "worst" to "least bad" the violent events in their ancestral history that may have contributed to "intergenerational trauma"? I told the Dean that context was important. Didn't she agree, I asked, that context was important? I reminded her that I was not, as far as I was aware, being investigated for having seduced and molested *any* of my students who had been plunged into a state of unimaginable interior chaos and psychic disintegration after the suicide of a parent. What? the Dean said. When might I expect to hear definitively about my contract? I asked. We're hoping to have it all cleared up by next month, she replied. What a coincidence, I told her—my birthday was in April. Next month I would be twenty-nine years old. The Dean politely wished me a happy early birthday. There came a firm knock at the door. I watched the inner knob rotating with the sense that it moved of its own will. Donna poked her head into the office. Sorry to interrupt, she said, but your two o'clock is here. She coughed; looked at me; coughed; retreated. Don't let me keep you, I told the Dean. I found it difficult to lift myself from the depths of the armchair. I was engaging my core, tensing the long muscles in my thighs, pushing off with both hands. I was plunging and heaving. I was almost groaning. It was wonderful chatting, the Dean said, watching me struggle to escape my seat. She would be in touch with updates about my contract. She walked me to the door, her slender hand hovering just above my shoulder. Humiliation crashed over me like water.

Thomas smiled at me from where he stood in the waiting area. His nose was more prominent than I remembered, his lips thinner, his earlobes longer; I pictured them flapping against the soft back hinge of his jaw in a strong wind. His hair was parted on the wrong side of his skull, his cheeks lightly freckled where I had imagined them unmarked. He was not wearing his Invisalign braces. The texture of his newly shaven chin made me think of wet bathroom tile. I watched the Dean's face go girlish and flushed when she saw him. Was Thomas truly handsome? Any man, I decided, could be handsome if I wanted him to be. The Dean's teeth clenched, then relaxed. Her lips parted. She patted at the base of her neat updo. I loomed over her and felt the heft of my body, my big dangling arms, my organs weighing me down from the inside.

Mercedes, Thomas said, still smiling.

He leaned in and brushed his lips against each of the Dean's cheeks. She allowed her face to remain pressed against his a second too long.

Nice to meet you, I said loudly, are you French?

We've met, actually—briefly, I think, Thomas told me. He shook my hand. Thomas Nelson, he said, remind me of your name? His head drooped like a cut flower as he spoke; because I was taller than him, his wilted gaze ended up fixed in the vicinity of my pelvis. For the first time I thought I detected a faint accent at the edge of his speech, a hint of a lisp or lilt around the dark vowels—was it German?—but as soon as I attempted to place it, it evaporated. It was nice to see me, he said, he hoped I was well. His eyes drifted back to the Dean. There were several photos of his erect penis stored on my phone. A small brown stain saturated his thickly woven cream-colored button-down, next to his right nipple. I told him it was nice to see him, too, but no one was attending to me any longer. I considered slamming my head against the wall and concussing myself, to test my hypothesis that I would be more sexually attractive to men if I suffered mild but irreversible brain damage; Thomas followed the Dean into her office. I regarded his smug cowboy's gait, his not turning back to look at me. Donna remained at her desk, typing and coughing. There was no trace of bird residue on the window. The landscaper must have mounted his ladder and squeegeed it away during my meeting. For a moment I stood, letting my sneakers sink into the plush rug. I looked at Donna and engaged in vague thoughts of impermanence—conceptually—and time—conceptually—of the conceptual past and the conceptual future. I remembered several things that happened to me in my childhood and several other things that happened later, in my adolescence, and a few things that happened to me as an adult. I considered the possibility that everything in this world could be one, with no outside from which to observe it; that everything could be water; that everything could be fire. Philosophy proper begins, someone had once told me, when we move beyond the observation of phenomena and into the realm of pure thought—blah blah blah blah blah, I said. He giggled. Armchair philosophy, he said, because you're just sitting there. I love just sitting there, I said. The world of the mind, he said. I love the world of the mind, I said. I know you do, he said. Should we have salmon for dinner, I asked. Ooooooh, he said. Should I make bok choy, he said. Bok choy of the mind? he said. Should I do some sweet potato, I said. Should we watch a movie, he said. Ooooooh, I said. Should we watch a noir. Should we watch a paranoid thriller. Should we watch a documentary about the Irish. Should we do a Mike Leigh. Should we do something Soviet. Should we do an Elaine May. Should we make banana bread. Should we get ice cream. Should we check the freezer. Should we wash the sheets tomorrow. Should we go to the beach. Should we start eating more fruit. Should we stop using Teflon. Should we have a baby in eight or ten years. Should we start a book club, just the two of us. Should we read the *Iliad*. Would that be fun. Should we go for a walk.

Let's go for a walk.

I want to get taken for a walk.

From the office I heard the Dean telling Thomas to have a seat. Her voice sounded husky, verging on drunk. The door hung ajar, perhaps for my benefit. Through the opening I watched Thomas scrape a wooden stool toward the desk, avoiding the armchair. The Dean met my eyes as she reached to pull the door shut. For several seconds I listened to the raucous laughter unspooling from within, modulating up and down in a perfect minor third. Then there came a dense and impenetrable silence.

Bye, Donna, I said.

Outside, the world was dead and cold. Endless winter, I thought, winter everywhere, winter following me, winter the only thing horny for me. Wah wah, I thought, my whole life winter. Brittle grass crunched underfoot, brown as dirt. All around were the deadbeat trees, bare-branched and ashen. My coat, my scarf, my hat. From the ocean, the wind came up and laid itself onto me. Everything was what it had been for months. In the auditorium, students were taking their exams: trigonometry and modern world history, physics and French. They were scratching at wide-ruled booklets with inky blue pens. They were gawking at the shudder of the clock's second hand. *The modern city,* they were writing, *is characterized by new forms of social relation in which the other is apprehended only via a passing glimpse, so that in the literature of the city the formal question of "flat" and "round" characters can be recast as an ontological rather than aesthetic problem, which I will examine through a close reading of the awesome spontaneous combustion scene in Charles Dickens's most ambitious novel* Bleak House—

They wrote *I think fog represents the idea of not being able to see—*

They wrote *There can be such a thing as an interior beauty so fine and so strong that it radiates outward like a bright light from something we might, for argument's sake, call the soul—*

I pulled out my phone and opened my messaging application. Do u think this is a duck or a goose, I read. I zoomed in on the accompanying image, muddy and blurred, as if it had been snapped while jogging. Ok just found out it is a hideous type of duck, I read. Ew, I typed. Disgusting, I typed. My brain cells were swelling. I put away my phone. I changed my mind. I sent another message.

Would you rather a) all is water or b) all is fire or c) all is one, it said.

I wandered in the direction of the cafeteria. It was too cold to eat outside, the picnic tables unoccupied but one, at which sat a middle-aged woman and, across from her, an adolescent boy. Looking at him, I realized I hadn't encountered a non-adult male in months. He might have been twelve, or a childish fifteen. His cowlicked hair spurted away from his head at the roots; his lips were pouted in the center of his soft face. He wore an oversized silver parka, its dangling hood trimmed in matted faux fur and its upper sleeve emblazoned with a logo that brought to mind a military armband. In his lap he cradled something, tenderly, with both hands. The woman—his mother, I assumed—was leaning over the table and speaking rapidly, not to her son but to the object he held. I knew at once what it was, what it had to be. The boy was holding the little red bird that had smashed into Donna's window. He had watched the creature collapse from suicidal heights. He had rushed to gather it up in his gloved hands. He was attempting now to resuscitate it, pulsing his thumbs into its tiny chest. Maybe he had found a video online to direct him. Or his kindly mother was providing aid. Perhaps she was a veterinarian by profession. And when his efforts inevitably failed, when the reality that the bird had been lifeless from the start, that there had never been any hope, that it never stood a chance, at last erupted into the boy's consciousness, he would grieve, stoically and appropriately, and then, with his mother's help, give the bird a proper burial on campus. Boys were so sensitive, I thought, so much more sensitive than girls. I stepped closer, thinking that I might find a way to enter into conversation with the pair by offering a warning about the dangers of avian diseases—for instance, avian influenza or, less notoriously, avian tuberculosis—until I was near enough to admire the length of the boy's lashes. I opened my mouth. I looked into his lap.

He was not holding a dead bird. He was holding a portable gaming system. It gleamed a bright plastic teal against his thighs. The boy's pudgy fingers dashed among the device's knobs and buttons while his mother watched, egging him on in a language whose cadences snagged on me like a net. Behind me, I heard the cafeteria doors swing open. I turned to see Petar emerging, clutching three compostable to-go containers against his sherpa-lined denim jacket. The boy glanced up, ignored both me and Petar, then continued to poke and jab and squeeze at the buttons in his lap. I was standing too close to deny that I had been approaching with meaningful intention. The woman stared at me. I just wanted to tell your son how much I adore his coat, I said, so chic! I waved heartily at Petar to make clear that I was a beloved figure in these parts and not a perverted stranger advancing upon her child in a pedophilic way. Okay, she said, TJ Maxx. I pretended to note "TJ Maxx" down in my phone. Petar reached us. He straddled the picnic bench and set down his boxes. The woman grabbed a container, opened it, sniffed, and pushed it away. My family, Petar said to me, smiling, you've met them? Elena—his wife shook my hand—and Georgi. The boy squinted at me and returned to his game.

I asked when they had arrived in town. About two weeks ago, Elena told me. Without removing her eyes from mine, she muttered a sentence firmly in Bulgarian to Georgi, who grunted and placed his gaming system on the table. And how were they liking it here so far, I asked. It's small, she said, but good, of course. Of course it's good to be together again. You need your family, Petar agreed, nodding. Georgi was swinging his legs violently back and forth beneath the picnic table, seeming not to notice when he kicked my shins. He began to huff and rub his hands together like he could only now feel the cold. My mother is from Lithuania, I said. That is nice, said Elena. Immigrating to the States, oh boy, I said, shaking my head. Mm, Elena said. I turned my attention to Georgi. So, do you like the USA? I asked. He kicked my shin. Sure, he mumbled, I don't know. Pretty crazy here, right? I said. Gun violence, right? No sidewalks, right? Do you like the grocery stores? I asked. What do you mean, he said. I told him that I personally enjoyed shopping at grocery stores in other countries, browsing the aisles, surveying the myriad varieties of packaged and processed and frozen foods. I don't really care, he said, it's basically the same. Ugh, yeah, there's probably a ton of hegemonic American influence in Bulgaria anyway, I said. What? he said. Did he have a girlfriend back home, by the way, I asked, a girlfriend he longed for? No, Georgi said, he did not have a girlfriend back home. That's cool, I said.

So how did he feel about the Soviet Union? I was curious—had his school in Plovdiv discussed all the ways that Bulgaria had been a loyal, faithful satellite country of Iosif Vissarionovich Stalin's USSR? Did Premier Chervenkov's hilarious nickname of "Little Stalin" ever come up in class? So sweet, I confided, and both leaders sadly accused of fostering "personality cults," when Iosif, at least, had by many accounts been a modest man of simple tastes and negligible vanity, a world-historical power with gentle brown eyes who, despite enduring years of abuse, managed to bend the future to his will, whose humility, given the circumstances, had been nothing short of extraordinary—

I trailed off. I looked down. I heard the silence, the gulls, the air that touched the trees. I did not feel I had much left to say.

I thought your game was a dead bird, I told him.

Elena put a hand on her son's wrist. Georgi, she said, don't you have homework? She shrugged at me affably, as if I, too, were Georgi's mother, or as if I might have important homework of my own to complete. They never want to do anything, do they, she said, rumpling Georgi's hair. You have children?

No, I told her. I did not have children. Though it could be argued that, in a way, each one of the girls at the Academy was like a daughter to me.

The wind was picking up. It fussed one end of Elena's scarf. Petar stacked the to-go containers neatly in front of him, like someone putting together a puzzle. Too cold to sit, he said, whether to me or to his family I couldn't tell. Georgi rose and slipped his gaming system into his parka. Elena spat in her hand and smoothed down the boy's hair, then lifted his hood over his head and zipped his coat up to the chin. He stood motionless, gazing dully into the distance while she worked at him.

It was so nice to meet you, I said. They nodded in response. Enjoy your lunch, Elena told me, though I was not holding any food.

I watched the three of them walk down the Academy's hill, toward their housing unit. Their hands were stuffed into their pockets: six identical bulges. For a few seconds I could make out the rise and fall of their speech, their voices lapping at each other like waves. Then the sound receded. I thought about the city in which I had grown up, where my weather application had told me a snowstorm would land that night. My mother, father, and sister would be buying groceries now, preparing for the storm, and even so, even as the snow blew in, soon enough my mother would begin to plant her seedlings in rinsed-out yogurt tubs, leaning over the containers to whisper endearments in Russian and Yiddish, waking early and kneeling on the recently finished floors to construct cages out of wire mesh sheets purchased at the hardware store, which would later keep her fragile sprouts safe from the ravenous rabbits and squirrels that scampered through the garden while she screamed down from the terrace, threatening to shoot them with a gun she did not own.

Above me, a flock of birds wheeled and squawked, maneuvering toward the sea, where the afternoon shadows were spreading like a stain. I turned back for a glimpse of the Dean's office, but the curtains had been drawn across the window.

I pulled out my phone. It looked the same as it always did. I made a noise with my mouth. I had a new text that said:

all is one all is one all is one!!!!

# 4

*

As the school year draws to a close, I said, I thought we might spend the last fifteen minutes of the period reflecting on our experiences in and of this course.

I wrote "Time to Reflect!" on the whiteboard. Three of my students blew their noses, two into tissues and one directly into her hand, wiping the snot on her thigh. Anita wrinkled her face at her classmates, pretended to gag, and dragged her desk to a window, throwing it wide. For weeks there had been a cold going around the junior dorm. I can't get sick, she muttered, I have an interview next week. She gasped at the air, which flowed moist and mild into the room. For a highly competitive unpaid internship, she said more loudly, then beckoned Thales, who looked nervously my way before scraping a desk along the floor to join her.

Divya raised her hand. Don't we still have a month of school left, she said.

Thank you, Divya, I replied, for that thoughtful observation. Yes, I told the class, angling my body away from Anita and Thales, as Divya had wisely pointed out, the year was not yet over; but in truth a month was barely enough time for the task I'd set us, given how lengthy a process reflection could be. "Reflection," I said, from the Latin *reflectere*: to bend back—the pursuit of a lifetime. Even if we were to dedicate the final fifteen minutes of every remaining session to reflection, I doubted we would get very far. We do not know ourselves, I continued, raising a finger for emphasis. Each one of us is a pit, a pit brimming with slime and muck—I wrote "muck pit" on the whiteboard—and that, though it may be painful to hear, included Divya herself. But I could excuse her hubris. Seventeen was an impressionable age, a formative age. I, however, was almost thirty years old.

I turned to the rest of my girls and asked if they felt they had been deeply changed by the experience of studying The Literature of the City this year.

Changed like how? Kyla asked.

I told her that she was free to define "changed" as she saw fit: the clearing up of neurotic disturbance, a shift in moral perception—

You mean like what did I learn in this class? she said.

Sure, I said.

I'd like to publicly state that I thought the exam was unfairly graded, Anita called from her seat by the window. I also believe it to have been sexist, as it did not feature representation of any identity apart from Charles Dickens.

Thank you, Anita, I said. Rest assured that the Dean of Academics has made note of your feelings and shared them with me.

Sasha raised her hand. I learned that the Soviet project lives on in the hearts of all the noble workers of the world, she choked out, her voice hoarse. Also that there is no primordial unity to which we can return, which is sad enough that it makes some people mentally ill.

Fabulous, I said. I scribbled a note on my roster to raise Sasha's final grade from a B+ to an A-. Across the room, Thales's hand was half-raised, but as soon as I turned toward her, she lowered it. I called on her anyway. She was silent for a second, then began to mumble rapidly in such hushed tones that I could not make out a word. Could you please speak up? I shouted. Anita placed a protective hand on her knee. Thales inhaled.

When I started this class, she said, fixing her eyes on her desk, I did not know what a blacking factory was. I did not know about the Court of Chancery. I did not know of the gross thing that would happen to Mr. Krook. I thought smallpox was a made-up disease. I did not know how to pronounce the word "Thames." I did not know that Anita's family friend was the CFO of a rideshare company, and now Anita and I are really close. I'm going to spend the summer with her family in Los Angeles. My parents are having marital issues and will be attending a marital retreat. I did not have a relationship with the divinity when I started this class but now I have a strong relationship with the divinity. My parents are having sexual problems. I learned that I should never become a lawyer or get too involved in certain spiritually corrosive court cases and that it's okay if I just say I don't feel well enough to come to class without specifying diarrhea or menarche.

Thales's breathing was shallow. She grabbed her hair with both hands and tugged. Her roots, I noticed, had grown in brown.

It was the longest speech I had ever heard her make. Perhaps she had recently been prescribed methamphetamine's cousin. On the other side of the room, Cordelia was humming, almost inaudibly. Thales raised her eyes to meet mine, and I nodded at her.

Thank you for that deeply felt reflection, Thales, I said.

I glanced at the clock, then back at the class. All my girls were leaning forward in their chairs, like jockeys at the gate of a horse race. Used tissues littered the floor.

That's all for today, I said.

Even before I finished my sentence, there was a generalized leaping to the feet, a grabbing of jackets, a mad rush toward the stairs, a few hands waving goodbye to me. No homework, I called out, but please be prepared for an in-class writing exercise on the meaning of "reflection."

I zipped my backpack. Cordelia approached my desk.

Would you mind if we had our conference outside? I asked her. I could use some fresh air.

We left campus and walked down Main Street in the five o'clock light. For a time neither of us spoke. Seabirds let out desultory screams, winding their great sweeping arcs over the bay. In front of the town hall, hedges of forsythia bloomed liquid yellow; crocuses pushed up tiny clods of soil; the trees breathed open their buds. It was spring. The air was a softening blue. A fat wasp twitched out its death on the sidewalk.

It's not enough, Cordelia said at last. It's not enough of a reason to be here.

We turned left into a graveled lot where no cars ever parked, at the end of which stood two picnic tables overlooking the water. Their wood was gray and rotted and leaning, their legs sunk partway into sand. Beyond them, wind flustered the dune grass, half-submerged and full of ticks I feared but never saw. The tide had swollen and drowned the bottom planks of the rickety stairway that led to the beach. We sat across from one another, each seeking the patches where our benches had been warmed by the afternoon sun.

I can't put my whole life into it, she said. I want something that I can put my whole life into.

I watched the light slip over her face. The water foamed a little, as if shaken up in a jar.

Cordelia, I said, when you say "it," I don't know what you mean. You have to give me an antecedent.

I unzipped my backpack and pulled out Cordelia's exam booklet, Cordelia's reading log, Cordelia's most recent take-home essay—Cordelia's brain, transmuted into her awful handwriting, like the body of Christ whooshing its way into all those slivers of old bread. Hers was my last student conference of the semester. I could no longer remember if this had happened naturally or if I had planned it. Across from me, her knee jittered, tenting her overlong pleated skirt. In the world of the mind I could feel myself preparing to step through time's hoop, as I had so often in the past. When I emerged on the other side, I thought, everything would be different; everything would be exactly the same.

A thin-legged spider scuttled across the table and Cordelia brushed it away with the back of her hand. I flipped slowly through her reading log.

Your work has been strong this year, I said. Really impressive.

She thanked me.

And I'm happy to see you got around to reading *Lolita*—I pointed at the open page—a profound, tragic novel that idiots all over the world, losers with soft confused brains, cretins and neanderthals who have never once looked life in its face, often mistake for salacious pro-pedophile smut.

It's a very fine book, Cordelia said, I appreciated the recommendation.

The spider had returned to the table. This time I smashed it with my fist.

I was curious, I said, if Cordelia had an idea of what she wanted to study in college. Did she have a sense of her general ambitions for the future? It was true that the humanities were dying, I admitted, but wasn't it also true that *everything* was dying—I aimed my finger up at the sky in an oblique gesture meant to encompass the death of all things—that everything good in the world was currently and had always been dying? Wasn't everything-good-always-dying the inevitable outcome of a class society? And wasn't the history of all hitherto existing human society the history of class struggles? But we mustn't forget that even if everything good was always dying, everything good was also always being born anew—which was why,

I concluded, I believed that Cordelia should think seriously about pursuing an undergraduate degree in English literature! As one handsome, sensitive, politically engaged though possibly overexcitable thinker had put it, *writers are the engineers of human souls*—were they not? Cordelia's natural aptitude as a scholar was obvious; she was clearly able to delineate between art and garbage, a rare quality these days, especially in students her age; and while she and I may have had our differences in the classroom, I hoped she understood that I maintained a deep and abiding respect for her intellect—

There's a school in the city where I can do my senior year, Cordelia said.

I looked up from her reading log. She sat angled toward the bay so that her face appeared to me in profile, like it was emblazoned on a coin: the smudged curve of the nose, the eyelid puffed and half-hooded, the stringy hair flailing in the breeze. I watched her nostril flare as she inhaled. I inhaled, too, and the air that entered me was so overwhelmingly sour and alive, I thought I might faint. I understood that Cordelia had not been listening to a word I said. When she spoke now, she wasn't talking to me at all, but to whatever she must have believed lay hidden behind or beyond me, as if she thought her soul could be transfigured through language, handed off somewhere, then elsewhere, then elsewhere once again, until eventually the words she said out loud would find their way to the one person who could really hear her—who could make her *feel real*. But I was the only other person there.

You're leaving the Academy, I said.

She shrugged, met my gaze, then released it and turned back toward the bay. The school in the city had a strong choral program, she said. She had worked with its director before, and she was friendly with a few rising seniors from the music camp she attended each summer in the middle of the country. They were nice, she said, all quite nice. Her voice remained in its lowest register as she spoke, her vowels throbbing in the damp cave of her mouth, her consonants neat and tight: the quick flick of a fingernail against a hard surface. She would have a chance to be section leader, she looked forward to that. For the altos? I asked. Cordelia nodded. I had been an alto too, I said, for some years, until I stopped singing—she would get to compete nationally, she said, which couldn't happen with the Academy's choir. And she planned to submit a music portfolio alongside her college applications, maybe even apply to a few conservatories or dual-degree programs, so it would be advantageous to resume her private voice lessons in the city.

She admitted that it was strange to leave the Academy so late, when there was only one year left to muddle through, but these past few months had been a transformative period for her—an almost sacred period—and in their aftermath she felt that she was looking down upon the unscrolling map of her life from a vast distance. She was a gigantic balloon surging into the cosmos, untethered. She saw clearly where she needed to go, what she needed to do. She understood the ceaseless, undulating flow of time, the time that lived inside of her, her body time made physical, like she was an hourglass packed with sand; and she knew that she could at last chart the terrain of her existence without doubt or fear. So cool! I said. What had transpired, exactly, to transform her, metaphorically speaking, into both a big balloon and an hourglass? Cordelia blinked, startled, as if she had forgotten I was there. The details were too much to get into, she said, waving her hand. But the takeaway was that this transformative period, during which she had come to see that she was and always had been a being made of time, had concluded with her discovering how desperately she needed space from the things that had happened to her while she was here at the Academy. How an atmosphere could seep into your skin; how a place could throttle you. It had descended upon her, this knowledge, she said, like a great rain crashing down from a cloudless blue sky. *I close my eyes and see a seagull in the desert,* I quoted. Everything was the same, she said, everything was different. She understood that she needed to move beyond this school, this town and the people who inhabited it, her classmates, her dormmates, even her younger sister, whom she loved—she did love her—but who was driving her, especially recently, insane. Had I met Eliza, Cordelia asked, she was a freshman?

No, I didn't think so.

Cordelia fingered the string of her hoodie. She and Eliza were close, she said, but it was a sisterly closeness that papered over a pit of barely submerged violence, which roiled right there beneath the surface, simmering and burbling and threatening to erupt. As children, they had often played a game wherein one sister would punch the other in the stomach; the other would then return the first sister's punch; and the two would go back and forth like this for a period, while their parents attended board meetings and galas and gallery openings and fundraisers that lasted late into the night. Because Cordelia was older, bigger, and buffer than her sister, with more muscular hands and forearms, her punches made a greater impact. One evening she had jammed her fist into Eliza's belly with such force that Eliza had been unable to breathe for somewhere between seven and ten seconds—or so, at least, Eliza had later claimed to their mother. As revenge for such incidents, Eliza would strip to her underpants, flip Cordelia's huge stuffed bear—the size of an overweight toddler, won for Cordelia by their father at a street fair—onto its stomach, and mount it from behind, grasping its floppy ears and thrusting her pelvis energetically into its backside. I'm raping you, I'm raping you, her sister would shout, and then she would squeak in the voice of the bear, I'm getting raped, oh no, oh help, I'm getting raped, its furry legs splayed side to side while she humped and scissored at them. I'm about to have trauma, the bear would squeal, uh-oh, I'm about to have sexual trauma. I muttered that everyone's sisters did that—it wasn't a big deal—sisters punched each other, puked together, shat together, raped each other's toys—violated each other, brought each other down, ruined each other's lives—anyway, Cordelia said, since their father's death, the sororal dynamic between the two had become even more thorny, more obscure and unmanageable. These days Eliza had taken to composing long, handwritten letters in which she detailed the enviable qualities of Cordelia's body, Cordelia's nipples in particular, and claimed that she would do anything in the world to make Cordelia happy. She would weasel her way into Cordelia's dorm room when she was in class and slide the folded sheets of paper under her pillow, letters that were in their own way more vicious and unsettling than the bear rapes had ever been. To me, I said, those letters sounded sweet and thoughtful; I wasn't sure I saw the problem. It was not sweet and thoughtful, Cordelia said. It was lunatic behavior. It was a relief that her sister would be staying at the Academy when Cordelia left. She could write someone else letters. She could find someone else.

Cordelia paused. Her face was flushed from the exertion of speaking.

I have to leave this place, she said—not to me. I have to go. I want to be more than the fact that my dad jumped off a bridge.

The air was getting cooler, the wind uncoiling across the surface of the bay. I buttoned my jacket and raised my hood over my head. The tide had begun to recede, pulling back into itself as if tugged by a colossal hand. On the picnic table the exam booklet flapped open to a blank page. Cordelia gathered her hair into a ponytail. Two ripe pimples shone along the side of her nose. Clumps of mascara had coagulated on her lower lashes. She was seventeen years old, and I was telling her that all of the past and all of the future lived inside of the present, that everything that had ever happened to her would stay forever twisted in her center, like a wasp in a fig, no matter where she went or what she believed she was leaving behind; it was *banal,* I was saying, to want to be more than the things that had happened to you, it was *cliché,* it was *trite,* it was *adolescent,* and though she imagined she wanted that, one day she would be almost thirty—almost-thirty would arrive for her, as it arrived for us all—and I guaranteed that she would no longer wish to be more than the fact that her dad jumped off a bridge; she would not wish to be *more* than anything; she would be focused solely on dragging her body, mind, and spirit through the barren terrain of her life, like Moses limping across the desert—

Like Moses? Cordelia asked, her eyebrows raised.

I looked down at my phone.

It's getting late, I said, we should head back to campus, you don't want to miss dinner.

I handed over her reading log, her most recent take-home essay, her exam booklet. I thought your paper on the concept of contagion in *Bleak House* was particularly well done, I said. We both stood. I watched her remove her phone from her jacket pocket and frame the bay for a photo, the dimpled water mirroring the sky and its bands of dying translucent daylight: pink and apricot, yellow, an endless receding blue. On the other side of the peninsula, the sun would soon meet the horizon; behind us, past the long highway, the tidal flats, the dunes. I didn't need to see them to know that they were there. The sand that stretched toward the bay was shadowed an austere gray. The wind pushed through the water. Cordelia moved her phone to take in the distant lighthouse, not yet illuminated, and then the camera was pointed at me.

It's a video, she said, say hi.

Hi, I said.

She turned the camera to her own face. She smiled, waved, tucked her hair behind her ear. Hi, she said. She slipped the device back into her pocket. She was almost my height. We could have passed for sisters, I thought. I like your necklace, she said, peering at my throat, is that a whale? I took the charm between my fingers. It was, I said, though not at all anatomically accurate, sadly, the tail too small—but I liked it too. It had been a gift. She nodded and slung her backpack over her shoulder. Of course there's a lot I'll miss, she said. Living by the ocean. The birds, I like the birds. Mr. Nelson's going to offer his Flâneurs et Flâneuses seminar for seniors next year. I've wanted to take it since I was a freshman. But he's going to send me the syllabus, and I'll try to read along, at least, if I have the time. I'm not sure how demanding my new schedule is going to be.

You've been in touch, recently? I asked.

On and off this year, Cordelia said. He did fall off the map for a bit, when he was spending a lot of time in the hospital with his dad. Aren't you two friends? she asked. He said you were friends.

We're friendly, I said.

It was almost dusk. Our backs were to the water. Our feet crunched the gravel. We left the lot and turned right.

Mr. Nelson's father, Cordelia said, and once more I sensed that she was talking to something that wasn't me, was a really toxic person, a really abusive person. What Mr. Nelson went through when he was a kid—it helped, having someone who understood, someone older, when all that stuff was happening with my dad.

You two talked about that a lot? I said.

Yes, she said, we did.

Just the two of you? I said.

Yes, sometimes.

Well, I said, Mr. Nelson's dad is dead now.

I know, said Cordelia.

We walked up Main Street on our way back to campus. We passed the town hall, the post office, the library, their facades holding onto the ebbing light of day, an alien glow against the deepening sky. The first tourists of the season strolled down the sidewalk and into the road, clinging curbside despite the lack of traffic. I watched the slow forward shamble of an elderly couple, each gripping the rubber handle of a cane. They were laughing. Behind them, a healthy family of four toddled along in matching orange sneakers. A young boy slurped at his soft serve, his face radiating elemental terror with every dart of his tongue toward the cone.

This flâneur class, I said to Cordelia, sounded similar to The Literature of the City, didn't she think? It was one of the forms of the urban novel, surely—flâneurs were merely men who wandered around cities, wearing hats, pointing at stuff, telling protracted boring stories about narrow side streets, childhood memories, encroaching modernity—he's been teaching it for years, Cordelia said, and it's pretty different from your class, he has students read four or five novels, not just one. Around us, the streetlamps came to life. Cordelia's eyes shone in the sudden halogen mist. It's an interesting topic, actually, she said, a feminist unpacking of the flâneur archetype—you know, who can walk around the city alone—because of course in that era if a woman was walking through the city unaccompanied, she was likely a prostitute—and maybe a woman can't maintain true anonymity when she walks through the city even today—and maybe anonymity is a prerequisite for a flâneur—if a flâneur is a cipher for the world—if there's a necessary blankness onto which the world can project itself—so you'll read Woolf, I said. Yes, they would read Woolf. And Rhys? No, she didn't think Rhys was on the syllabus. That was a shame, I said. Our gaits were in step. Our hoods were both raised. Cordelia's knees cracked as she walked, the sound of hollow seeds being crushed underfoot.

He stepped out of a bookstore at the end of the block, the only one open through the offseason. From his wrist dangled a green umbrella, Velcroed shut, though I didn't think there was any threat of rain. His other hand grasped the twine handle of a paper shopping bag. He looked innocent, healthy, a little younger than my parents. Next to me, Cordelia's pace was quickening. Her face was slackening, tightening, rupturing. She was a long tunnel; she was a river; she was an open door. She was stepping through a birch forest into a basin of light. She was completely regular, a completely average teenager. She was smiling.

Hey, she called, Mr. Nelson.

He grinned and waved, then jogged to catch up with us. Soon we were all huddled together in the middle of the sidewalk. Thomas swung his arms over Cordelia in a firm, paternal hug. I watched his body make contact with hers, his chest against hers, their cheeks very close. There was no fear in his face. He released her and touched my arm with his friendly hand. I only got back yesterday, he said. Back for good—for now—it's hard to believe. A handsome pierced couple stepped into the street to make their way around us, and we all called toward them—Oh, we said, sorry—speaking with one voice. We began to walk, Thomas falling easily into the rhythm Cordelia and I had established. He was between us. I told him I was sorry about his father. He thanked me. And thank you, both of you, for the cards, he said, turning to Cordelia. I called your mother, but will you let her know again how generous it was, that food she sent, it could have fed an army, we didn't have to cook for a week. I'll text her, Cordelia said. She blushed and cast her eyes at the sidewalk. It was my idea, actually, the food, she muttered. Thomas smiled. The Academy is going to miss this one, he said to me, clapping Cordelia fondly on the back.

Yes, I said, it was clear that the Academy would miss that one.

How was the funeral? Cordelia asked. Thomas pushed his hair back from his face. He looked tan, though his father, as far as I knew, lived in a city with the same climate as this town. His Invisalign braces gave his speech a soft, pleasant lisp. Honestly, I barely remember it, he said, I must have blocked it out. She understood, said Cordelia. Except, he continued, I *do* remember what we sang—guess, Cordelia, you'll like this. Thomas's bag of books knocked against my shin with each step. Cordelia grinned. She flung open her mouth and her voice made a pure cut into the air.

And was Jerusalem builded here, she sang, Among those dark Satanic Mills?

Brava! Thomas cried. They both laughed. Blake, I said; what a strange hymn; were they aware that *dark Satanic Mills* was widely interpreted as a reference to the Industrial Revolution; a fascinating poem, a weird little shapeshifter of a poem—Bring me my Bow of burning gold, they both trumpeted, pumping their arms. Bring me my Arrows of desire. Thomas's voice was a fine rich baritone. They curled and rolled their *r*s triumphantly as they sang. Across the street, a family swiveled their heads in our direction. I made eye contact with a toddler, gnawing on the hoof of a stuffed hog and weeping. Cordelia and Thomas dissolved into laughter once more. Sorry, Thomas gasped at me, sorry, too much to get into, we have this whole insane history with "Jerusalem." Insane, Cordelia agreed, almost in tears. I laughed, too. They stopped laughing. Had either of them ever heard Paul Robeson sing it? I asked. No, they hadn't. The way he interprets it, I said. He had this gorgeous rendition, too, of the

Soviet National Anthem—what a voice, what a bass—certain recordings did, unfortunately, cut out the second verse's reference to Iosif Stalin's faithful and inspiring leadership of the people, which was too bad, because it was an interesting moment, lyrically and sonically—

It was nice to be back, Thomas said in reply to a question no one had asked, but at the same time strange, to try to absorb that the ordeal of the last year had finally ended. There was an unreal quality to the whole situation. He found that he could only talk about the past in the vaguest terms: events had occurred, and then, at a certain point, those events had stopped occurring and others had begun to occur instead. When he had first decided to go on leave, he'd been unsure if he would return to the Academy. He couldn't have predicted how the time with his father would unfold, how the illness would progress; he couldn't have envisioned what kind of person he himself might become, what he would want, the choices he would make, whether he would be deeply changed by the experience of watching his dad—this figure that had loomed so mightily at the edges of his consciousness—die. But these days it almost felt like the sickness, deterioration, and eventual passing of his father had taken place long ago: that they were memories from earliest childhood, even from the womb, some inchoate mind-world, the ether of the universe. It seemed this past year had been only a blip, a scratch on life's surface, a hairline crack that he would easily spackle over. Come autumn, he would resume teaching at the Academy. He would return to the rhythms he had established eight years ago, when he first made this town his home, when his daughter was still in college. She was not yet a lesbian then, he said. And now she was a lesbian. Now his father's house was on the market. And soon it would sell. He would pack up the photo albums and the stained-glass lamps and the fragile wood boxes he had admired since his youth, and the rest of his father's objects he would hawk to strangers on the internet. The past had melted away.

And *you're* out of here soon, he said to Cordelia. How does that feel?

Good, she said, I think it feels good. She paused.

I'm ready, she said.

We had reached the cross street that snaked the Academy's hill to campus. Above us tilted the familiar ring of cottages, shrouded in the dusk. There was my own classroom's window. The faculty housing building. I gazed up at the gleaming rectangles of yellow light, rooms in which people I knew were tearing open snack wrappers and scrolling on their phones, and felt overcome by a surge of affection for my apartment here—its rollable floors, its plump red corduroy couch, its sad artery of a hallway. I could love it, I knew, from the outside. For a time we lingered, and then a sudden panic rose in me, a conviction that Thomas and Cordelia would walk away together, leaving me behind to stand at this corner, staring longingly at the Academy on its hill for all eternity. I no longer feared what the two of them would do with each other. I only feared that I would be completely uninvolved. Soon real darkness would fall. I tried to convince myself that I was looking forward to the constellations—but I couldn't remember any of their names.

Cordelia thanked me for meeting with her. She had enjoyed my class, she said. She had enjoyed the Dickens. Dickens had not been a writer she believed she would feel a kinship with, but she had surprised herself. Yes, I said, I knew what that was like. She asked if I had plans for the upcoming year, and I said that I wasn't sure. She asked if I remembered what was on the cafeteria menu tonight, and I said I believed it was meat lasagna and grilled asparagus. Oh, good, she said. She liked lasagna. I told her to go on ahead; I would probably eat at home tonight. I'd see her in class on Tuesday. I paused. I was sure she would be very missed at the Academy, but I wanted her to know that I was impressed by the way she was choosing to wrangle her own life. Like a horse, I said.

She thanked me again.

I'll email you that reading list, Thomas told her, smiling, and we'll get a coffee before you go.

I watched Cordelia begin her slow trudge up the hill, toward all those little lights. Her skirt swished around her calves. Her hood slipped down; her hair caught the wind. She put in her wireless earbuds and bobbed her head to a music I couldn't hear.

Shall we walk for a minute? Thomas asked.

We turned back the way we came, in the direction of his apartment. He was sorry that his return to the Academy meant I was out of a job. It was awkward, he said, I don't know what else to say, it's just awkward. He wished there had been another position in the department available. I did ask, I'd like you to know, I did try to make a case for you. I told him that was okay. I was not certain that I was ready to devote my life to women's education, anyway. It was true that all year I had been concerned about my contract; it was true that I'd had the future sitting on my shoulders like a bag of dripping ice. But when I learned that the contract wasn't going to be renewed, I had felt nothing but a warm flood of inevitability, as if this were the ending I had written long ago to a story I was telling myself.

Also, I'm not a very good teacher, I said. I knew he and Cordelia were close—maybe she had mentioned that.

He shook his head. She never said anything of the sort, he told me.

We passed the Old Pilgrim, where a musician was plucking out a folk song I loved on a poorly tuned guitar. The sound washed into the street. We both peered in at the performer, who yodeled grandly at a microphone set too close to his mouth. His long blond beard was wrapped in an impressive coil around the microphone stand, like a snake. Distorted glottal stops careened into the air. Suddenly he ceased his singing.

Get in or keep moving, he shrieked at us through the window.

We continued walking.

You're probably sad that she's leaving the Academy, I said, right as you're coming back. It was difficult, he shrugged, sure. Cordelia was almost like a daughter to him. I reminded Thomas that he already had a daughter. He reminded me that it was possible to have two daughters; in fact, many people did. In any case, he was proud of Cordelia. And he was accustomed to this dynamic, more than most. His life as a teacher involved constant repetitions of loss, constant rehashings, constantly beginning anew. So he would move into my apartment on campus after I moved out? I asked. That was right. And what about me? Did I have any idea of where I might go next?

I told him I had not quite decided. I had the option of staying with my parents in the city in the middle of the country where I had grown up while I searched for another job. That was always something I could do. Always within the realm of technical feasibility. Don't cry, he said, and I said that I wasn't crying.

Across the street from Thomas's apartment the motel pool sat uncovered and unfilled, a massive bathtub carved into the earth. In its corners lay miniature mountains of trash and debris, fruit peels, candy wrappers, dead leaves—leftovers from the autumn, when I had first arrived in town. Do you want to come up, Thomas said, we could have sex, I'm kind of hard right now? I thanked him for the offer, but I had some grading I needed to get done that night. You know how the end of the semester gets, I said. He laughed. He did know. But that was fine. He would see me soon. Yes, I said, I was sure he would. Before he turned into the lobby, I stared intently at his face, wanting to memorize it this time, to keep it with me as it really was, not as I imagined it to be—and then I gasped, because all at once I saw him, as if the only thing I had ever needed to do was look. He was instantly so distinctive, so frighteningly odd, so craggy and crooked and feral and alive, thrusting and glistening and yellow and pure, pulsing, gaping, full of holes that led all the way to the dark damp interior, that it was impossible to believe I had ever found his features difficult to remember. I looked at him, and I knew that for the rest of my life, this was the face I would meet in my deepest dreams; this was the mouth that would open and tell me it was time to step down into the water. It was time to swim across the lake. It was nighttime. And the stars are above you and the stars are below you. And on the other shore there are rows of wooden chairs. There are beautiful string lights. There are some people you know. Yes, the lake is cold. Yes, it's always winter. Your feet are wet. You're up to your knees in it.

Then he went inside and I blinked and I could no longer recall what he looked like.

When I arrived home, all the lamps in my apartment had been switched off.

Hey, I called.

I kicked away my orthotic sneakers with their special lumps to correct my chronic overpronation. I unbuttoned my fuzzy insulated jacket and lobbed it at an armchair and watched its slow tumble from the cushion to the floor.

Sorry, that took longer than I thought, I called.

Hello? I called.

Hey? I called.

He bumped open the bathroom door with his hip.

HAPPY BIRTHDAY TO YOU, he sang.

Oh my god, I said.

HAPPY BIRTHDAY TO YOU, he sang.

He held the cake out in front of him like a crown in a coronation procession. It was one layer, the size of a dinner plate, its surface slanted and globbed with thick slabs of green frosting. Beyond its wavering ring of flames, his face was shining. It was a male face, the face of a man my age. I can't describe it further—can't or won't, one of those. He shuffled toward me and his socks made gentle squeaking sounds against the hardwood, like mice.

I lit these on the toilet! he said.

He set the cake down on the kitchen table. I contracted my diaphragm and drew air into my lungs and made the room go dark with one breath. In the dark I asked him what time he had to leave tomorrow. Early, I think, he said. I made a noise with my mouth. I can make the drive in two days, he said, but I need to get the car back because the chickens have to go to the vet. Again? I asked. Worms, he said, always worms. Everyone says hi, by the way, and happy birthday. Do you think I was their least favorite roommate of all time, I asked, and he said no, because remember that guy, oh, oh, I said, that guy, that Italian guy, was that it? Was he Italian? The guy who kept saying the Jews? The Jews, the Jews! They had hated that guy. We giggled. That guy *loved* Mussolini. Like, he actually did. Yeah, he actually did. The *fascisti*, I said. The *fascisti*, he said. I stopped giggling. Are you crying? he asked. Yeah, I said. Are you crying? I asked. Yeah, he said, because I'm still not sure whether you're coming back, or where else you're going to go if not. I have trauma, I said, and he said, blah blah blah blah blah, and I laughed and said, blah blah blah blah blah blah blah blah, and we each ate a bite of cake.

It's not enough, I said after swallowing. It's not enough of a reason to be here.

He stood from the table. I lay down on the sagging couch and balanced my plate on my chest.

I can't put my whole life into it, I said. I want something that I can put my whole life into.

He walked around the room and flicked the lights back on, one by one. He settled beside me on the couch. He stole a chunk of my cake with his fingers and propped his legs over mine. His body was hot. The room was bright. Outside there were dark shapes and darker shapes, the strong wind, the sea. There was a smear of frosting on his chin, as beautiful as a painting. I could feel my brain cells swelling against my skull.

No, I couldn't.

I don't really know what you mean by "it," he said.

He said, Your whole life?

Sure, I said, why not. My whole life.

5

*

My whole life. Again my books were in boxes, sixteen by fourteen by twelve, their glossy cardboard walls reinforced to support the transportation of flavored vodkas in the trucks that lumbered year-round along the only highway to town. Cherry, passionfruit, mango, lime. With a permanent marker I had slashed ominous black *X*s through the companies' logos, a requirement for media shipments in this country—one of the state's few pathetic pretenses at separating art from garbage, I thought. My kitchen cabinets were thrown ecstatically open, as if they expected someone small but important to climb in. On the shelves, my Academy-provided dishes sat clean and neatly stacked.

The apartment's walls were bare. Only a spot of sticky residue remained, from the strip of tape I had used to paste up my photograph of a young Iosif Vissarionovich Stalin, which was tucked now into my annotated copy of *Bleak House* and thus protected from wrinkling, crunching, spillage, all the possible damage a flimsy object might have inflicted upon it during travel. In the center of the living room, my suitcase gaped. Sweaters, pants, T-shirts, and socks. A heavy wool dress I hadn't worn all year. The suitcase's zipper lay twisted and warped along the perimeter; several of its metal teeth were badly bent and the mechanism was prone to sticking, so that each time I tried to zip the suitcase shut I had to saw the slider back and forth like a bow across a string.

I sank into the couch and withdrew *Bleak House* from my backpack. The book fell open to my photograph of Iosif Stalin, its edge lodged cozily in the binding. I took the picture between my fingers and rubbed. My thumbpads made fuzzy prints on the grain. With my fingernail I traced Iosif's long ears, the shadowed cleft beneath his lower lip. One of his eyebrows appeared to be slightly thicker than the other. He was cocky and handsome, full of faith in what was to come, a vision of futural alternatives, the urge to bend the world to his will, practical considerations regarding forced collectivization, the economic power of the kulaks, nationalism, purges, mass murders, assassinations, prison camps, etcetera—it was only a photograph, and he looked very different in others taken around the same time. I found it impossible to say exactly what he meant to me. His father had beaten him with a shoe, probably.

On the back of the image I had written out a few lines from a poem he had published in his youth.

*Know for certain that once*
*Struck down to the ground, an oppressed man*
*Strives again to reach the pure mountain,*
*When exalted by hope.*

The poem had been composed in direct address to the moon. To the moon, Iosif was providing an explanation; he was offering the moon some advice.

I looked at the open page in *Bleak House* and read a passage that had been obscured by Iosif's photograph.

> *Mr. Vholes is a very respectable man. He has not a large business, but he is a very respectable man. He is allowed by the greater attorneys who have made good fortunes or are making them to be a most respectable man. He never misses a chance in his practice, which is a mark of respectability. He never takes any pleasure, which is another mark of respectability. He is reserved and serious, which is another mark of respectability. His digestion is impaired, which is highly respectable.*

His digestion is impaired, which is highly respectable, I whispered. It was a wonderful sentence. I uncapped a pen and drew in the margin a small star, then a large exclamation point. There came a knock at my front door; I returned the photograph to the book and *Bleak House* to my backpack.

My history-teacher neighbor stood on my apartment's entry ramp, weeping and clutching the railing with both hands. His cheeks were an aggressive mottled pink. He wore a gorgeous seersucker suit onto whose wide lapels his tears dropped, fat as coins. The sky above him lofted glorious and clear; against it, seabirds preened, screeching insults, pumping out their ceaseless laps to and from the beach. In town the ferry was running again. Each afternoon it pulled into the harbor to disgorge its nauseated tourists, who promptly vomited into the trash cans that, perhaps for this purpose, lined the dock, then swarmed the streets—wearing hats, slurping chowder out of paper cups, pointing at stuff. The season had begun. On every tree, flimsy leaves fluttered the palest green.

Would you like to come in? I asked my neighbor.

No, he gasped, no—that's all right. I just wanted to give you this.

He handed me a sheet of yellow construction paper folded in two. The front read ONTO GREENER PASTURES in childish bubble lettering. I opened the card; the lefthand side was blank. On the right my neighbor had drawn an obese pack mule, burdened by bulging bundles. The animal was rendered mid-lope, with one front leg crooked in the air to signify the anguished effort of its movement. It was stepping in the direction of a wimpy stack of hay, far in the distance, that I doubted it would ever reach. The mule's expression was one of sheer exhaustion, desperate thirst, and a total lack of faith in the future. Next to a gargantuan sun, whose pulsating heat was represented by a series of violent pen strokes, slashing across the paper to ruin the mule's life, my neighbor had written: I WILL MISS YOU.

I thanked him for the lovely card.

The end of the school year gets me emotional, my neighbor said, hiccupping. From his mouth leaked the warm, vinegary smell of alcohol and spit. I drew my face away, but he leaned closer in response, still clinging to the railing, like a person stuck at a dizzying height. It brought him back to his own time in college, he said, his senior year in particular, an overwhelming and transformative period, during which, several nights each week, a young man with whom he had been casually acquainted—small and squirrelly, with fine blond hair like a bowl of silk—would bang relentlessly on his door, begging to be let in. When my neighbor at last opened up, the young man would be revealed trembling on his feet, in tears, sipping a Big Gulp full of gin and threatening to kill himself if my neighbor did not allow him to give him a blow job. Under these dire circumstances my neighbor felt obligated to acquiesce to the young man's request—and so the young man would suck my neighbor off in his dorm room, his bony knees digging into the linoleum, one dainty hand gripping the frame of my neighbor's twin XL bed for stability, and on occasion my neighbor would afterward take the young man to the hospital to get his stomach pumped so that he did not die of alcohol poisoning. Some evenings, when my neighbor's girlfriend at the time was spending the night, the young man would recognize her car in the dormitory's cul-de-sac, and he would stand ankle-deep in the flowerbeds, throwing trash and twigs and pebbles at my neighbor's window and screaming, Is that pig in there with you right now? Are you fucking that pig right now? The Academy's graduation day always reminded my neighbor of that period in his life, he said; a period that in some ways still felt so present but was in fact over. My neighbor sighed wistfully. Completely over, he said.

I thanked my neighbor for sharing this tale of his college years with me. I appreciated his openness, I told him, in discussing what sounded like a time of profound internal tumult. My neighbor asked if I would sit next to him during the graduation ceremony that afternoon. It had been so meaningful getting to know me this year. He began crying hard once more. Oh, I said. Sure. My neighbor hoped I would stay in touch after I left. He knew people always said that, but he really meant it. Did I have his number? No, I said, I didn't think I did. He waited for me to pull out my phone, then spoke the digits aloud, slowly, pausing to expel his musty hiccups and burps while I dutifully punched his information into my contacts. Give me a call, he said. He wished me all the best in my future endeavors. He stumbled in the direction of his own unit, then stopped and turned back to me. What had I been singing that morning, by the way? he asked. This morning? I said. The alto part from Thomas Tallis's "If Ye Love Me," a motet for four voices. I apologized if I had been too loud. Would I sing it to him now, he asked, weeping. No, I said. The alto line alone was boring and not worth listening to. But I could recommend a recording I liked, if he wanted. Text me, he said, text it to me. He returned to his unit and I to mine. I pulled *Bleak House* from my backpack and tucked his card safely between its pages. Several minutes later, through my apartment wall, there came the sound of three or four women's guttural moans, groans, screams, screeches, fuzzy and distorted at the high end because the volume had been jacked up, interspersed with my neighbor's wracking sobs. Anything, I thought, repeated enough times could become a kind of comfort. That was the whole problem.

I made a peanut butter sandwich, then loaded my boxes onto the rolling cart I had borrowed from the administrative cottage and tugged it out the front door.

I found Billy in the alley behind the post office. He was sitting on his khaki jacket, his knees raised and his back pressed to the building. In one hand he clutched a half-eaten hamburger, in the other a lit cigarette. Beyond him, the sea thrashed. He didn't need to see it to know that it was there. On the beach a child tossed a kite at the sky. Two people in love shared a meatball sub. A pretty young woman dipped a toe into the water, screamed as if she were being raped, then glanced around to see if anyone had noticed. When it was clear that no one cared, she stopped screaming and kicked sullenly at the sand. I parked my cart to the side of the alley and asked Billy if he could please spare a smoke. His hair had been shorn like a lamb's; it formed a sweet halo-like fuzz over his skull. Even in my T-shirt, I was uncomfortably warm. My breath emerged in baggy huffs from the strain of pulling along my packages.

Sure, Billy said. He wrapped his hamburger in its foil, set it down, and stood, his own cigarette dangling from the corner of his mouth. I leaned over his hands, cupped tenderly around the flame to protect it from the snuffing wind. I inhaled and sputtered. Billy laughed.

That's perique tobacco, he said. You ever had perique tobacco?

No, I said, never. I took another drag and hacked out a cough. Wow, I said. That's strong. Full-bodied, full-flavor.

Yeah, Billy said, real wet. That's the good stuff. You can only grow that stuff in Louisiana. I used to live down there, in New Orleans. You ever lived down there? he asked.

I had not, I said, though once I had visited for Mardi Gras.

Crazy down there. He shook his head. Lots of things I could tell you about New Orleans, he continued, staring at me hard. In the sunlight his eyes shone the watery green of submerged seagrass. The things I could tell you, he whispered, his face almost touching mine.

But not today! he cried happily. He hopped back. It's a beautiful day, isn't it? He spread his arms and threw his head skyward and took a triumphant gulp of the endless salty air.

It was a beautiful day, I agreed, an absolutely perfect day.

He stuck out his hand. He told me that his name was Billy, and I introduced myself. He asked where I was coming from. I said that I was actually going, not coming—not today, but later in the week. I had been teaching at the Academy—I fluttered my wrist toward campus's hill, away from the beach—but I wouldn't be returning in the fall. In a few days I would take the ferry to the closest coastal metropolis, then a train to the city in the middle of the country where I had grown up. I would stay at my parents' house for a couple of weeks, while they were out of town. To get my bearings. And then I would probably go somewhere else.

Probably? Billy said, and I said, yes, probably.

Somewhere else? he said.

Somewhere else, I said.

It was strange, I told him, to think that I would never experience the town in the height of its real season, that I would never see its true face; but then again, maybe the on-season was no more real than the off. Still, I felt a bit like a ghost, watching the streets come to life around me—the butcher paper pulled down from the shopfront windows, the restaurant floors swept and mopped and scrubbed by Bulgarian and Jamaican and, on occasion, Serbian workers—right as I was preparing to depart. I had the sense that I was living inside of a time that was separate from everyone else's, a time that had been deflated, but that nonetheless managed to drag itself along, even if only for another second or two. I knew that for most people here, this was a beginning. I could feel it in the air, an anticipatory wildness, like humidity about to crack open, an untrained voice sustaining one note for many measures—but for me, it was an ending. Or maybe just a different point on the same circle.

I began to describe to Billy the fictional probate case of Jarndyce and Jarndyce in Charles Dickens's greatest novel *Bleak House*, the interminable court proceedings that structured the book's plot, the soggy muck of bureaucracy inducing insanity in all those who attempted to untangle its dense network of capital and law—Jarndyce and Jarndyce, I said, which sucks up everything, collapses everything, destroys everything, makes one guy spontaneously combust—Jarndyce and Jarndyce, the foothold of modernity, the precursor to Kafka, to modernism, the systems novel—Jarndyce and Jarndyce, which, at book's end, is punctured in the purest and most crystalline of anticlimaxes when the entire estate at stake in the case is absorbed by the costs of litigation, so that, I explained, as the selfless and sagacious doctor Allan Woodcourt puts it, *thus the suit lapses and melts away*—the phrasing of which can't but bring to mind Marx's formulation that *all that is solid melts into air*—Jarndyce and Jarndyce, I concluded, was what my departure from the Academy had me thinking about. In the end the lawyers gather their papers and hobble off and it is as if there never had been a Jarndyce and Jarndyce at all. And soon I, too, would be hobbling home. My presence here would lapse and melt away; maybe it had lapsed and melted away already. Billy nodded emphatically. He understood, he said. Personally, he explained, he had never smoked crack, but that didn't mean he had something against anyone who did. It was a *personal* choice, he said. He used his cigarette to wave ambiguously toward the sky, as if that were the place where the majority of personal choices were made. I told him I agreed completely. He asked me if I had ever smoked crack, and I said no, I had never personally smoked crack, but that I appreciated his checking. I told him I was Jewish. I thanked him for the cigarette. I'd better go drop off my packages, I said, pointing to my cart. Before I left, I asked Billy if he planned to stay in town all season. Yes, he did. It was magnificent here in the summers, he said, unlike any other place in the world, a sliver of light at the edge of the cosmos. And sometimes there were dolphins!

I told Billy that I did not care for dolphins, due to their controversial affinity for rape. But still, maybe one day I would come see the town in the summer. He nodded. If I did return, Billy said, I should find him. He was usually around this alley, here behind the post office. I should feel free to stop by anytime. He had been coming to this town for years, he said, in the warmer months.

I passed my boxes off to the bureaucrats at the post office. By the time I'd finished, Billy had disappeared from the alley. Where he had been sitting only a ball of hamburger foil remained. I studied it briefly. Then I turned around to tug my empty cart down Main Street, making a right toward the bay, its wheels furrowing the soft sand. Birds called in my direction. My phone buzzed in my pocket. The wind was all over me, as it had been so many times before.

One second, I said, it's too bright, I can't see much. Let me find some shade.

I held my phone loosely, transmitting images of the beach and my own knees as I stepped under a restaurant's overhanging porch. Above me, tourists nibbled on strips of fried fish, engaging in existential thoughts induced by the endless surge of swollen, slimy water. It was a beautiful day, a perfect day.

Okay, I said, that's better. I sat down and crossed my legs in the cold sand. To my right, a piping plover buried its head in the hollow carcass of a crab, seeking meat. I looked at my mother.

Can you see? she said in Russian. Her face filled the screen.

Yes, I said, I see you.

Let me change it, she said, ow, ow, let me move it.

She poked at her phone several times before she managed to flip the camera.

Look, she said.

It was drizzling or it had recently rained, I couldn't tell which. It was dusk. The pavement reflected the glow of the streetlights. My mother's camera showed an unkempt triangle of grass, flattened by precipitation; several scraggled trees rose in its center, their branches drooping. The grass was hemmed in by a concrete barrier and the concrete barrier was hemmed in by parked cars of different makes and colors, compact, gleaming, their windows fogged. Look, she said. Move your phone more slowly, I told her, I can't see, you're shaking it. It's my house, she said, look. I looked. I saw a number in the pavement, set in red and black ceramic tiles. I saw a thick wooden double door. One, nine, one; the final digit may have been a two or a three, I couldn't make it out, its lower half appeared to have crumbled away long ago. Look, my mother said cheerfully, totally decrepit, a piece of shit. She panned to the top of a three-story building, its tan brick facade dulled with age, mold, moisture damage, other assaults I couldn't imagine. On a small wrought-iron balcony, a line of sopping laundry flapped, flinging water. I saw a woman's dress, a child's shirt. The camera zoomed in on an unlit window until my screen was a rectangle of reflective darkness. Mirrored in the window I could see the sky, big and low, with its great sturdy slabs of Baltic cloud. Look, where my mother and father slept, my mother said. The camera shook and blurred and whipped around, and again darkness filled my screen, again the sky's reflection. And here was my sister's room, she said, my parents used to force-feed her like a goose—you get out of the camps and have a baby and you stuff it like you're making foie gras. She zoomed out. We had returned to the narrow shining street. Look, she said, say hello to your daughter; my father smiled and waved from across the road, next to a glistening green car whose roof reached his chin. He had a guidebook in his hand, a warm brown sweater draping his shoulders. His hair was damp. The camera trembled as my mother shuffled to the side of the building, her gait slower than I remembered, into an alleyway lined with terracotta pots containing dead or dying plants. Look, she said, my bedroom window. She pointed the camera. Slow down, I said, can you please slow down? Once again a dark and empty rectangle filled my screen, though this time it reflected not the sky but a taller apartment building, likely constructed after my mother's family had emigrated, with a yellowed plaster facade and curved balconies adorning each unit. For fifty-four years I've dreamt of that window, my mother said, fifty-four years of my life. For fifty-four years I've woken up at two in the morning and thought, that is the window I will never see again. And now I'm here and it's like, it's a window, get over it. Looks like shit! she said. She thrust the camera at the alley-side of the building—and this part wasn't stucco then, she explained, it was all brick, like the front; the nice lady who lives here told me most of the apartments are short-term rentals. Antisemites, my mother said vaguely. Let's go. We walked down the road and turned right. The camera was angled upward, and I could now make out the clouds themselves, bulbous and ripe, looming over the city as if to swallow the distant church spires. A lamp flicked on in a window. Behind it all, I saw my own bright crisp daylight, my rolling American ocean, my seagull lunging its fat head into a bag of potato chips. I picked up a fistful of sand. Look, the KGB building, my mother said, it was right by our house, when my parents were trying to forge those documents, can you imagine. Look, in that square used to be Lenin's big statue. No more Lenin, persona non grata these days, like Christopher Columbus, it's sad. And if you keep walking back that way it was the ghetto. And there used to be the synagogue before the Nazis burned it and the Soviets finished off the job and tore it down. And over there it's the river Neris, which by the way I walked along every single weekday when I was little, going to school, three miles round-trip, all by myself, seven years old, and I had a twitch in my eye from anxiety, a terrible twitch, and I couldn't stop throwing up, so they gave me a special medicine to take each morning—tranquilizers? I asked—look, my mother said, if you go that way there is a very nice and very clean H&M, it's huge! The beautiful river Neris, she said. I wish I could show you the Baltic Sea. I wish I could show you Palanga. Look, the stairway to that church, all the way down there, you see, it was built out of Jewish headstones, looted from the cemetery. Not that church, my father called out, it's a different one, that one's normal, I think. Look, let's go to the grocery store, my mother said, I'll tell your father to hurry up. A pair of automatic doors flung open, and we stepped into a pool of pure fluorescence. I heard announcements in a language I didn't understand, the shrill beep of the checkout machine, my mother making apologetic noises to a shopper I couldn't see. Look at this yogurt, she said to me in Russian, that's the best yogurt. She held the yogurt to the camera. We moved to another aisle. Look at all these sausages, she said. Every kind of sausage, look. She held up one package of pink sausages, then another. And we took the train to Kovno but we couldn't find the big grave, the mass grave, we couldn't find it, did I tell you? I explained that the mass grave was a twenty-minute drive outside of the city center, that you had to know what you were looking for. But you said Kaddish there? my mother asked, and I said yes, years ago I had said Kaddish there, but it had been a windy day and the candles I'd brought wouldn't stay lit, and we didn't have a minyan, and actually I didn't know the prayer, I didn't know the Aramaic, so someone else had recited the words on my behalf while I struck the matches to light the candles that were then immediately extinguished, over and over again, four or five times I tried, four or five times they blew out, so who could say if it really counted. Yitgadal v'yitkadash sh'mei raba b'alma di-v'ra chirutei, v'yamlich malchutei b'chayeichon uvyomeichon uvchayei d'chol beit yisrael, ba'agala uvizman kariv, v'im'ru, amen, my mother said. Look at this good black bread, dirt cheap, isn't that your favorite? she asked in Russian. Yes, I replied in English, she was right, it was my favorite. Just like my mother, she told me. Good black bread with butter, my mother said. Yummy. The camera zoomed in on the loaf of bread, swaddled in shrink-wrap. Do you want me to bring you back some? she asked. I looked at my screen, filled with the bread's pasted-on label, out of focus and jittering so that the text was illegible—though I couldn't have read it even if the words were clear.

I will bring you some, my mother said. I will bring some home for you.

The air-conditioning in the auditorium was broken. The thick afternoon sun that poured in from the west-facing windows humidified the room like a greenhouse. I looked down my row—all of us poaching together like eggs, all of our sweat running into all of our mouths, all of our pits wet, our necks, the undersides of our knees. We all gazed longingly outside, where the breeze passed through the trees and, farther away, the dune grass, the sand, the ocean and everything that lay beyond it. My history-teacher neighbor placed a sweaty hand on my bare and sweaty thigh. When I nudged it away, it felt like peeling off a sticker.

It is never easy, the Head of School said from her podium. It is never an easy day. Her pure white hair was gathered into a low bun; sweat streamed down her temples and glistened above her upper lip, catching the light like jewels. Today, she said, we cast these young people forth into the world. We hope we have prepared them to move with courage and integrity through whatever is to come. We look at them, and what we see is the future. We look at them!

Like one many-headed creature, we all craned our necks to look at the seniors where they sat onstage, arranged in alphabetical order on three staggered risers. Their maroon gowns slouched open to reveal a sea of matching dresses in virginal white, tight polyester that clung to their breasts and indented their shoulders at the straps. On their feet they wore lustrous white stilettos; seated, the added height elevated their knees close to their ribs, giving them the gawky angularity of praying mantises. Many of the seniors were already weeping, or pretending to—it doesn't matter which one it was. Sloppily applied mascara dribbled down their cheeks. Their mouths were a series of vague pink holes, blurred from melting lipstick.

But as the future sweeps our girls away, the Head continued, fanning out her arm in a gesture of futural sweepage, what will become of those who have been left behind? She urged us, she said, to take a moment to honor the ones who *stayed:* parents and teachers, younger siblings, even administrators—she tittered, and the crowd tittered in response—whose work was not the work of beginning anew, as it would soon be for these impressive young women, but rather the work of soldiering on in the face of loss; the work of remaining; of mourning; of comprehending; of dissolving the past into the future and the future into the past; of remembering, she said, that the owl of Minerva takes flight only at dusk!

Behind me, someone hurrahed softly, and then the audience burst into a sudden, raucous applause. I turned in my seat. A group of parents near the exits had gotten to their feet. Those who were still sitting pounded their fists violently against the arms of their chairs, as if they were at a political meeting. They wore well-cut suits, loafers, linen dresses hemmed just above the knee. Their hair looked so clean. I rubbed at my own sticky scalp; I feared I might have a tick. Two rows in front of the standing parents, Thomas was clapping politely in his chair, legs crossed. I caught his eye; he smiled and lifted his hand, exposing the dark, damp patch in his armpit. I waved back. My history-teacher neighbor draped an arm around my shoulder, and this time I decided to let him keep it there. He was weeping again, and making kissing faces at the girls onstage. At the end of my row, Petar stood, tugging at his son's elbow in an effort to force him to his feet. Georgi ignored him and stared at the floor, his arms folded solidly across his chest, a shimmer of teal plastic visible in his lap. He had on a blazer, a size or two too small, over a T-shirt depicting a cartoon shark in sunglasses and a sideways baseball cap. Onstage, a senior shoved through her classmates, leapt from the riser, flung off her heels, and sprinted barefoot down the aisle toward a trash can, into which she proceeded to loudly vomit. Bulimia, my history-teacher neighbor whispered, she was in my fascism class. I told him I was not sure that was how bulimia worked, and he shrugged. Maybe heat stroke, then, he said.

Do you think now is a good time to pee? I asked.

I worked my way along the row, apologizing as I went. At the podium, the Head of School was starting to beckon the piano-playing French teacher and the Academy's choral director to the stage. Soon there would be singing. I hurried, hunching my shoulders and stooping in the hopes that this would render me invisible to the parents of my students, with whom I would never again interact. I passed the trash can. It oozed a familiar scent of bile and vomit. A few of my juniors were scattered throughout the audience: Divya seated alongside her family, her head on her father's shoulder, her mother's braids identical to hers, Kyla asleep in a row of freshmen, Anita with her knees pulled into her chest and her feet lodged against a seatback. Next to her was Thales, who had dyed her hair firetruck red; she held Anita's hand on their shared armrest, like lovers at the cinema. Our eyes met. She flapped her unoccupied wrist at me in terror. A few seats down, a girl I didn't know withdrew a bag of candies from her purse and shook it at her friends, laughing. We could have been sisters. No—she was Cordelia's, I realized. I followed her glance toward the front of the auditorium, and there sat Cordelia herself, solemn in her black choir gown, surrounded by a group of students in matching dresses, all of their heads bowed, as if in prayer. Her hair stuck to the sweat on the back of her skull. I knew she didn't see me. She was a being made of time. She was probably humming. I moved farther down the aisle, out of view of my juniors, each one of them like a daughter to me. In a few years they would not remember my first name. Someone in another state was making my phone buzz in my pocket. All was water. All was one. I would go home. I would go somewhere else. I would call him back soon. I pushed through the auditorium doors into the sudden silence of the hallway.

I stopped for a second.

Then I kept walking, past the gender-neutral bathrooms, past the stairway, past the security desk, through the double doors, until I was standing outside, where everything was the same. I looked at the lake. It wasn't really there. It was as blue as the sea.

# Acknowledgments

Endless thanks to Emily Bell, dream editor and kindred spirit, and to Kent Wolf, brilliant agent. I am grateful to the whole team at Astra House—Alexis Nowicki, Rachael Small, Tiffany Gonzalez, Ben Schrank, Jane Handa, Suzanne Lander, Toni Willis, Alissa Theodor, Lisa Taylor, Frankie DiGiovanni, and Rodrigo Corral—as well as to all those who helped bring this book to life in the UK—Alexa von Hirschberg, Rachel Clements, Elizabeth Allen, Kate Moreton, Javerya Iqbal, Sienna Wadhwani, Alistair Thompson, Jenny Lord, Alice Graham, and everyone at W&N. For two beautiful covers, thank you to Chloe Scheffe, Ola Galewicz, and Rebecca Aldernet.

The unnamed text from which this novel's narrator plagiarizes during her lectures is Raymond Williams's *The Country and the City*. *Offseason* owes a debt to Raymond Williams's and Terry Eagleton's wonderful writings on Dickens, particularly Eagleton's *The English Novel: An Introduction*. Details are drawn from Ian Grey's biography *Stalin: Man of History*. The unattributed quotation in the narrator's final conversation with Cordelia is from "P.S." by Franz Wright. The translation of Stalin's poem "To the Moon" is Donald Rayfield's. I'm grateful to the Institute of

Psychoanalysis for allowing me to use James Strachey's translation of Freud as an epigraph in this novel's UK edition.

Thank you to the friends who read and helped me think about this book: Emily, Claire, Lev, Henry, Jonah, and Niyi. Thank you to my parents, for believing in art, and to my sister, Nomi. Thank you to Hedgie, for her awesome mind; my teachers, especially Elizabeth McCracken, Jessica Anthony, and Sally Bachner; my mother-in-law, Jackie, for sharing her home; and Asli, for walking with me through the dark.

This book would not exist without the support of the Fine Arts Work Center in Provincetown. I am indebted to everyone at the FAWC, especially Sharon Polli, Naya Bricher, Jerome Greene, Josh Willis, Nat Doane, and Joe Fish. Many thanks to Matt Null and to my fellowship cohort, one and all. Thanks are also owed to Yaddo for the gift of seven weeks to finish this novel (and for the friends), and to everyone—faculty and staff and workshopmates—at the Michener Center for Writers and the New Writers Project.

Finally, thank you to Jason, who makes everything different, and whose love has changed my life.